OLIVER TWIST AND THE MYSTERY OF THROATE MANOR

DAVID STUART DAVIES

OLIVER TWIST

AND The Mystery of Throate Manor

Urbane
PUBLICATIONS

First published in Great Britain in 2018 by Urbane Publications Ltd
Suite 3, Brown Europe House, 33/34 Gleaming Wood Drive, Chatham, Kent
ME5 8RZ

A CIP catalogue record for this book is available from the British Library.

ISBN 978-1-911583-54-7

MOBI 978-1-911583-55-4

Design and Typeset by The Invisible Man
Cover by The Invisible Man

Printed and bound by 4edge UK

Urbane
PUBLICATIONS

urbanepublications.com

DEDICATION

To my darling Katie - again!

CHAPTER ONE

Evening came. The sun began to slide slowly behind the darkening horizon. Thickening shadows, riding on the warm air, rolled across the green meadows of Surrey, nimbly scaling stone walls and riffling over hedges, reaching out to engulf the large isolated house that fronted the great expanse of open countryside.

This man-made intrusion on the pastoral scene was Throate Manor, the ancestral home of Sir Ebenezer Throate. The house was a strange mixture of styles. Students of architecture were less circumspect in their description of the property, regarding it as a monstrosity with the fashion of one period clamped unceremoniously on to another without finesse or any consideration of aesthetics. The first ennobled Throate, Sir Willoughby, built the main body of the dwelling in 1067 in his own image: bluff, sturdy and somewhat ungainly. Very much the epitome of Norman ingenuity mixed with rough frugality, it stood, rounded grey stone sitting firmly on rounded grey stone; a brutish blot on the lush green countryside.

The structure was added to in the reign of Elizabeth I by Sir Percival Throate, who had sailed with Raleigh until inveterate *mal de mer* brought an abrupt end to his short and undistinguished naval career. He returned to Throate Manor under an embarrassed cloud and kept sheep and cultivated his gout until the latter brought about his early demise. His lasting memorial was the creation of an ungainly wing in the Elizabethan style with high arched windows and labyrinthine draughty corridors.

The property had lain untouched by succeeding generations until the present incumbent of Throate Manor had a large orangery and a third wing built in the popular Gothic mode. The house was a monument to the longevity, eccentricity and lack of taste of the British aristocracy. It was also exceedingly cold. One could pass from one end of the property to the other and journey through seven hundred years of English history while catching a severe chill into the bargain.

As the sun slipped even further behind the far horizon, Sir Ebenezer was ensconced in the orangery with his first brandy and soda of the evening and a book of dubious content resting on his lap. As the last rays of amber sunlight squeezed their way through the palm fronds, tigering the walls of the orangery, Sir Ebenezer grew uneasy, the lines on his ancient features deepened with worry. The onset of night, that dark uncertain segment of our twenty four hour day which cloaks so much from the eye of man and when, it is said, evil things walk abroad, caused the baronet much consternation. As though it would physically ward off the coming darkness, Sir Ebenezer drained his brandy in one erratic gulp and then with some effort clambered to his feet, allowing the book to slide to the floor with a loud thump – a noise that caused him further unease.

In the manner of a somnambulist, Sir Ebenezer made his way to the great hall. He was seeking company – the solace and safety of being with another human being as night began to ambush the land. In preference, he would have liked to encounter his secretary, Roger Lightwood. His ready smile, kind features and warm brown eyes, which still sparkled with the unsullied enthusiasm of youth, would have brought comfort to the curmudgeonly baronet, would have helped to ward off the tendrils of creeping fear that were slowly entwining themselves around his tremulous soul with every darkening moment. Sir Ebenezer would have found great comfort in the company of Roger Lightwood, but the young man had taken a brief leave of absence to spend some days at the coast where he hoped the unfettered sea air would blow away a persistent cold which had been brought on by the severe draughts generated by Throate Manor even in the summer time.

Sir Ebenezer's second choice for company, a poor second choice, he had to admit, was Bulstrode, his man servant, a fellow of few words but always a felt presence. However, as it happened, on reaching the hall, Amelia Throate, Sir Ebenezer's wife and constant irritation, was the first person he encountered as she descended the staircase in a high stately manner as though she were attending her own coronation. As these two individuals glanced at each other with practised disdain, their memory did not for one instant take them back to their youth – to one of those idyllic moments when they were both lithe of body, smooth of skin, and nimble of mind. A time before age, illness and over familiarity had not deformed their once bright natures. Amelia had completely forgotten the occasion when a tall willowy fellow, with attractively unruly hair cascading around his forehead like blonde watch springs and the possessor of a broad captivating smile, had punted her down the river, serenading her with songs of romance and exotic climes. Oh, how her young heart had fluttered when he bent low to kiss her chastely on the cheek. Such memories had long been exorcised. They had seeped from her mind like sand through an hour glass. Her thoughts of Sir Ebenezer were now prompted solely by what she saw before her: a fat, bald fellow whose several chins resembled a pile of biscuits which overflowed his collar and whose rheumy eyes and stained teeth suggested an apparition that had been released from a gluttonous netherworld. A creature to whom she was shackled by the insidious chain of marriage vows until death.

In a similar fashion, Sir Ebenezer never recollected the occasion of Lady Dartmouth's ball in the spring so many yesterdays ago when he spied a magnificent girl by the punch bowl in conversation with a young soldier. Her shining hair shimmered like a chestnut halo in the muted candlelight; her smooth pink cheeks dimpled delightfully as she smiled and her bright blue intelligent eyes flashed with enthusiasm as she expressed a point with fervour. It was on that magical moment of first seeing her that he had determined to meet the girl, woo her and marry her. He now had no recollection of the evening nor the young beauty who stole his heart, despite the fact that her older self now faced him and her blue eyes, although dimmed a little now by the passing years, still held the fierce spark of intelligence.

Sir Ebenezer and Lady Amelia were now intolerant strangers isolated upon the tiny barren desert island of their marriage, forever castaways with no hope of rescue.

'Oh, it's you,' observed Sir Ebenezer with a charmless warble.

'Yes, it is I,' replied Lady Amelia, making no effort to disguise the sneer and sarcasm in her voice. 'You were perhaps expecting someone else?'

Sir Ebenezer shivered with genuine fear at the suggestion.

Without further converse, they made their way to the dining room, a great draughty chamber where a meagre log fire struggled to keep itself alight, its puny yellow limbs stretching upwards towards the sooty maw of the chimney. But as these feeble flames lacked the power to remain dancing above the thick damp logs they sank down out of sight before they could make their presence felt. Two candelabrum placed at either end of the long dining table provided the main source of illumination. Like a visiting spirit from the afterlife, Bulstrode emerged from the shadows, where he had been disguising himself as a piece of darkness, to draw Lady Amelia's chair from the table in order for her to be seated. Once this task had been completed, he moved swiftly as though on castors to the other end of the table where Sir Ebenezer was waiting for the same operation to be performed for him. It was a nightly ritual as was everything about the meal. Master and mistress sat at either end of the long table, hardly able to discern each other's face let alone indulge in any conversation. Indeed, conversation had not been practised in the house for many years. Brief utterances and wry observations were all that could be managed now. There was a time coming, they both realised, when even those would dry up and they would become mime artists in their own home.

Soup was the first course. Soup was always the first course. Sir Ebenezer took one spoonful as usual, grunted slightly and laid the spoon aside before taking a gulp of red wine. Lady Amelia took an infuriatingly long time to sip, sip, sip, sip, sip, sip and sip the soup. Sir Ebenezer filled in the interval by downing two more glasses of wine. For a moment he gazed sideways towards the high windows and saw that the sky was now a thick indigo broken only by the appearance of a thin slice of pale yellow moon surrounded by a sprinkling of a few timid stars. Night was here and with it the arrival of his terrors. As though to acknowledge the fact, he gestured to Bulstrode to replenish his glass yet again.

Tonight the main course was lamb. Sir Ebenezer dropped one slice into his mouth whole, the thin gravy dribbling down his chin. He sneered at the potatoes, grimaced at the vegetables and lifted his glass once more.

Lady Amelia sliced the meat thinly and then conveyed numerous dainty portions to her mouth, which she nibbled and chewed and chomped and then nibbled and chewed and chomped once more before swallowing. She repeated the process with the potatoes and then with the vegetables. Sir Ebenezer began to doze while this tedious ritual of mastication was performed. A sharp crack emanating from the fire brought him fully back into consciousness and once more the icy hand of fear touched him gently but irresolutely on the shoulder. With a gesture grown large with nerves and alcohol he beckoned Bulstrode to refill his glass once more, which he then proceeded to empty again without pause.

Once Lizzie Barnes, the housekeeper and cook, had cleared the dinner plates, there was a ten minute interval before the pudding was served. During this period neither diner felt the least inclination to acknowledge the other. That mechanism, in any form, had failed years ago, the little cogs of spontaneity were jammed and the great wheels of thought had rusted completely. Instead, each lost themselves in their own private contemplations. Lady Amelia was thinking it was time she made a trip to Town to indulge in some shopping and visit the theatre. In other words, to experience a little life.

Sir Ebenezer's thoughts were less pleasurable. He was conscious that soon he would have to retire to his bedchamber and face the night terrors again. He had already contemplated the possibility that he was going mad. Eccentricity rather than madness was a family trait but perhaps he was the first of his breed to step across the line from idiosyncrasy into lunacy. His stomach churned at the thought of it. Because all forms of intimacy between he and his wife had long ceased, he had not confided in her what he feared or what he had seen.

He was alone in his bewildered misery.

Pudding arrived. Sir Ebenezer ignored it. He never had a liking for sweet things and now the alcohol had shrivelled his taste buds so that they only appreciated … alcohol. Therefore while Lady Amelia dallied with the apple pudding, sucking, chomping and grinding, Sir Ebenezer sent Bulstrode off the cellars for a decent brandy. Because this was a nightly request, Bulstrode was sharp and seasoned enough to have a bottle already stowed, like Polonius, behind the arras and returned with remarkable speed with the cobwebby bottle.

And so the evening and indeed the whole tedious dining experience of this time-ravaged couple drew to a close. The passing years, disillusion, fate, infirmity and a whole collection of unidentifiable elements had wrought such a change on Ebenezer and Amelia who, once upon a time had been lovers and life partners who would have laid down their life for the other. Now they were mechanical shadows bonded by a religious ceremony they had indulged in with enthusiasm nearly forty years ago. How those mischievous cupids floating on the clouds on high must be filled with merriment at this gloomy consequence.

* * *

Sir Ebenezer entered his bedchamber some time later. His brain and perceptions were suitably softened by drink, but not enough to make him forget the possible peril that might befall him. In a lumbering, arthritic fashion he began to disrobe, stopping every now and then to stare at the shadows on the wall created by the flickering candles on his bedside table. They danced and assumed shapes that he did not like. He drew the curtain sealing out the night, the moon and the stars. Pulling on his long woolly nightcap until it came down to his eyebrows, he approached the monster four poster bed. It was, his slightly befuddled mind acknowledged, the bed in which, almost certainly, he would die, as had his father and his father's father and his father's father's father. It was the family death bed. This insidious thought sobered the old baronet up somewhat for it carried with it the supplementary notion that this may well be the night when that fateful event took place. The night when he was frightened to death.

CHAPTER TWO

As the hands of the various timepieces in Throate Manor tick-tocked their way past the hour of midnight, Lady Amelia was deep in a pleasing slumber, dreaming of new fashionable dresses from various smart London emporiums that she would visit on her trip to Town. On the other hand, in another chamber, her husband, Sir Ebenezer, lay scrunched in a foetal position beneath his fine bedclothes quite awake, his ears attuned to the night sounds, wondering, wondering if it would happen again tonight.

Would he be visited again?

He had told no one about his recent nocturnal experiences. This was partly due to the fact that he wasn't sure if he believed in them himself. After all he had no proof. It could very well be that his own fevered imagination had conjured up this waking nightmare. That and guilt perhaps. Sadly there was no recourse to logic and he knew that to confess to another human being was possibly the quickest way to gain entry to Bedlam.

Sir Ebenezer had drawn all the side curtains on the four poster not merely in a vain attempt to prevent the passage of the fierce sneaking draughts across the counterpane but also to block out any unpleasant sights that may manifest themselves in the room. He was conscious that this was a futile procedure for should he hear any disconcerting noise beyond the curtains, he was well aware that he would not be able to resist the temptation to sweep them back to gaze upon whatever was out there.

It was around the hour of two in the morning when the sound came. It was like the cooing of a pigeon at first, gentle, melodic but nonetheless eerie. Sir Ebenezer knew that whatever was making the noise, which was growing in intensity by the moment, the thing was but a few feet away. His curiosity overcame his fear and, struggling forward, he flung back the curtain at the foot of the bed and stared out. It was as he supposed. There by the window was the strange figure again, draped in a white shroud-like garment which was swathed about it from head to foot thus not only covering the face but also hiding the creature's gender. It held a single candle in its left hand. He had seen this thing before. It had visited him on several nights over the last two weeks. It was, he supposed, a ghost, a dead soul who had come haunting him for some purpose or other.

Each night when the apparition appeared cooing in that strange musical fashion, he had attempted to speak to it, to challenge it, to question its purpose. And each night when the apparition appeared, fear robbed him of speech. His throat dried like an old river bed and converse was denied him. Tonight, however, he was determined to overcome his fright. It may have been the extra brandy he had consumed after dinner while waiting for his wife to devour the apple pie that fired up his spirits. It was to his amazement that he heard himself croak out, 'What do you want with me?'

The spirit grew silent and bent its head towards him. In the candlelight, the shroud-like drapings around the head took on the appearance of an awful countenance, malformed and ribbed with age, like some ancient mummified creature that had been re-animated.

'What do I want with you?' the apparition murmured the baronet's words back at him.

But now the river bed had dried up again and Sir Ebenezer could only nod.

'I want justice,' the apparition said, the voice husky and sexless. 'Justice. Remember your child. Remember your special son in your will. If you do not, you will be damned. Damned, d'you hear?'

At the word 'damned', Sir Ebenezer felt a sharp stabbing pain in the chest and even before he was able clasp his hands to his heart, the curtain of dark unconsciousness fell about him.

* * *

Mr Hubert Faddle struggled up the very narrow staircase which led from the ground floor of The Saracen's Head, a nondescript inn situated south of the River Thames. Nevertheless, as the landlord, it was an establishment in which Faddle took great pride. He made his way up to the small chamber situated above the bar. His progress was slow due to his prodigious girth scraping the wall on one side and the banister rail on the other, while he was balancing a large bottle of brandy and six glasses on a narrow wooden tray.

On reaching the landing he allowed himself a tight smile and licked the sweat from his top lip. He entered the dim chamber, illuminated only by a series of guttering candles. Five men sat around a circular table and turned their gaze upon him as he made his way towards them.

'Excellent fellow,' cried a smiling young man as he spied the brandy. It was he who had ordered the drink for his fellow gamblers. It hadn't been an entirely altruistic gesture. He knew that a tipsy gambler is a careless gambler. It had been a ploy of his to encourage his comrades to imbibe liberally, while he sipped slowly and kept a cool head. It was a procedure that he had used on many previous occasions to his advantage.

He swept the brandy bottle from the tray and relieved it of its cork. 'Glasses, gentlemen,' said the young man. The glasses filled to the brim, their benefactor proposed a toast. 'To Lady Luck,' he cried with a bold gesture, which allowed him to spill a liberal amount of alcohol from his own glass, it ran along his arm and dampened his shirt sleeve. The men drank and emptied their glasses as it seemed so did the young man, but then his had been less than half full. They all drank, that is, all but one. A tall thin fellow whose face resided in deep shadow left his drink untouched. His skeletal fingers played idly around the stem of the glass as he stared stoically at the pack of cards in the middle of the table as though mesmerised by them.

With a grin Mr Faddle replenished the glasses. At this rate he may well sell another bottle.

In the flickering, amber gloom, the game commenced. The stakes were high, as the smiling young man liked. These were all serious gamblers to whom coppers and shillings were of no consequence. The guinea was their currency and plenty of them. The room was stuffy and sepulchral and the men were studied and sweaty. Thin sheens of perspiration glimmered in the candlelight on their collective foreheads. The shadows played idly on the walls, stretching towards the ceiling and then dashing away again on a flickering whim.

One man, an importer of items from the Far East, clad in a thick tweed suit more suited to grouse hunting on the Yorkshire moors than a steamy gambling den, allowed himself a brief sweaty smile as he studied his hand; the rest wore emotionless masks, tired eyes peering forth from damp faces. The game proceeded in comparative silence broken only by grunted demands to the dealer and the chink of coins. Stakes were raised. Players fell by the wayside, much lighter of pocket than when they had started. Eventually, there were just two gladiators facing each other across the table, across the great pile of cash accumulated out of men's hope and greed. One was the generous young man who had ordered the brandy and the other was the tall thin fellow whose face still remained partially in shadow. An automaton of a man with a faint rasping voice as though his vocal chords had been corrupted through lack of use. He shifted easily in his chair with the lithe sinewy movements of a practised gambler. For a brief moment he allowed himself a rare smile. It was lupine and predatory. The young man failed to notice it.

All eyes in the room were now on these two and the considerable fortune that lay between them. The temperature seemed to soar in that stuffy chamber and the discomfited young man loosened his necktie as the sweat began to trickle down the side of his face in rivulets. The face of his opponent, however, was dry, the features relaxed while the eyes hinted at amusement.

'Now sir,' he said in that curious rasping tone of his. 'Why do we not make this wager a little more interesting?' The words were easy and simple but the implications were great.

The young man twitched with apprehension. He leaned forward and with some difficulty he managed to raise an eyebrow of enquiry.

'Let us double the stakes on this last hand,' his opponent explained. 'One hundred guineas.' There was a united murmur of surprise around the table. All eyes swivelled towards the young man whose lips quivered with some undecipherable emotions. Was it fear? Was it pleasure? Was it shock?

It was fear.

With a great effort of determination, the young man forced his recalcitrant lips into a smile. 'A fine wager,' he said, the words not quite matching the tone of his querulous voice. 'But,' he added swiftly, 'I am afraid I do not have sufficient funds about my person.'

His opponent smiled easily. 'I am prepared to take a note of credit. We are all gentlemen here. Our word is as good as our bond, surely.'

'Of course,' said the young man readily, stepping further on to the web. 'Of course.'

'Then you accept the wager? Double the stake. One hundred guineas?'

'Of course.'

A steely silence settled on the room as the cards were dealt. Even the wayward shadows settled down to a gentle meandering around the walls.

The skittish young man's hands shook as he took his hand and scrutinised the cards.

'Earlier this evening, my dear sir,' said his opponent, 'you toasted Lady Luck. I thank you for such a gesture for it would seem that she has landed on my shoulders.' With a smooth, eloquent gesture he placed his cards down on the table.

It was a royal flush.

'And your cards, sir?'

The young man's cards spluttered from his fingers on to the rough-grained wood of the table. They were pathetic impostors to the crown. He sat frozen to the spot, the model for a horrified statue.

'The game is mine,' said his opponent casually, racking over the coins and notes to his side of the table. 'And now if I can trouble you for that credit note which I trust you will honour within seven days.'

'Seven days,' the young man gasped, the voice just managing to scrabble its way out from a constricted larynx.

'As in the usual terms,' came the smooth reply. He passed over his card. The despondent loser cast an eye over it. It belonged to a Mr Eugene Trench who resided at an address in Islington.

A sheet of paper with pen and ink miraculously appeared on the table in front of the young man who was unusually less composed at this moment. The supplier of these items was the beaming landlord who was used to such occasions and prided himself on being prepared.

With quivering hand, the young man scribbled out the credit note to Mr Eugene Trench for one hundred... the hand faltered seriously here and several of the observers took an intake of breath.

'G-U-I-N-E-A-S,' prompted Mr Trench.

A spark, a demon spark of anger glowed momentarily in the young man's eyes and his free hand curved itself into a claw. But common sense and a kind of innate decorum won the day and the spark faded and the fingers relaxed. With a flourish, the young man signed his name: Jeremiah Throate Esq.

'And where do you reside, young sir?' enquired Mr Trench after retrieving the note and blowing on the paper to dry the ink.

'I have rooms at the Albany but my country seat is Throate Manor,' said the young man, pushing back his chair. 'And now gentlemen, I bid you good night.'

* * *

By the time he had reached the street, Jeremiah Throate had lost all his swagger and bravado and the saturnine qualities that he had exuded earlier in the evening had been overtaken by those of despair and anguish. 'What am I to do?' he wailed as he staggered forth in the dark midnight streets. His predicament was simple. He had lost all his money in that game, money that had accrued from his meagre allowance and from a successful series of card games – success that had given him the sense of invincibility that had proved false. Now, like an overeager railway engine, he had hit the buffers. The loss of all his money was bad enough, but now he owed a further hundred guineas to a practised card sharp. A hundred guineas which he did not possess.

His fingers scrabbled for his hip flask and leaning against the railings, he poured a liberal quantity of brandy down his throat. It made him choke for a moment but then strangely, as the alcohol seeped into his system, it helped to clear his head and steady his nerves. No problem is insurmountable if one was clever, he told himself. He had the brains, the courage, the cunning and the immorality to ensure that the problem could be eradicated. Indeed something must be done and something would be done; the only question was the nature of this something.

* * *

Approximately, at the same time as Jeremiah Throate was contemplating his future actions, his benighted father, having regained consciousness from his brief fainting fit was quivering beneath his bedsheets, too fearful to peep out to see whether the dreaded apparition had actually departed and faded into the moonlight. The words of the sprit echoed within his brain: 'Remember your special son in your will.' Of course he knew of the true import of this command and he would be more than happy to obey it. But he could not for the simple reason that he did not know where his special child was or if, indeed, it was still alive.

* * *

Back at The Saracen's Head, the gamblers had all departed homeward, lighter of pocket and weary of heart. All that is apart from Mr Eugene Trench who was savouring a final nightcap at a table close by the dying embers of the fire in the bar parlour. His companion was the well-upholstered landlord, Hubert Faddle, who rested a generous mug of porter on his equally generous stomach while his mouth formed itself into a crescent mooned grin.

'A very successful evening for you, my dear sir. A very successful and profitable evening,' he said raising his mug in a spirited toast.

Mr Trench, who was not given to displaying any kinds of emotion, merely nodded, but cast over a quantity of sovereigns to his host. 'For your pains.'

'Oh, I assure you there was no pain involved.' Faddle laughed at his own observation. 'Pleasure, more like. It is always a treat to watch you at work, my dear Mr Trench. The way you palm the cards is sheer poetry, a work of art.' Another thought occurred to him. 'You weave magic. That's what it is. Indeed you are a magician, a sorcerer with those pieces of pasteboard... and I am merely the sorcerer's apprentice.' Delighted with this allusion, he took a large gulp of porter.

'Your assistance is always most welcome,' said Trench. 'More so than usual tonight. It was pleasing to me to bring that arrogant puppy down a peg or two.'

'Do you think you'll get the rest of the money? The fellow looked somewhat distraught as he departed.'

'I suspect he'll go home to the family seat and beg for the cash from his rich papa. I am sure he has done it before. They all do. Dogs of that breed. If not, it will give me equal pleasure to set my men upon him. Rest assured, Mr Faddle, either way, Jeremiah Throate will pay.' He gazed into the fading coals and allowed himself a rare smile. The lips parted slightly and the eyes glittered more intently, but it was a cold thing, a bitter thing, a thing lacking in human kindness was Eugene Trench's smile.

CHAPTER THREE

It is one of the great failings of human nature that we cannot escape from our Unpleasant Past. It lies festering like some graveyard ghoul in those dark regions of the brain where our cheerful thoughts never care to wander for they have brisk, cheerful and uplifting business to be concerned about elsewhere. But our Unpleasant Past waits in the gloomy, craggy corners, in the slimy recesses, patiently humming some little discordant, self-satisfied tune while it bides its time until it is the moment to strike; the moment to remind us of how it was, how unpleasant, painful and demoralising it was. It only needs an image, a place, a word, a taste, a smell, a touch, a smile, a laugh, a blow or any of a thousand other trifles to prompt it into action. It only needs a very little thing.

Or, indeed, a dream.

For it is in dreams that the dark unconscious has full reign. In that sleeping time of night, our moral protectors are dormant, wrapped in their own comforting nightgowns and are at rest. At this time, past midnight, when the stars are at their fiercest in the heavens, our Unpleasant Past leaves its secret place and rides forth, unhindered by any restraint, to feed our minds with those bad memories.

Thus it was with Oliver Twist whose brain, during the daylight hours, is so full of business and love, optimism and anticipation, care and consideration, jollity and extravagance, enthusiasm and patience that the past, unpleasant though it was, and it was very unpleasant indeed, does not come to bother him. The shield of goodness which surrounds him is too strong for the darts of his Unpleasant Past. In the daytime, that is.

But at night, there is a different story to tell. The good Mr Twist, a young fellow of twenty eight years old, is placed on the rack of bad dreams and experiences again in the perspiring dark of his feverish bed the torments of his childhood. Out of the bedroom shadows come figures from his past, animated by imagination and fear, to taunt him. Here the fearful Bill Sikes is conjured up, apparently alive and just as vicious, his hand grasping for Oliver's neck. Oliver can see him, hear him, can smell and almost touch him. And then comes the dangling form of the hanged Fagin, dancing in sprightly fashion on the gallows as though he were part of a music hall troupe, his bright avaricious eyes, wide open and shining like two puddles caught in the moonlight.

On the occasions of these nocturnal visions, Oliver Twist would rise from his bed, drenched in perspiration, weak with fatigue and fearful to return to the uncharted regions of sleep in case the nightmare demons finally had their way with him. Thankfully such occasions are not frequent, but when they come they have a dual effect. They make him gloriously thankful to the Lord for the influence, beneficence and love of the recently deceased Mr Brownlow who rescued him from the dark world of Fagin and Bill Sikes; but they also rob him of energy and brightness of mind for a day or two, after which the memory of the night fears fades… until the next time

Oliver woke one morning bright and early, and despite emerging from a peaceful and dreamless slumber into that strange limbo state where sleep is retreating over one border while consciousness is forging ahead over the other, old apprehensions still disturbed the young fellow. As his eyes attempted to focus on the dark dressing gown hanging behind the door, in the half-light of the bedroom it seemed to manifest itself into the old sinner himself. The garment appeared to shimmer with movement and Oliver expected Fagin's gaunt, greedy face to loom out from the folds of the dressing gown collar, grinning maliciously. He blinked hard and the illusion disappeared as illusions do. And in its place was a mundane dressing gown.

Oliver's own innate mental strength allowed him, rather like the proverbial duck and water, to shake off these moments quickly without any ill effect. To dwell on them, he knew, would lead him down dark and dangerous pathways.

As his sharp razor smoothed his chin some five minutes later, Oliver had forgotten the sinister image of the dressing gown and was considering the prospect of breakfast, which he knew would be waiting for him when he made his way downstairs. The face that stared back at him in the shaving mirror was an attractive one with its firm set jaw, pale blue eyes and feathery blond hair. It was only his slightly crooked nose, a trifle too large for his slim features that robbed him of the appellation of 'handsome'. Although it has to be said that certain ladies considered this prominent feature the most pleasing aspect of his appearance.

His ablutions completed and dressed for the day, he descended to the dining room. Despite being a rising young lawyer in the firm of Gripwind and Biddle and secure in the comfortable inheritance left to him by his beloved benefactor, Mr Brownlow, Oliver did not engage an army of servants to rally to his beck and call. He was not only conscious of his penurious past but his natural modesty forbade such pampering notions. However he did employ the services of a housekeeper, Mrs Ada Clout. She was a demure twinkling angel of a woman in prospect but as sharp as a tack and ruthless as a lion when dealing with tradesmen. She cared for Oliver as if he had been her own son – the son she lost to diphtheria some thirty years before. Whatever time Oliver Twist entered the dining room in the morning, Mrs Clout, by some strange telepathic process, would be bringing in the coffee pot to be placed on the table as Oliver took his seat. She would then disappear and return in a trice with a plate of scrambled eggs and bacon just as her master was taking his first sip of coffee. And such was the case today.

'Lovely morning, sir,' she observed.

'It is,' said Oliver, a man of few words at this time of day.

Mrs Clout left her master to his victuals.

As Oliver devoured his breakfast, he took time to count his blessings. He knew he was a lucky man in so many ways. He had his health, his comfort and his career was flourishing. They were very pleased with him at Gripwind and Biddle where he was a junior partner. And indeed as the fulsome and barrel-shaped senior partner Horatio Gripwind was accustomed to observe – 'but not junior, for much longer, Master Twist, if I get my little way. A full blown partner is what you'll be, if I get my way, Master Twist'.

But Oliver had to admit, as he laid his cutlery down on an empty plate, there was something missing in his life. He wasn't quite sure what, but there was a little gap. The nearest definition he could supply for this missing segment was in the words 'excitement' and 'romance'. Things were too placid for him. After the turbulent seas of his Fagin days, his ship of life had become becalmed rather like the ancient mariner in Mr Coleridge's poem:

'As idle as a painted ship
Upon a painted ocean.'

Oliver wanted, indeed he felt he *needed* something dramatic to happen in his life.

Fate, it would seem, had the same idea.

* * *

Oliver Twist was sitting at his desk poring over some critical but very boring documents when there was a gentle tap at his door. Oliver not only recognised the tap, or to be more precise, the owner of the tap, the tapper himself if you like, but through experience and familiarity he could ascertain the mood and tone of the tap. On this occasion he deduced that it was apprehensive mixed with a tinge of guilt. The perpetrator of the taps was Jack Dawkins.

Oliver bade the tapper enter.

The door swung open and did indeed reveal the figure of Jack Dawkins, whom to Oliver would always be the Artful Dodger, that ragged companion of his youth when both boys were in the thrall of Fagin. Despite the weight of years removing the youthful bloom from his features and gaining a certain respectability, which caused him to behave – on the whole – as an upright law abiding citizen, there was still the air of the attractive rogue about Jack. After many years of not seeing each other, the two childhood comrades had been reunited earlier that year when Jack had sought out Oliver to help him with a spot of serious bother in which, with Dawkins-like aplomb, he had landed himself. With a different kind of aplomb but equally efficacious, Oliver had managed to extricate his old friend from the mire. Not only that but Oliver had taken it upon himself to assume the role of guardian for this now very vulnerable fellow, despite him being several years Jack's junior. Oliver had persuaded Messrs Gripwind and Biddle to employ his old acquaintance Jack Dawkins as his clerk – a rather grand title for what in reality was the role of dogsbody. Jack's remuneration was meagre but Oliver kindly offered to supplement it from his own salary. And then Oliver had set about educating the supposedly reformed reprobate in order that he might carry out his professional duties more effectively and with more accuracy.

As the months passed, Jack Dawkins had grown more respectable, more articulate and more literate, but Oliver knew that his old friend still harboured certain wayward inclinations, which were deeply ingrained within his character. It was part of his nature and Oliver knew that it was also part of the fellow's charm and he did not want to eliminate that altogether. Nevertheless, he was aware there would be occasions when the old Dodger would rise up, elbowing the smarter, tidier Dawkins out of the way, so that he could go on the rampage. From Jack's hunched position as he stood in the doorway now wearing that familiar guilty hangdog expression, Oliver deduced that this was likely to be one of those occasions.

'I am mightily sorry for attending work later than the appointed hour, my dear Oliver, but I find myself in rather unfortunate circumstances.' The voice was humble and hushed and coated with a thick layer of theatricality.

'And what unfortunate circumstances might they be?' asked Oliver Twist tartly.

'I've been thrown out of my lodgings.'

Oliver pursed his lips and allowed his eyes to roll a little in their sockets. 'And why is that?'

'Well, in simple terms…'

'Those are the best.'

'In simple terms: I am a little behind with my rent.'

Oliver knew that the Dodger was as practised in the art of litotes as well as hyperbole. In this case he was convinced that he was shrinking the truth rather than expanding upon it.

'By how much?'

'I owe nearly three months.'

'Nearly three months!' Oliver found that not only had he raised his voice but he had also raised himself from his desk into a standing position. 'Oh, Dodger,' he cried, lapsing into the old appellation, 'how did you let this happen? You have a regular, albeit modest, income here and are certainly more than financially capable of paying the rent required of you.'

'I just let it slip,' replied Jack lowering his head further in an approximation of shame. 'I suppose I was enjoying myself too much to relinquish my hard earned shekels for the privilege of laying my head in a dusty old room in a dingy old tenement. So, I spent the money on myself.'

'In what particular fashion?'

Jack gave a little shrug, but there was the hint of a twinkle in the eye and a suggestion of a smile hovering about his thin lips. 'Food, drink and a little gambling. Well, if the truth be known… a lot of gambling.'

Oliver Twist shook his head sadly and resumed his seat. 'Presumably you were warned of your eviction and yet ignored the warnings.'

The suggestion of a smile now manifested itself into a broad grin which Jack Dawkins flashed at his friend who received it with a stony glance. The grin vanished with the same speed at which it had appeared. 'You can read me like a book, Oliver.'

'A book that is read in the debtor's prison, no doubt,' snapped Oliver, not the least amused or beguiled by his friend's confession.

Oliver's cold stare caused the Dodger to wince. 'I'm mightily sorry, my dear Oliver. I have let you down. You, who snatched me from the clutches of the law and set about making an honest and respectable citizen of me.'

'I seem to have failed.'

Dodger shook his head violently from side to side. For a brief moment Oliver thought that he had been struck by some convulsive malady.

'No, no, do not say that,' cried Jack Dawkins and this time the emotion was genuine. 'I ain't stolen any money or done anything what is illegal. It's just I ain't paid my rent.'

On this point Oliver felt obliged to agree with him, although he maintained his stern mask of disapproval.

'I am heartily sorry, Oliver, my friend. Heartily sorry that I didn't cough up to the landlord, but more heartily sorry that I have let you down. Please, I beg you, give me another chance.'

Oliver sighed again. 'You are irresponsible, penniless and homeless…'

Jack nodded. 'That is a very accurate summation of the situation.'

Oliver turned towards the window where the bright morning sun was creating fine shafts of yellow light filled with myriad dancing particles of dust. He gazed at them as though fascinated by their errant and yet elegant rotations, while he pondered, turning thoughts over in his mind. At length, he swung round to face his repentant friend again.

'It seems to me that there is only one solution to the conundrum that you present me with Mr Dawkins,' he said formally as though he were addressing a jury. 'You will have to come and live under my roof where I can keep a weather eye on you.'

Oliver had hardly uttered these words before Jack Dawkins' eyes lit up like two bright coals set in a cheery fire. His mouth gaped open with delight and he took a step forward, raising his arms as though he was about to embrace his friend. Oliver froze his actions with a stern glance and a swift commanding raise of his hand. 'I do not do this out of charity, Mr Dawkins. There must be no more further episodes of falling by the wayside. I have a commodious basement in my house which with a little ingenuity and effort can be converted into comfortable quarters for you, for which you will pay the same rent as required by your previous landlord. And you will pay the said rent regularly and accurately. Is that understood?'

Jack Dawkins by now had transmogrified into a naughty school boy. He stood head bowed, each skeletal hand clutching the other before him, his voice hoarse with humility. 'It is understood,' he said.

Oliver's features relaxed a little. 'Do not let me down.'

Jack indulged once more in an orgy of head shaking.

Just at this moment there came a loud bang at the door. On this occasion Oliver had no time to determine the nature of the knock or indeed its owner before he burst into the room. He was a tall fellow with a large girth. Indeed the man's stomach was prodigious. His watch fob, instead of hanging down from its chain with ease and having the freedom to swing to and fro as it saw fit, was firmly lodged on a generous shelf produced by the material of the gentleman's waistcoat which was rucked into large folds because of the enormity of flesh pressing against it. As he moved, the shiny buttons on the aforementioned garment rippled erratically as though they were in danger of being forced from their moorings and would spin into space at any moment. This rotund gentleman was Horatio Gripwind, the senior partner in the firm of Gripwind and Biddle.

The enormous appetite for food and drink which was the cause of the gentleman's size had made investments in his facial features also. He was the owner of a very round face that seemed not to have in its possession a neck of any kind, merely a large fold of flesh which wobbled down from his prodigious chin on to his chest.

His complexion followed accurately the dictionary definition of the word 'ruddy' and his golden pince nez rested on a thick bulbous nose reminiscent of a fine beef sausage. The exception to these physical excesses were Horatio Gripwind's eyes, which were small, like tiny blue buttons, but they were eyes that twinkled with good nature, kindness and fierce intelligence.

He stood on the threshold of the room, the exertion of leaving his own domain upstairs and journeying to Oliver's office having produced a thin sheen of perspiration on his face and a wheezy shortness of breath.

'Ah, Master Twist, I am sorry to interrupt. I know you are hard at work on those infernal, and may I say, eternal Mallory papers, but...' He paused having espied Jack Dawkins, who had slid to the side of the room to make himself less conspicuous. 'Ah, Dawkins. A little late this morning I observed.'

Jack nodded and tried to apologise for his tardiness, but his voice failed him. Instead he edged his way further back until he was up against the wall.

'As I was saying,' continued Gripwind, swinging his attention back to Oliver, 'the Mallory business is important but we have this morning received a communication from Sir Ebenezer Throate, one of our most treasured and noble clients. He wishes to make certain alterations to his financial matters and I thought this was an ideal opportunity for you, Master Twist, to have some experience of dealing with the landed gentry. The fact is Sir Ebenezer does not come up to town these days and so it means that someone will have to travel to Throate Manor, his family seat, to conduct the business.' Gripwind bestowed one of his beaming benevolent smiles on his young junior partner. 'And as you are rather fleeter of foot than either I or Mister Biddle it naturally falls to you to attend to the matter. And so, Master Twist, abandon your current concerns - for this relief much thanks, eh? - and make preparations to travel to Throate Manor in the county of Surrey.'

CHAPTER FOUR

The sun rose in the azure sky, establishing its dominance, illuminating cobwebs, exposing imperfections and brandishing the hope of a new beginning for those in desperate need of one.

By mid-morning the promenade at Brighton was already a kaleidoscope of colour with ladies in dazzling summer dresses, bright parasols twirling recklessly in the growing heat; gentlemen in gaily striped blazers and cream flannels with straw boaters tipped precariously at a jaunty angle; the various tradesmen selling their wares from pies to whelks to various garish sweet confections; and little boys in sailor suits haring in front of their parents in search of excitement and mischief. There was, however, one solitary figure who was not an integral part of this colourful animated pageant, this vibrant whirligig of humanity. He was a young man, soberly dressed and static, leaning on the balustrade staring out to sea, his gaze reaching beyond the throng of people on the beach, the row of bathing huts and the smattering of early bathers in colourful costumes playing a chasing game with the waves. It was on the far horizon where the sky melted into the water that his eyes were focused, his thin but handsome face set in a melancholic mask. He was troubled and the trouble was that he could not fathom any reason why he should be troubled. He carried around with him a permanent cloud of depression, which constantly manifested itself in minor afflictions. At the moment it was a heavy cold which had plagued him for weeks and seemed to be immune to physic, exercise, early bedtimes and now, good sea air. In the past it had been inexplicable aches, insomnia, strange rashes, blinding headaches, inflammations, chronic stomach cramps, bowel disorders and boils.

Perhaps, somewhere out there, beyond that line where the water ends and the sky begins lay the answer. Certainly doctors could not explain his disorders. He viewed these various afflictions rather like applicants for a situation to be filled. They waited in some outer office until the current candidate had run his course and then it was another's opportunity to discomfort him. The sore throat has gone so now it is the turn of lumbago to be followed by shingles. But none of these fellows had been summoned. They turned up of their own volition and barged their way into his life without any invitation.

One doctor suggested that it was something within him, installed in his mind, that was prompting these illnesses. He had been informed that these complaints were a manifestation of some deep distress that he was keeping hidden even from himself. 'The mind is both a sensitive and powerful organ and controls our well-being and our lives,' said the doctor. 'If it wants us to go blind or see snakes crawling out of the wall then we will lose our sight or perceive those slimy reptiles. It is as simple and as complicated as that.' The medic smiled sympathetically. 'That will be two guineas,' he added, the smile broadening.

The young man had considered this diagnosis seriously. He had begun his life anonymously, knowing neither parent and never experiencing the love and tender comfort that a caring home life could give. He was the typical 'workhouse brat' who in his early years had never experienced anything but disdain, but there were thousands of those unfortunates around and they didn't seem to be the prey of myriad disorders. But nevertheless this young man possessed a determined and ambitious streak which drove him on to 'better himself' until he had been seduced by the demon gambling – the short cut to comfortable living or so he had thought. It had been the deceptive slide to penury and ruin. If he had not metaphorically been scooped out of the gutter by Sir Ebenezer Throate who knows where he would have ended up. A permanent skivvy at The Saracens Head no doubt. But Sir Ebenezer had taken an immediate liking to the young man and after a very brief acquaintance the baronet had offered him the post of private secretary with a very pleasing salary. And so Roger Lightwood, orphan, spawn of the workhouse, had taken up residence at Throate Manor. He had a comfortable home at last and the entry to all the amenities and luxuries one could ever wish for. He even developed a fondness for the old man, pompous and self-obsessed though he was. For the first time in his life he had dared to be happy. And then like a biblical plague, the illnesses began. It was a bad back at first – 'lumbago' the local quack called it – and then it was the croup – 'the croup' the local quack called it – and then... Well, Roger had lost track now. And sometime soon it would be Death (it's Death, the quack would call it); and then the whole thing would be over. He bit his lip with annoyance. He shouldn't be so morbid. He had a great deal to be thankful for – if only he could persuade his mind to accept that and stop presenting him with one incapacity after another.

He sneezed. It was as though he had received a reply.

Despite the warmth of the day, he shivered. Time for a warming drink and another powder for my cold, he thought. There was a little café near his hotel which he had frequented on a number of occasions and felt comfortable there. He would repair there for a café noir and take his medication.

Turning away from the sea he mingled with the throng of promenaders as he made his way to the café. He crossed the road and moved into the shadows which seemed to please him more than the bright, glaring sunshine. As he mounted the pavement with more alacrity than he had planned, he bumped into a young lady with such force that she staggered backwards in surprise.

'I am most awfully sorry,' said Roger, raising his hat.

The young lady was shocked but not angry. She smiled sweetly in response to Roger's apology but before she was able to reply, her eyelids fluttered erratically and she collapsed to the ground.

Roger was horrified. What had he done?

'Is she a dead 'un?' asked a burly passer-by with more a note of relish than concern in his voice.

Roger knelt by the young lady as a small chattering crowd swarmed around him. He took her pulse and – heavens be praised - there was one. Roger cradled her head and stroked her cheek and as he did so her eyes opened slowly. For a moment the mist of unconscious befogged her memory and then with a little gasp she sat upright. This dramatic movement brought a muted round of applause from the crowd who then began to drift away, the drama now being over, disappointed perhaps that it had resulted in a happy ending rather than a tragedy.

'I am so terribly sorry,' the young lady said irrationally.

'It is I who am sorry. It was very clumsy of me, bumping into you in such an oafish fashion. Do you feel strong enough to stand?'

'I think so.' And with the young man's assistance she rose to her feet. She smiled in triumph. 'There now,' she said straightening her skirt. 'I'm fine.'

'You look at little pale. Are you sure you do not need medical assistance?'

'No, no. I am fully recovered, thank you.'

It was at this point that Roger Lightwood first realised how pretty the girl was. She had delicate doll-like features, smooth, perfect and wonderfully balanced with a pair of light blue eyes which sparkled brightly. The sight of such delicate beauty unnerved him. He had never spoken to such an attractive creature before, let alone knocked one down and then helped her to her feet. For a moment he stood before the girl in a state of suspended animation, his mouth ready to open and speak but held in frozen motion by her enchanting gaze. There was no anger, irritation or a sense of blame in her expression. She just looked at him sweetly with a hint of enquiry in those lustrous eyes.

As no comment appeared to be forthcoming, the young lady smiled one more and said, 'I must be on my way or I shall be late.'

As she made to move past him, something sparked within Roger Lightwood's soul and very gently and cautiously he barred her way. 'Please, I beg of you, let me accompany you to your destination so that I may be assured that you suffered no ill effects from your fall.'

She lowered her lashes and grinned. 'I assure you I am perfectly all right, but if you wish you may come along with me. I have not far to go. To the Royal Court Hotel.'

Roger nodded eagerly. 'I know it.'

The two young people fell in step with each other.

'Are you in Brighton on holiday?' asked Roger, having some difficulty keeping up the brisk pace of his companion.

'In a manner of speaking. I am the companion to Lady Wilhelmina Whitestone who is staying here for a few days for the sea air. However, she has yet to venture from her room. It is either too bright, too warm, too still or too windy.'

'A difficult lady to please.'

'Impossible.'

They both laughed.

'I am Roger Lightwood. Whom do I have the pleasure...?'

'Ah, here we are,' cried the girl, rushing forward towards the carpeted steps of the imposing hotel. 'Thank you for your kindness,' she said turning to him with a smile. 'As you can see I am fully recovered. I must go now and attend to my mistress, Lady Whitestone.'

And then with a cheery wave, she vanished into the whirl of the revolving door.

It had all happened so quickly that Roger had once again been struck dumb and immobile. She had come into his life without warning and had left it in the same fashion. He didn't even know her name. However there were two things he was conscious of: that he was in love with this delightful creature and that his cold had left him altogether.

CHAPTER FIVE

Matthew Varney was just completing his morning ablutions as the sun rose over the canopy of a busy London reaching its noon time high. As usual Varney had been late to bed, very late to bed. As he had climbed the stairs to his shabby apartment, the morning light was already beginning to streak the sky and street sweepers were preparing to brandish their brushes in readiness for another day of drudgery along the thoroughfares of the city. Tired as he was, he had slept badly. The night had not been good for him. His run of bad luck had extended itself further. More losses. More debt. More threats. More misery. As the razor dragged over his recalcitrant whiskers, he contemplated the possibility of escaping London into the country, somewhere deep and rural, somewhere anonymous, where no one knew him and where those to whom he owed money could not find him.

As he struggled into his grubby shirt he mused on the possible benefits of such a move. There would still be gambling out there in the pastoral hinterland and although the stakes would hardly be very high, he would have no problems running rings around his opponents, inbred yokels who thought that the moon was made of cheese. For the first time in many days, he managed a weak smile. This could be his answer. His salvation. Perhaps he should pack and leave today. Why hesitate?

The decision was made. The sense of it was overwhelming as was the realisation that if he stayed disaster would certainly strike. In a hurried and desperate fashion he began to grab what few possessions he had and stuff them into a canvas bag in preparation for his swift departure when there was a knock at the door. It shattered the silence and pierced his heart. He froze with fear. He never had visitors. He had no family, friends nor acquaintances. Such encumbrances were a hindrance. The only cause a person or persons would have to knock on his door would be to collect money owed to them. Money that he did not have.

The knock came again. It was brutish and loud and the door shook with the force of it. It wasn't the landlord for he had a key and entered without ceremony. It was no doubt one of the legion to whom he owed a gambling debt.

They had found out his lair.

The small knot of fear inside him that had been instigated by the first knock on his door developed into a thick bowline knot. It inflated his stomach and forced his heart to beat faster than a racing engine. On instinct he ran to the window and threw it open and gazed out. A panorama of slated canopies and drunken chimney pots spread out before him like vast uneven carpet. If he clambered out and dropped down to the roof below perhaps he could effect his escape that way, gradually scrambling from rooftop to rooftop and thus eventually to the street and safety.

There was no time to ponder the practicalities of such a plan: it was his only option. He pulled a rickety chair to the window, clambered on to it and was about to put one leg over the sill when there was an almighty explosion and groaning of splintering wood as door of his room burst open. It swung violently to one side and came to rest at an angle, the top pair of hinges having come completely adrift from the frame. On the threshold were two swarthy characters, short but bulky. Their faces had been stolen from a pair of gargoyles. One carried a cudgel, the other an iron bar. Varney had never seen these creatures before and indeed he wished that he was not seeing them now. Their mean spirited scowls and small belligerent eyes told him they were men of neither reason nor compromise. Behind this ugly couple he observed another figure, tall and gaunt with a grey face and dark piercing glance. This was a face he did know. It belonged to a man he loathed and feared – feared far more than his grisly companions.

Varney took in this tableau in an instant and then quickly returned to his task of leaving the room by the window. Now there was an even more desperate need to escape. But before he could launch himself on to the roof below, the two burly intruders had grabbed his arms and hauled him like a sack of grain, back into the room where they dumped him with some force on to the floor.

He gave a cry. Whether it was of pain or fear not even Varney himself could be certain.

The tall thin man entered the room and gazed down upon the wretch Varney. He loured over him like the very Devil himself.

'I am so sorry to interrupt your morning constitutional, Mr Varney,' he said in his strange rasping fashion, 'but I call on a matter of business. Urgent business.'

'You'll get your money, Mr Trench,' replied Varney, his voice as well as his limbs shaking in terror.

Eugene Trench allowed himself a small false chuckle. It was purely for effect; there really was no humour in the situation at all. And besides Mr Trench had no time for humour, it was a folly and a waste of time.

'Please give me a few more days,' begged Varney, scrabbling into a sitting position.

'It is the usual bleat that I have heard from you on numerous occasions. Over the last three months you have given me your oath many times to pay your debt but you have failed. You have lied, cheated and to be frank sir, you have severely incommoded me.'

'Just a few more days. That is all I ask.'

Trench shook his head. 'Search him,' he snapped, addressing his vicious minions. They obeyed, tearing and wrenching at Varney's clothing until they had taken everything that was about his person: a cheap pocket watch, a pack of cards, a voluminous and heavily stained paisley handkerchief and a small purse that contained a few coins of meagre value.

'You miserable dog,' sneered Trench, a faint flush suffusing his ashen features. 'There is nothing for me at all.'

'Just a few more days,' repeated Varney, his voice now reduced to a squeak. 'I promise I'll repay you everything.'

Trench sighed and turned away from Varney and addressed his companions. 'Kill him,' he said.

Varney felt the first blow, one made by the cudgel before the everlasting darkness of death took him. The second blow made by the iron bar smashed his skull so violently that parts of his brain began to dribble out on to the threadbare carpet.

Trench scribbled a few words on a sheet of paper and then laid it on the dead body.

CHAPTER SIX

'This is a bit of an adventure ain't… er…isn't it, eh, Oliver?'

Jack Dawkins looked out of the coach window at the lush Surrey countryside as it rolled by, providing a remarkable green backdrop to this final portion of the journey from London. They were now rocking along in Sir Ebenezer Throate's own private coach which had collected them from The Rising Sun, the main coaching inn in the quaint town of Dorking in the edge of the Surrey hills.

This trip was not Mr Oliver Twist's notion of 'a bit of adventure'. He perceived it as an inconvenient interruption to his normal work back at the office in the City. Having to travel into the depths of the country to draw up a client's will, stay the night in his draughty old house – Mr Gripwind had warned him of the errant gusts, 'Take a thick nightgown and several scarves m'boy' - and then spend another morning rocking and juddering in a coach back to London was no adventure. It was a tedious enterprise. Why couldn't Sir Ebenezer Throate come up to town himself and visit our offices, Oliver mused, then it would only take an hour or two at the most to set the matter right. Still he was the junior in the firm and if someone has to undertake this 'adventure' as Jack put it, then it had to be him.

Oliver smiled indulgently at his companion. 'I suppose anything that takes us away from the familiar is a bit of an adventure,' he said with admirable restraint.

Jack rubbed his hands together with pleasure. 'Never been inside a big manor house before. It'll be like parading around in Buckingham Palace.'

Oliver chuckled. 'Not quite,' he said softly, almost to himself. He glanced at his pocket watch and sighed. He estimated there was at least another half an hour's journey to go before they reached their destination.

At last Throate Manor finally hove into view. Even Jack, who, leaning out of the coach window in child-like anticipation and spied the Manor first, could see that it was not the most elegant of buildings. It looked to him as though it had been designed by a child with a deficient attention span. It stood bold, brash and ugly on the horizon, surrounded by the generous and lush sweep of uninhabited countryside.

'There she blows, cap'n,' said Jack, affecting a nautical tone. Oliver peered out of the window at his side of the coach and caught his first sight of the country seat of Sir Ebenezer Throate glistening in the late afternoon sun.

Within ten minutes the coach had driven up the long winding drive to the front entrance. Here the weary travellers were met by a tall imposing figure of funereal appearance who introduced himself as Bulstrode the butler.

Jack bowed and then held out his hand. 'Charmed I'm sure,' he said in a voice that was not quite his own.

Bulstrode ignored the gesture. 'Allow me to show you to your rooms, gentlemen, and then Sir Ebenezer will be happy to see you in the orangery.'

'Thank you,' said Oliver.

A liveried youth appeared from nowhere and proceeded to carry the luggage from the coach ahead of them as Bulstrode led them into the house.

As they progressed through the great hall, up the broad curved staircase and along a baffling series of corridors, Jack Dawkins' mouth remained open in wonder at the sumptuous furnishings, the shiny vases of oriental origin and impressive works of art adorning the walls. Something of the old Dodger stirred within him. Here was rich pickings indeed. A choice selection of some of these knick-knacks in his possession and he would never want again. His little horned alter ego concocted a nefarious plan but the new reformed Jack quickly if not easily squashed it.

Oliver, ignorant of his companion's moral tussle, was gazing with equal admiration at the sumptuous dressing of this eccentric house. Inherited wealth was a magical thing to him. Riches conjured out of thin air. While the lot of mankind was to struggle and scrape, to sweat and labour to attain whatever livelihood and possessions their industry, talent and abilities were able to obtain and sustain, the landed gentry sat back, held out their hands and great wealth, comfort and property were bestowed upon them without exercising a muscle, engaging a brain cell (if they had one) or carrying out any deserving action. It did not make Oliver so much angry as sad – sad that the scales of fortune, in both senses of the word, were so unfairly balanced.

Some thirty minutes later, having swilled away the grime of the journey and donned a fresh collar, Oliver, accompanied by Jack Dawkins, was led by Bulstrode back down the same baffling series of corridors to the great hallway once more and thence to the orangery.

As they approached, Oliver observed two figures, glimpsed through the fine tracery of foliage which splayed against the glass of the chamber. One, seated on a large chair, was Sir Ebenezer. He recognised him from Mr Gripwind's description: a corpulent man of pale complexion, save for the raspberry qualities of his nose, the possessor of a pair bulging rheumy eyes, with the round summit of a bald head emerging through the clouds of unruly white hair. The description had an artist's accuracy. The other occupant of the orangery was a tall, dark-haired man with sharp features and saturnine looks. He was pacing to and fro in an angry, agitated manner. Both men were conversing with raised voices. Oliver could not hear the specifics of the conversation but it was being carried out with much heat.

Observing this spectacle, Bulstrode seemed for a moment

discomfited. On reaching the entrance to the orangery he halted and turned deferentially to Oliver. 'If you would care to wait here, sir,' he said in his usual stoical manner, 'I will ascertain whether Sir Ebenezer is ready to receive you now.'

Oliver nodded in agreement.

Jack who had also noted the altercation taking place, nudged Oliver and rolled his eyes while allowing himself a little smirk. Oliver did not respond.

Bulstrode knocked discreetly on the door and entered. As he did so, Sir Ebenezer could be plainly heard bellowing, 'No, sir. How many more times? Not again. No, sir!'

And then the door was closed and muffled sounds only could be perceived.

'Quite a little hullaballoo in there, Oliver,' said Jack with some pleasure. 'So, not everything is rosy in paradise, eh?'

'So it would seem,' replied Oliver, straining his ears to catch the gist. However, Bulstrode's intrusion appeared to burst the balloon of this particular altercation and with a roar of frustration, the saturnine young man burst from the room, pushing past Oliver with a gruff, 'Out of my way, sir.' He strode off down the corridor as though he were competing in some form of demonic walking race.

There was further exchange of raised eyebrows between the two friends.

'A bird with severely ruffled plumage there, my dear,' observed Jack with a satisfied grin. He enjoyed the spectacle of the higher orders being discomfited.

Bulstrode returned, still serene and stoic, as though unaware that any disconcerting ripples had disturbed the placid surface of life at Throate Manor.

'Sir Ebenezer will see you now, gentlemen,' he said, beckoning us to enter the orangery.

His lordship bade them take seats close to him.

'I am indulging in my first brandy and soda of the evening. Would you gentlemen care to join me?'

Jack nodded vigorously but Oliver declined. 'Later perhaps, after we have discussed business,' he said, respectfully.

'Keeping a clear head, eh? Well, I am sure you're wise to do so but the days when I weighed wisdom against intoxication are over. Now I choose the latter every the time.' He chuckled grimly at his own aphorism.

Bulstrode supplied Jack with a drink and then replenished Sir Ebenezer's glass liberally with brandy and a mean whisper of soda.

Sir Ebenezer took a large gulp and then relaxed back in his chair. 'So,' he said expansively, his raspberry nose twitching, 'you are the bright young man at Gripwind and Biddle.'

'Modesty forbids that I claim such a title, sir, but I am the junior partner there and measured against my superiors I am young.'

The baronet chuckled. 'A discreet answer. I like you, Twist. I like you already.' With this he gave a studied glance at Jack Dawkins. 'This is a most delicate and private business, perhaps it would be well if we conducted it alone.'

Jack frowned but made as if to rise. Oliver halted him with a small eloquent gesture of his hand. 'Mr Dawkins is my clerk and is privy to all my legal affairs. You can rely on his discretion.' As he was saying these words, Oliver Twist threw up a brief prayer to Heaven requesting that this very suspect statement proved to be correct.

Sir Ebenezer paused a moment, took another sip of brandy and then nodded in acceptance of Oliver's claim. 'Very well. Let us begin. Let me impress upon you that what I am about to discuss with you is a very private and personal matter and I rely on you – on you both - to treat it with discretion.'

'Of course,' said Oliver.

'Definitely,' agreed Jack cheerily.

'Very well. As you know I wish to make some alterations to my will…'

Oliver withdrew several sheets of parchment from the case he was carrying and spread them out on his knee. 'I have your original Last Will and Testament here, completed just under five years ago. I have studied it closely.'

'It was composed in rather a hurry. I had a severe bout of

pneumonia at the time and it was feared – or hoped by some – that I would be carried off very shortly. But I rallied. I have since had time to consider the matter with more care.'

Oliver nodded and waited for the old baronet to continue.

'A wise move,' chipped in Jack but his observation was ignored by the two men.

'I wish to make a considerable allowance for my younger son.'

Oliver frowned and glanced at the document on his knee. 'As I recall, you have already willed the bulk of your estate to your son.'

Sir Ebenezer's eyes narrowed and his lips pursed. 'And they said you were a bright young man. Take note of my words, Mr Twist. My *younger* son.'

'But you have only one son, Mr Jeremiah Throate, whom I believe we had the… occasion to see just now.'

'This is where we move into delicate territory, Mr Twist. Jeremiah is not my only son. He is my legitimate son, the son of my wife and I. However, I have another son. The result of a foolish lapse some twenty five years ago. A brief encounter with a serving girl when drink and passion overtook me. Moments of madness can have dire consequences. The girl fell pregnant…'

Sir Ebenezer turned away and seemed to be studying the intricate fronds of one of the great palms at the rear of the chamber.

Oliver knew to wait. It would be inappropriate to either interrupt or prompt his client. With a severe shake of the head, he indicated as much to Jack who appeared to be on the verge of interrogating the baronet.

When Sir Ebenezer turned to face them once more, his eyes were moist with tears.

'I am ashamed to say that I behaved abominably. I paid the girl off and effectively washed my hands of her and her… our offspring. I later learned that she gave birth to a boy whom she deposited with some charitable institution in the city. I never saw her again and I never saw my son. Mr Twist, I cannot tell you how guilt has wracked and haunted me all these years, to cast both the girl and my son out on to the stormy sea of life, taking no effort to support them, care for them. I cannot tell you …'

Sir Ebenezer's voice faded. He shifted awkwardly in his seat again and another inspection of one of the palms was taken. Oliver observed that the baronet's shoulders rose and fell with repressed sobbing. And then all at once the old man seemed to pull himself together. He wiped his ripe bulbous nose with a large silk handkerchief and continued in a more robust fashion.

'However, now I feel strangely compelled…' The image of the apparition that made nocturnal visits to his bedroom flashed upon his inner eye and his mouth dried as a consequence. Brandy was administered, allowing him to continue. 'I hope it is not too late to make some amends to the boy by providing for him in my will.'

'That is perfectly possible,' said Oliver.

Sir Ebenezer gave Oliver a sour smile. 'It is not so easy as that, Mr Twist. If only it were. You see I have no idea where or who my son is. Therefore I am asking you to find him. To bring him to me.'

'Cor blimey,' cried Jack Dawkins involuntarily before his jaw dropped with the weight of his surprise.

'But sir,' responded Oliver in a tone of gentle protest, 'I am a lawyer not a policeman. Surely it is the official police whom you need to engage in this matter.'

'You really think I could go to the police with my dilemma?' In a desperate act of theatricality, Sir Ebenezer gazed around the room as though he were in frantic search of something. 'Where, oh where,' he cried with more than a note of anger in his voice, 'is that smart young man from Gripwind and Biddle whom I was promised would visit me.'

'Oh, he is here,' said Jack, pointing at Oliver. 'Mr Twist is a bright 'un all right.'

'Then, sir,' the baronet said to Oliver as though it was he who had made the claim, 'you will realise that I cannot go to the police or engage a detective of the private sort and risk exposure. Above all the name of the Throate family must remain untainted and respected. I know I can trust the old firm of Gripwind and Biddle who have handled the family's business for generations. Find the boy, sir, and bring him to me.'

Oliver was momentarily struck dumb by this unexpected request. This order. As a representative of Gripwind and Biddle, he knew he could not refuse this commission from one of its most important of clients. 'As you wish, sir. I will do what I can,' he replied at length with feigned enthusiasm, his soul already heavy with the weight of such a responsibility.

CHAPTER SEVEN

'My answer is the same as your father's: no.' Lady Amelia Throate gazed at her son over the folds of her fan with more than a modicum of distaste. In fact she despised the boy. She had disliked him as an infant and as his avaricious, selfish character formed, she had grown more and more disgusted by her own offspring, but she had been prepared to succour and cosset him because she was aware of her responsibilities: she was his mother and, God help her, he was the heir to the Throate estate. But now he was fully grown and all those embryonic malevolent aspects of his character had reached an ugly maturity and in her eyes he had become a monster. In return he had demonstrated no respect or affection for either of his parents, using his father solely as a source of cash to fund his obsession with the turn of a card or the throw of a dice. Now he was badgering her in her own boudoir for more money.

'If you had your way you would bleed this family dry to pay off your gambling debts and we should end up in the bankruptcy courts,' she said coolly.

Jeremiah Throate began pacing again. It was the only outlet for his agitation. He knew that while he could rant at his father, he must at all costs present a civilised and reasonable front to his mother. 'I will end up in court or worse if I do not pay this money. Mother, you cannot allow such things to happen to me,' he said with a soft passion, his voice hardly stronger than a whisper.

'You are mistaken. It seems that I can. Perhaps it will teach you a lesson.'

'It may well be a lesson from which I am unable to benefit.'

'What can you mean by that, pray?'

Jeremiah saw this query as a small chink in her armour. She was intrigued, a little uncertain. Now was the time to strike. He rushed to her side and knelt down by her. 'Mother, the man to whom I owe this money is an unscrupulous fellow. A blackguard. If I do not pay him the hundred guineas, he will not take me to court. He will merely take my life.'

Lady Amelia chuckled. 'What nonsense. Now you bring a penny dreadful melodrama into play in order to persuade me to finance your shabby pastime.'

'Mother, it is the truth!'

He raised his voice for the first time and Lady Amelia stiffened with anger.

'I have heard enough. You have your allowance. You must live on that or gain employment to subsidise your passion for the cards. You will not get another penny from either your father or I as long as we are alive. When we are dead the estate will be yours and then you will be at liberty to squander that away to your heart's content.'

Her cool and implacable obstinacy to his pleas caused Jeremiah Throate's temper to snap. A wave of desperation crashed over him and he grabbed hold of his mother's arms and shook her violently.

'The man will kill me. Do you hear me? Kill me. Kill your son. You must help me.'

Far from being frightened or intimidated by this ferocious and violent outburst, Lady Amelia's anger rose to the same level as her son's. Her eyes blazed and her body stiffened. With a determined gesture she thrust him from her and smote him across the face with her fan.

'How dare you! How dare you assault me! You are nothing more than a common ruffian. A guttersnipe with no morals. If this man is bent on killing you, then I say, let him do it. The world will be a sweeter place without you in it. You are my son, I know, but I feel no connection to you, no warmth, no love. You are an alien creature to me. You have long since smothered any maternal feelings within me by your cruel thoughtless actions and disregard for the sensibilities and honour of your family. We only see you now when you need money. Well, no more will you get forty pieces of silver from me or your father. Now go! Leave this house. You are no longer welcome here.'

With these words, Lady Amelia Throate rose regally from her chair and strode from the room.

For some moments her son stood as though petrified by her fierce words and then breaking this spell he strode to the window and gazed out at the green parkland beyond, seeing nothing but dark clouds of despair. He shuddered with emotion at the thought of what might, what would happen to him.

Was this really the end?

Trench would seek him out wherever he tried to hide. And when he found him…

Was there no answer? No reprieve?

If only his father would take it upon himself to meet his maker.

If only.

He turned slowly and gazed at his mother's sumptuous bedchamber and then suddenly something caught his attention. Like a jackdaw, his eyes focused on the bright object. Sitting on the dressing table, shining in the candlelight was a silver box; trailing out of it on to the tapestry cover was the end of a necklace. A lustrous pearl necklace.

CHAPTER EIGHT

The day was dwindling and the sky darkened into a soft purple dusk. The candlelight in the orangery cast eerie shadows amongst the palms as though strange jungle beasts were lurking there ready, with the flicker of a flame, to pounce.

Reluctantly having accepted Sir Ebenezer's mission to discover the whereabouts of his illegitimate offspring, Oliver Twist had extracted a notebook from his document satchel and was trying to ascertain as many facts as he could regarding the case in order to aid him in this needle in a haystack affair.

Sir Ebenezer was reluctant and vague. Oliver remembered Fagin using an expression 'like pulling hen's teeth' in relation to trying to extract information from an unwilling source. To a young boy this seemed a nonsensical and rather bizarre simile. After all hens do not possess teeth and therefore the task was an impossible one. But now Oliver knew exactly what the old scoundrel meant.

'Let's start again, sir,' said Oliver with a sigh. 'Exactly what year was the child born?'

'As I told you,' replied the baronet, crustily, 'about twenty-five years ago.' In truth it wasn't that he could not be accurate as to details but he was both embarrassed and ashamed to be discussing the matter with a stranger, a young man who was not much older than the son he was desirous to locate. A man of his class and breeding did not expose one's private life with all its peccadilloes to the lower orders.

Oliver sighed again and realised that the only way to progress was to be bold and forthright. He took a deep breath and addressed his client in a stern confident manner. 'Sir Ebenezer, the task you have set me is a difficult and onerous one and the only chance I have in succeeding is if I have detailed and accurate information to work upon. 'About' twenty five years will not do. I need specifics and a great deal of them. You must give me as much information as you possess concerning this matter. Either that or the venture is doomed to failure.'

It took a great effort on Jack Dawkins' part not to burst into a round of spontaneous applause. However he managed to contain himself thus far, but he did utter the words, 'He's right, Sir Ebenezer' in a wheezy undertone.

For a brief moment Sir Ebenezer's face moulded itself into a mask of great indignation. He was not used to being spoken to in such a challenging manner but then common sense overruled his petty aristocratic sensibilities. His features softened and he gave a nod of submission. 'Very well,' he said, gazing at his empty brandy glass like a child whose favourite toy has just broken. 'If you would be so kind as to replenish my glass, I'll tell you all you need to know. At least all that I am able.'

Before Oliver could move a muscle, Jack Dawkins was on his feet and had snatched the brandy bottle from the nearby table. With the swift and nimble action of a practised pickpocket, he splashed a generous quantity into Sir Ebenezer's glass.

'Now, sir,' said Oliver, once the baronet was sitting back in his chair, cradling his glass of brandy, 'exactly what year was your second son born?'

'1832.'

'Do you know the date?'

Sir Ebenezer shook his head. 'Not the exact birth date but I believe it was August.'

Oliver noted these details down in his notebook.

What was the mother's name?'

'Her name was Louise Clerihew.' He said the name warmly and the craggy old features softened for an instant as he recalled the girl, the slight frame, the tumbling chestnut hair, the simple but kind eyes and the beguiling smile. And then she faded like a figure disappearing into the mist on an autumn day. Soon there was just empty greyness and a dull ache in his heart.

'And she surrendered the child up to…'

'An orphanage in Battersea. Tranton House, I believe it was called. She left the child on the doorstep with a note begging them to look after the baby. She wrote to me to inform me of the fact.' He delivered this information as though he were chewing on a tough, indigestible bit of beef.

'You have the letter? The handwriting could be of help.'

'I do not, sir. I burnt it on receipt.'

'Did the mother name the child?'

'If she did, she did not impart that information to me. She wrote that it was a healthy child, a boy and that was all.'

'No mention of the colour of its eyes or any other distinguishing feature.'

'None.' And then the old man hesitated. 'She did write that… that he was his father's child.'

'What did you understand she meant by that?'

Sir Ebenezer gave a mild shrug. 'I suppose she meant it looked somewhat like me, but how a mewling blob can look like anyone at that age is beyond me.'

Oliver Twist nodded. His client was completely unaware how emotionally unsettled Oliver was by the story he was unravelling. It bore such similarities to his own history – unmarried mother, child left in care of disinterested strangers… That word 'care' had many interpretations but for a child in that situation they were all dark, unpleasant ones.

'And you have no idea what became of the child or the mother.'

Sir Ebenezer shook his head. 'None.'

'Over the intervening years has anyone contacted you claiming to be either the mother or your child?'

The words 'has anyone contacted you' sent a chill running up the curved spine of the old aristocrat. He certainly had no intention of revealing the details of his nocturnal visitations in case he was considered insane. He took another gulp of brandy to cover his nerves.

'No,' he said at length.

Oliver gazed at the scant notes which failed to fill a page in his small notebook. There was hardly sufficient material there to weave a pair of gloves for a mouse let alone discover the whereabouts of a long lost son and heir to the Throate fortune.

'Is there anything else you can think of which may be of help to me? Anything at all?'

Sir Ebenezer took the question seriously and cudgelled what was left of his tired, geriatric brain. 'Well,' he said at length, keen to present some morsel, however insignificant, to this young fellow Twist, 'I gave the girl a locket, a gold locket, as a keepsake. It may be she left it with the child.'

'Or pawned it for cash,' observed Jack, with a knowing wink.

Sir Ebenezer knew the fellow could be right but he ignored him. He looked smart and bright enough but he radiated an aura that was discomfiting to him.

'What did this locket look like?' asked Oliver, still making notes.

'It was in the shape of a heart and bore the Throate coat of arms on the back.'

'May I ask you, sir, why, after all these years you have suddenly decided to try and track down your son?'

Once again the images of the ghostly figure that haunted his room at night reared up in his imagination. With an effort of will and the aid of a further gulp of brandy, he managed to banish the vision from his mind. 'As a man grows older and nears that time when he knows that he must leave this world, he is able to look back over the years with a kind of detached view to consider his mistakes and failings – to review the pain he has administered and the people he has wronged. It is a sad and melancholy occupation for there is very little a man can do about the hurts inflicted and injustices performed at this late stage of his life apart from shed a few tears and say his prayers, asking the good Lord for forgiveness. But in this instance there is something I can do about it. With your help. If I am able share some of my wealth with this young ill-used creature it will make my going all the sweeter. He didn't ask to be born and certainly he did not deserve to end up in a workhouse somewhere… So Master Twist you will be doing a great Christian deed if you can restore my son to me.'

Oliver fought hard with his emotions, desperately trying to extricate his personal feelings provoked by this far from comfortable scenario presented to him by Sir Ebenezer, which cruelly paralleled his own situation far too closely for comfort.

'Mr Dawkins and I will do what we can.'

'Very good.' Sir Ebenezer gave a heavy sigh as though some great burden had been lifted from his soul. 'I would ask one further boon of you. As I intimated earlier, this is a secret matter and what I have revealed must go no further. No other soul must know of it. I have kept the secret close to my chest all these years and I have revealed it to only one other person, my secretary, Roger Lightwood who knows of my plan to try and find my lost heir. No one else must know. And, gentlemen, that includes Lady Amelia. Do I make myself clear?'

Oliver and Jack nodded in unison.

'Good. And now dinner, gentlemen. I am sure after your long journey you are ready for some vitals. The Throate table provides simple fare but it is plentiful and wholesome.'

Speaking for myself,' said Jack Dawkins, rubbing his hands together, 'I'm starving. I could eat a scabby horse.'

CHAPTER NINE

As dusk descended on Brighton, none of its gaiety diminished. In the warm evening air, with the sun dipping beyond the horizon, spilling its last golden shadows across the water, people still thronged the promenade while the cafés and restaurants resounded with noisy chatter. Barrel organs churned out simple melodies to punctuate the embryonic night. All was glamour, noise and ease.

Inside the foyer of the Royal Court Hotel, Roger Lightwood sat nervously in the corner by a large potted palm which he hoped would help to hide him from general view. He watched with fascination the constant flow of human traffic as it buzzed, paraded and gyrated past his vantage point. It was an ever changing cyclorama. From time to time he asked himself what on earth he was doing there. What did he hope to achieve? He had no fully formed plan in mind. He was simply following his desire to see the pretty young lady again, the pretty young lady whom he had knocked to the ground; the pretty young lady who had apparently cured his cold; the young lady with whom he was now madly in love.

He cursed himself for not obtaining her name. Was she forever destined to be, 'the pretty young lady'?

As the one static point amidst the cacophonous whirl of humanity that revolved around him in the foyer, he sometimes asked himself what he intended to do if this creature of his dreams should suddenly appear. He could hardly rush up to the girl and declare his love for her. How foolish he would seem. She would think he was some kind of mad man and call a policeman and have him arrested. But nevertheless, abandoning all logic, he stayed, constantly surveying the crowd, watching and waiting. He was prepared to be satisfied with merely a glimpse of that pretty face once again. This was the last night of his holiday and at least he could take that treasured memory back with him to Surrey.

The premise behind the proverb, 'everything comes to he who waits' is created out of the unsound notion that wishful thinking brings results rather than the realistic probability that it doesn't. However in Roger Lightwood's case the proverb proved to be accurate: the improbable came true. After two hours of sentinel duty his persistence was rewarded. The object of his affection materialised in the foyer as if out of thin air. He had willed her to appear – and here she was. She was dressed in a dark emerald outfit which highlighted her fair skin and chestnut hair. Instinctively Roger half rose from his chair, a broad beam wreathing his features. But then he hesitated as he observed that the girl was not alone. She was accompanied by a tall, aged woman, whose face was incredibly wrinkled as though she had left it in a bath of water for too long. She gazed about her in the most imperious fashion, observing the world with distaste through a lorgnette, her narrow eyes tightened with general disapproval. The thin lips were clamped together in repose giving every indication that their owner disapproved of everything and everyone. It seemed to Roger that her mouth had never been utilised in the act of smiling. A grin would be an alien response to those thin, hard lips. This, he supposed, was Lady Whitestone, the girl's employer, and thus it became quite clear to the young man that the object of his affection was shackled to a gorgon.

The creature snapped some instruction to her companion, and then the pair moved towards the dining room. The girl's face was a mask of decorum, but Roger could tell from her eyes that she was unhappy, desperately unhappy. His heart went out to her but he remained where he was. He reasoned that any approach now would not only be futile but it may well land the girl in trouble with her disaffected employer. Within seconds they had disappeared into the dining room.

Had Roger Lightwood been privy to Felicity Waring's innermost thoughts he would have been shocked and dismayed. He had been accurate in his deduction that she was unhappy, but her unhappiness had nothing to do with her employer, Lady Wilhelmina Whitestone. After two years in her employ she had grown used to the ways and manners of the cheerless harridan and had learned to build an immunity against her carping and rudeness. Felicity regarded her as an ill-tempered pet one had been left to care for while the owner was on holiday. Ideally you would like to cage the beast and stow it in a dark cellar for the duration, but in deference to the owner one had to show it kindness and be prepared to tolerate its unpleasant and often hurtful behaviour.

The cause of Felicity Waring's unhappiness sprang from another source entirely. It was a source that would have wounded Roger Lightwood deeply. She was missing the man she loved. The man she hoped one day would marry her and, indeed, take her far away from the vituperate termagant who at this moment was seated opposite her at the dining table complaining about the soup.

From practice Felicity filtered out the irksome croaking voice with its interminable babbling criticisms and allowed her mind to wander back to Milford Mansion, Lady Wilhelmina's town house, and in particular to Arthur Wren, the leading footman there. Like a mirage, Arthur, tall, sandy haired with the neatest moustache imaginable, came wandering across the floor of the restaurant smiling at her. Or so it seemed, because she wished it. He had a manly military bearing, appropriate to his position, but he was also in possession of the kindest, sweetest nature.

Initially they had been brought together by a mutual loathing of their employer. Each in their own way was constantly derided by the aged shrew. They were close targets for her foul petulant temper and her irascible wounding outbursts. Then as time wore on, they had formed a bond of intimate friendship which in the contained hot house of Milford Park, eventually germinated and blossomed into deep affection.

'Do you hear me, child? Do stop daydreaming.' Lady Wilhelmina's harsh guillotine of a voice sliced through her daydream. Her ladyship thumped the table with vigour. 'Do pay attention to me. That's what I employ you for.'

'I beg your pardon,' said Felicity humbly. 'It must be this sea air. It's making me drowsy.'

'Nonsense,' came the reply. 'You are always slipping off into your own little daydream world. It is time you got a grip of yourself, my girl. I did not engage you to think of other things other than me.'

'Of course, Lady Whitestone.'

'Now attract the waiter's attention and see if it is possible to obtain a piece of fresh bread to accompany this cold, unappetising soup.'

Felicity did as she was bidden. She always did as she was bidden.

The meal progressed as all meals with Lady Whitestone progressed: with a barrage of complaints and criticisms. Things were too soft, too hard, too hot, too cold, too bland, or too spicy. There were insufficient portions, there was too much; the meat was tough; the chicken was tasteless, the pheasant was too gamey; the pork was too greasy. Felicity wondered at the range and variety of her employer's complaints. She never seemed to be at a loss in creating a fresh failing. And yet while she derided the inferior quality of the food, she always ate it.

'Do you think we shall take to the promenade tomorrow?' asked Felicity in an attempt to placate her employer.

'How on earth should I know?' came the churlish reply. 'It all depends upon the weather. I require a moderate temperature. If it is too hot like today, I would shrivel in the heat.'

It was an attractive image for Felicity.

The meal completed, all courses complained about by Lady Whitestone but all courses devoured completely leaving a series of shining clean dishes, she sat back in her chair with a sigh. 'Brighton is not like it used to be in my youth. There seems to be no society here at all, no culture, no people of breeding and refinement. Not one person in this hotel has come to pay their respects to me since I have been here. I may as well be just one of the ordinary guests.'

For all her guile and ingenuity, Felicity had no notion how to respond to this minor diatribe so she turned on her standard sympathetic smile of agreement. As usual Lady Whitestone ignored it. 'I tire,' she said, emitting a dramatic sigh. 'Come Miss Waring. It is time to return to our rooms.'

'Very well, Lady Whitestone.' Felicity rose quickly, circled the table and drawing back the chair, helped her employer from her seat. With the exaggerated stance of a female Moses parting the Red Sea, Lady Wilhelmina Whitestone made a theatrical exit from the dining room. Despite all her efforts, the majority of the diners did not notice. Those who did merely grinned at such clownish pomposity.

Lady Whitestone's routine of getting ready for bed was a long and tedious one. There were so many lotions and potions to administer to preserve 'her youthful good looks'. With patience Felicity Waring arranged the jars in order of application along the dressing table in her boudoir and applied the unguents to the appropriate location, be it her neck, her eyelids, her cheeks, her elbows or her hands. Then there was the session of hair brushing. Lady Whitestone unleashed the tangled grey web of hair from its elaborate and ridiculous arrangement until it fell free of the pins and slides which had kept it imprisoned during the day. Now it was kinked and wild, falling around her face not unlike a horse's tail both in shape and texture. It was then Felicity's task to brush in a constant rhythm for ten minutes.

Once ensconced in bed with a little gin and water, Lady Whitestone laid back while Felicity Waring read to her; read to her until the old crone began to snore. This could take up to half an hour or longer for when she seemed almost on the brink of slumber, she would struggle to regain consciousness in order to indulge in another sip of gin.

Eventually, sleep came to her and the rasping tones of her snores filled the chamber. It was then that Felicity Waring was released.

The chain was temporarily severed and she was a free woman until daylight when her incarceration began again with Lady Whitestone's morning ablutions which involved further potions and creams and the reversal of the hair procedure.

As the buzz-saw breath resonated around her, Felicity sat back in her chair, closed the volume from which she had been reading and gave an almighty sigh, while asking herself the question which she did nightly: how much longer could she put up with this drudgery. The answer was depressing and wretched; she would put up with it forever. She was a young lady in possession of no fortune or prospects. She was and always would be at the beck and call of Lady Whitestone or some other selfish, pampered creature like her for the rest of her life. Even if dear Arthur proposed marriage, financial constraints would dictate that they retained their current positions within the penitentiary of the moneyed monster. The future looked bleak.

Felicity turned down the lamp and repaired to her own modest bedroom next door. She gazed out of the window at the moon and shed a tear. She felt like a prisoner, gazing at freedom through her cell window.

And then a reckless thought struck her. She glanced at the clock on the mantel shelf. It was only nine o'clock. Nine o'clock on a summer's evening when the world was still at play, enjoying the pleasures and wonders of the night and she was relegated to go to bed. Go to bed! Why should she? Why must she? No, she would not. The spark of revolt flared within her. In an instant she had donned her bonnet and wrapped a light shawl about her shoulders and left her room. She carried out this procedure with great alacrity; her mind focused solely on the task in case cautious and sensible thoughts crept into her mind and robbed her of the courage to carry out her plan. In the great schemes of the world, this was the simplest, the most innocuous of plans and yet to Felicity Waring it was daring with an air of rebellion about it. She intended to walk a while along the promenade, to mingle with humanity, to listen to the rish-rushing of the waves and gaze at that bold yellow, serene face hanging in the heavens surrounded by a myriad of twinkling stars.

Of course, it was not the done thing for a respectable lady to take the air at such an hour unaccompanied, but for once Felicity was of a mind to do what was *not* done.

The air was still balmy along the promenade, despite the gentle breeze oozing in from the sea. And indeed there were still many people about who appeared to share a similar notion to Felicity's. They would stroll awhile and then stand and stare up at the moon in a kind of delighted wonder.

Felicity did not intend to wander far from the Royal Court. No matter how bold and determined she felt, she also maintained an element of protective common sense. However, so pleasant was the evening and so unfettered did she feel once she had left the confines of the hotel that she strayed further than she had planned. Suddenly she was aware that she had wandered beyond the crowds, the lights and the noise.

She turned on her heels to retrace her step when a gravelly voice came to her from out of the darkness. 'Hello, Miss,' it said. 'Lost yer way, 'ave yer?'

She could not see the person who spoke to her but the tone and nature of the enquiry told her quite clearly that this was a man she did not want to meet. Without a word, she moved on with greater speed only to bump into the owner of the voice, a tall, rough looking fellow dressed in the most eccentric manner as though he had borrowed his clothes from a series of disparate friends. He sported a grey top hat which had seen better days, a green checked jacket with a canary coloured waistcoat, brown jodhpurs and he carried a bamboo cane with a curled handle. Like his hat, his face had also seen better days. It was heavily lined and the pitted bulbous nose and bleary bloodshot eyes told of his liking for drink. A pair of decrepit whiskers lurked at either side of his unprepossessing face as though they were ashamed to make their presence known. At this moment in time, this gruesome fellow was grinning, revealing a graveyard of teeth. Those that still remained in situ were discoloured and pitched at an angle.

He raised his hat in a charade of politeness. 'As I was sayin'…
you lost yer way, have you, miss?'

Felicity shook her head and managed to murmur a reply. 'No,
thank you,' she said, before trying to sidestep the man and get past
him. Practised at foiling such manoeuvres, he sidestepped with her
and still remained a barrier.

'A young lady like yourself shouldn't be out this time o' night on
your own. Who knows what mischief might occur. There are some
very unpleasant coves about, I can tell you.'

'Please let me pass.' Felicity was surprised at the brusque
confidence of her tone. It was no doubt fear that prompted this
false courage.

'Not so fast, my lady. Not until you show me what you got in that
little bag of yours.'

'I have nothing that would interest you.'

'Come now, that can't be the case, can it? Smart lady like yourself.
Must have a few trinkets and some money in there.'

'No I do not. Now please let me go.'

'You can go when I've taken a peek in your bag.' A great hairy
hand appeared out of the shadows and took hold of her bag with
some force, but Felicity clasped it to her. The hand tugged harder
but she held fast.

The man's face crumpled into a scowl. 'Give it ter me or I'll do
yer,' he grunted, all false civility extinguished, his piggy, red-veined
eyes flashing with fury.

It was at this moment that Felicity gave a scream. So loud and
piercing was it, and so unexpected by the brute before her, that he
released his grip upon her bag in surprise.

Sensing her freedom, Felicity once more stepped to the side,
but again her assailant in a bizarrely delicate terpsichorean action
matched her movements and, casting his cane down on the ground,
once more grabbed her bag, this time with both hands. For a few
moments there was a farcical tug of war and then Felicity noticed
that a strange white growth had materialised on the fellow's shoulder.
It took her a few seconds to realise that this was in fact a hand – a

human hand. It belonged to a shadowy figure that had suddenly appeared behind the brute who was tugging at her handbag.

The hand gripped her assailant's shoulder and dragged him away from her and spun him round.

The shadowy figure then bellowed, 'You villain!' before hitting the thief squarely on the jaw. He gave a cry of surprise and his knees began to buckle as though someone had suddenly removed the bones from his legs, but he recovered sufficiently to rise to his full height again, snarl and utter an oath before striking wildly at his foe. His fist smote thin air. Once again his opponent smacked him on the jaw with a powerful uppercut. This time his hat flew off and he sank to his knees. In desperation he reached out for his cane lying on the ground just within his grasp, but the shadowy figure observed the gesture in time and stamped hard with his foot on both the cane and the villain's hand. He cried out in pain and surprise.

'Me 'and,' he bellowed, scrabbling to his feet. 'Me poor bleedin' 'and!' And with this testimony of his hurts, he disappeared swiftly into the darkness, leaving behind both his hat and cane.

The man stepped forward. 'Are you unharmed?' he said gently.

Still shaking from this most unpleasant and dramatic episode, Felicity shook her head. 'I am a little unnerved but I am not injured.'

'Thank heavens for that,' said the stranger moving closer.

She gazed up at her Sir Galahad and recognised him straight away. It was the young man who had bumped into her earlier in the day.

He beamed at her and raised his hat. 'We meet again, Miss…?'

On this occasion he was vouchsafed her name. 'Waring. Felicity Waring.'

'Roger Lightwood at your service,' he replied, bowing theatrically.

She smiled in amusement. 'I have much to thank you for, sir. If you had not chanced to come along at that moment…' The smile faded and she shuddered. 'I dread to think what would have happened.'

Little did she know that Roger Lightwood had not chanced to come along at that moment. He had been following her, watching her, longing to make contact with her and capricious Fate had provided the opportunity in the shape of Barney Rickles, the opportunist thief who at this very moment was heading for a nearby ale house nursing his bruised knuckles.

'I think it would be prudent if you allowed me to escort you back to your hotel. It is late and there are many more ruffians about at this time of night.'

'I would like that,' she demurred.

'Please, take my arm.'

She did as he requested.

And so the pair strolled quietly back along the promenade to the Royal Court Hotel. It took a mere ten minutes to reach the destination but in that ten minutes the lives of these young people changed forever. Sometimes there are brief moments when Fate creates a kind of electricity between two individuals, two lonely souls, which bonds them together for eternity. Such a magical process occurred between Roger Lightwood and Felicity Waring in that short perambulation. The conversation was light and tinged with awkward politeness, but both felt strong undercurrents that made them tingle and as they occasionally caught each other's glance, they both felt and knew what was happening.

By the time they entered the hotel, they had exchanged brief biographies, placing their lives in context. Suddenly all awkwardness fell away. Polite decorum was abandoned allowing a closer intimacy to sweep in.

Roger took Felicity's hand in his. 'Before you retire for the evening, would you take tea with me? I am sure it will help to calm your nerves.'

Felicity did not hesitate. 'Of course,' she said, her eyes flashing with pleasure.

CHAPTER TEN

For Oliver Twist, dinner that evening was a trial. To begin with, his mind was still awhirl with the implications of the task which had been set him by the respected client of Gripwind and Biddle, Sir Ebenezer Throate. It was a most surprising and onerous challenge. He had expected merely to review the details of the old man's will and return to London, the business all done and dusted and consigned to the shelves in the firm's vaults until it was time for his lordship to shuffle off this mortal coil. The prospect of finding the baronet's illegitimate son filled Oliver with dread.

Then there was the dinner itself. It was a stilted, excruciatingly formal affair in the draughtiest dining hall he ever had the misfortune to visit. From where he sat he was prey of the sharpest and most penetrating shaft of cold air that Throate Manor could conjure. Conversation was desultory. Sir Ebenezer barely uttered a word while eating little and drinking copiously. Lady Amelia exchanged a few stilted pleasantries initially but subsequently ran out of steam also.

On the other hand, Jack Dawkins seemed to find the occasion highly entertaining, apart from the dilemma of deciding which knife and fork to use for which course. He had been schooled by Oliver in the etiquette of cutlery but in his excitement the information had slipped from his mind. He cast his eyes to the other diners for clues but in the sepulchral lighting it was difficult to observe their faces let alone their hands.

This minor handicap did not spoil Jack's enjoyment of the occasion. He thrilled to the idea that he was sharing a dining table in the ancestral dining room with a living lord and lady. This excitement manifested itself in a permanent wide-eyed grin and a constant babble of nonsensical utterances.

However this almost somnambulistic culinary event took a turn for the dramatic half way through the main course when the door of the dining hall burst open and a tall figure entered the room in a melodramatic fashion.

It was Jeremiah Throate.

Immediately, it was clear to Oliver that he was the worse for drink. His swagger had a decided uncertainty to it. He strode towards the table in what would have been a threatening manner had he not stumbled along the way causing him to sway dangerously. For a moment Oliver believed he was going to lose his footing altogether but with a determined effort the young Throate managed to regain his balance. His face was suffused with alcohol and anger, he thumped the table with his fist and glared in turn at his mother and father.

'Where is my place set at the dining table?' he roared. 'Am I not welcome to take my last supper with you? I am your son after all. Your only offspring. The heir to the noble name of Throate. Where is my place?'

'You are in no fit state to be dining with us, Jeremiah,' said his mother imperiously. 'We have had our final interview where our views were made very clear. At present you are not welcome in this house.'

'But I am your son.'

'In name only. Your behaviour and attitude have alienated you to us.'

'Indeed, sir,' rejoined Sir Ebenezer, his words slurring softly.

Oliver observed that he would be hard pressed to judge which of the two, father or son, was the worse for drink. After this outburst Sir Ebenezer slumped back in his chair all energy and emotion spent.

Jeremiah Throate thumped the table once again in lieu of uttering some suitable response to this joint rejection. At length, he found the words he had been searching for.

'You cannot, indeed, you will not, get rid of me. If you have rejected me as your son, then you must accept me as your enemy.'

He turned to leave the room, but swivelled round too swiftly and tripped up on his own feet and sank to his knees.

Lady Amelia gave a snort of derision. 'Bulstrode, escort Master Jeremiah to his room and arrange a fresh horse for him in the morning so that he can return to London at first light.'

The funereal butler materialised from the gloom with a muted 'Very well, your ladyship', and proceeded to raise Jeremiah Throate from his recumbent position and help him from the room. The rebellious youth offered no resistance.

During this dramatic interlude, Jack Dawkins had watched events with great interest as though he were in a box at Drury Lane enjoying some highly coloured theatrical performance; but not for one instance did he stop eating. His knife and fork were in constant motion, as was his mouth. It was as though the food was an essential accompaniment to the spicy scenario being played out before him.

Oliver, on the other hand, watched with some sadness. How could it be that mother and father and son could have become so estranged? None of them seemed to care for the other. It was not surprising, therefore, that Sir Ebenezer wanted, in a sense, to start again with his unknown son. What the baronet had not perhaps considered was the possibility that his illegitimate offspring may well be just as rebellious and apparently unprincipled as Jeremiah. Indeed, it was not outside the bounds of probability that he may be even worse. It would seem that this was a risk that the aged aristocrat, who currently was drinking himself in to oblivion, had not considered.

Once Bulstrode and Jeremiah Throate had departed the chamber, Lady Amelia smiled graciously at her diners as though nothing untoward had occurred and then taking up a little bell from the table, she rang it brightly. The sharp clanging noise summoned the housekeeper to collect the dishes. She was a mature woman of some fifty summers, who wore a mob cap pulled down far over her forehead; straggles of grey hair escaped at irregular intervals. With her head bent low so that it was difficult discern her features, especially in the gloom, she moved with practised alacrity around the table collecting the plates and cutlery on to a large wooden tray.

'This is Lizzie,' said Lady Amelia, giving a nod towards the industrious skivvy. 'Our treasured housekeeper and cook. It is her apple pie you will be trying next. She is a wizard in the kitchen. I can assure you that you will find it delicious, eh Lizzie?'

The servant gave a nervous half smile, but said nothing. She seemed embarrassed by being brought to the attention of the guests and was obviously relieved when she was able to scurry away back to the kitchen.

Jack Dawkins leaned forward in a conspiratorial fashion. 'Apple pie's me favourite,' he said, as though he was revealing the secret to the location of a hidden hoard of treasure.

Sir Ebenezer burped.

The pie was indeed delicious, but it seemed to Oliver to have an unpleasant after-taste. Sir Ebenezer ate his mechanically and quickly, eager to return to his drinking. Despite her recommendation, Lady Amelia seemed to pick at her portion in a desultory fashion.

At last the ghastly experience drew to a close and Oliver was able to excuse himself, mumbling sentiments about a long day and a tiring journey. He rose somewhat unsteadily from his chair, a little surprised at how fatigued he felt. He had drunk little that evening and yet he experienced the strange softening sensation that over-indulgence in alcohol brings. Reality was held slightly out of focus and at a distance.

'Come, Mr Dawkins,' he found himself saying, the words echoing in his head.

Jack, who apparently seemed content to remain at the dining table, threw him a look of surprise before reluctantly rising to his feet. He too seemed a little the worse for wear and his raised eyebrows and twisted mouth told Oliver that he was also taken aback by how unsteady he felt.

However, their host hardly noticed their rather shambling departure from the dining hall. By now Sir Ebenezer's prodigious chins were resting on his chest and he was snoring gently while his wine glass was still gripped precariously in his hand. Lady Amelia seemed to be examining a piece of stray food which had landed on her napkin, a smile touching her thin lips and her usually bright eyes hooded with tiredness.

By the time Oliver and Jack had reached the first staircase, they were supporting each other in order to progress further. Like two antic clowns, they stumbled and wavered their way up the staircase and along the draughty corridors towards their rooms, each mumbling words to each other which neither of them understood.

Ten minutes later, Jack Dawkins staggered into his room and sat down on a chair in order to take his boots off but before he was able to unfasten one lace Morpheus ambushed him and he remained there in the chair frozen in sleep.

Next door, Oliver managed to reach the bed in his own room before collapsing on it. Just as sleep finally overtook him, one thought floated in his somewhat befuddled mind. 'I have been drugged,' he told himself.

* * *

Dark, moonless, starless night wrapped itself around Throate Manor, not in a protective sense but as an aid against discovery, an indigo curtain behind which evil deeds could take place unnoticed and undiscovered. Out beyond the confines of the house, an owl screeched its mad cry to the blank heavens: 'the fatal bellman which gives the stern'st goodnight'.

Within the great house, strange shadows shifted along the walls and muffled creaks and groans of the old timbers settling to rest filled the air. Sleep had shrouded most of its inhabitants for the duration.

But not all.

Unusually, as midnight struck, Sir Ebenezer was fast asleep. There were no qualms and quakes this night to trouble his mind about a spectral visitation. This may well have been because he had carried out the ghost's injunctions and set in motion a plan which he hoped would in time bring about a reunion with his lost child and to some extent make amends for his harsh and selfish actions an age ago. His conscience was eased and he felt at peace with himself, a state of affairs that was almost unique. It was also the case that he had consumed a great deal of wine that evening, partly out of relief and partly to celebrate the fact that he had taken action at last, action that he should have taken years before. As his mind crumbled and consciousness oozed out of his corpulent frame, he was convinced that his intake of claret had contributed to his sense of ease and his innate assurance that a night of untroubled sleep awaited him. However, if he had been able to think rationally – or, indeed, think at all - he would have realised that on previous evenings he had sometimes drunk far more than he had that night in order to anesthetise himself and ward off the night fears but yet he had shivered and trembled around midnight in his bed chamber cold sober with fear as he anticipated the arrival of his nocturnal spirit.

However, tonight he would not be visited by the spectral apparition but by a more formidable force with a dreadful purpose. Despite the silence of the chamber, the loud creaking of the door as it opened to admit the malefactor failed to pierce Sir Ebenezer's stupor. It is probable that an explosion of gunpowder at his bedside would not have roused him. He was, as some folk might say, and in this case with a morbid prescience, dead to the world.

The shadowy figure approached the bed where the baronet lay on his back, his mouth agape, snoring like a grizzling dog. From the folds of its cloak the figure produced a dagger - a sharp, long-bladed dagger which it raised high above its head. The figure paused for a moment and then with great determination and force it plunged the dagger deep into the chest of the sleeping master of Throate Manor.

A strange gurgling noise emanated from Sir Ebenezer's mouth and then the snoring ceased.

CHAPTER ELEVEN

That night, in their respective bedrooms, two young people lay in the gloom staring at the ceiling unable to sleep, their minds a whirlwind of emotions and thoughts. Roger Lightwood was warm in the conviction that he had found the love of his life and the girl of his dreams – goals which his over-sentimentalised and over-romanticised nature had been seeking since he had reached the state of manhood. His lonely childhood had led him to pine for the idolised form of domestic life: a pretty, adoring wife, two perfect children, a cottage somewhere in the country, far away from the foul vapours of the city all wrapped in the ribbon of financial security and domestic happiness. It was a fairly mundane dream, the fanciful aspirations of every hard pressed clerk and seamstress in the land – but for Roger it was a fantasy that he believed could be reality. His mind forever ignored the impracticalities, and improbability of such a situation actually happening. Now it seemed, after meeting Felicity Waring, that dream was within his grasp. He would marry her, with Sir Ebenezer's blessing, and be granted a cottage on the Throate estate where they would live happily ever after.

In her room in the Royal Hotel, Miss Waring was viewing the same scenario but with a more business-like and practical approach. She accepted without any reluctance that she had met the man she wanted to marry. He was good-looking (in a fey kind of way), kind, brave and caring. And had potential. What more could a girl require? The answer to this query was swift in coming. Wealth. That commodity which made the best use of all the others. What use is it to be tied to a man however handsome (in a fey kind of way), kind, brave and caring, if one has to live a penurious life? In this respect Roger Lightwood was not the ideal, but Felicity knew that in the real world the ideal was rarely if ever attainable. However, in gambling parlance, he was 'a good bet': he was ambitious and intelligent and already allied to the aristocracy. Certainly his role as private secretary to Sir Ebenezer Throate was a considerable number of rungs up the ladder from the position of footman to Lady Whitestone. Oh, she was fond of dear Arthur. He was a decent and loving man and had brought solace and comfort to her dreary existence with her Ladyship in that gloomy mausoleum in Chelsea but now she had met Roger she had come to realise that her fondness for Arthur had been based on gratitude and a kind of desperate relief to find a kindred spirit in the Whitestone desert. In simple terms, it was not the real thing, just a pretence conjured out of a desperate desire for that to be the case. She saw that now with a revelatory clarity. On the other hand, Roger, it seemed to her, was the real thing. It was practical and had potential. With Arthur, the potential was at best restricted and, if she was honest, realistically non-existent. In the brief time she and Roger had known each other, so much had been achieved. The usual social proprieties had been leap-frogged. In a strange, mystical unspoken fashion, both of them knew they were destined to be together.

This was a new and exciting chapter in her life. She hoped that within a year she would have slipped the Whitestone shackles and be ensconced on the Throate estate, living a life more in the manner which she believed was due to her, one in which she had autonomy and freedom. With these thoughts pleasantly settled in her mind, she surrendered her body to sleep, a gentle smile touching her lips.

CHAPTER TWELVE

Dawn came sluggishly, bringing with it a grey mist and a fine sheen of rain. Throate Manor loomed out of the gloom of the burgeoning day like some huge leviathan adrift on an undulating dark green sea. At precisely eight o'clock, Bulstrode entered his master's bedroom bearing a tray containing hot tea and toast. He placed it beside the bed and drew back the window curtains allowing the dreary reluctant beams of daylight to struggle in providing the chamber with a faint gloomy illumination. The butler then carried out the same procedure with the drapes around the bed, the metal curtain rings clanking eerily in the silence. The sight that met his eyes made him gasp and take two steps backwards. For the self-contained, unemotional Bulstrode this was a dramatic reaction. Had he been still holding the tray he certainly would have dropped it. On recollecting the scene later, the predominant impression was one of blood, bright red blood smeared, as it appeared to him, everywhere.

Sir Ebenezer was lying half out of bed, his arm dangling, fingers almost touching the floor, while his mouth was agape and his eyes closed. The top half of his nightgown, visible above the bedclothes was covered in blood. For some time Bulstrode stood mesmerised by the gruesome scene set before him. He seemed incapable of action as many thoughts crowded into his brain. Eventually the practical side of his nature took hold. He had to decide what to do now. Someone needed to be informed. Not her ladyship, he reasoned. Likely there would be tears and hysterics. Under normal circumstance he would have gone to Mr Lightwood but he was away and not due back until the following day. Certainly, Jeremiah should be informed but the butler had no wish to encounter this rash and unpredictable youth so early in the day. It would, therefore, have to be the lawyer, the young gentleman from London – a legal fellow like him would know the correct course of action to take.

Oliver was in mid-shave when there came a fierce rapping at his door. It caught him by surprise and he nicked his cheek with the razor just below his left ear. Clamping a damp towel to the wound he answered the door. Bulstrode, the butler, stood before him exhibiting more animation than Oliver had believed he was capable.

With eyes wide in a frenzied stare, he stated bluntly: 'Sir Ebenezer has been murdered.'

The statement seemed so bizarre and delivered in such a blunt melodramatic fashion that Oliver smiled.

'Surely not,' he said lightly, dabbing his cheek and then examining the towel to check if the bleeding had stopped.

'I tell you sir that the master has been killed. There's blood everywhere. Come and look for yourself.'

Oliver's smile faded. The fellow was serious. 'Very well,' he said. 'Show me.'

* * *

It was, thought Oliver, like a scene from one of Marie Tussaud's gruesome wax exhibits. Indeed the waxen features of Sir Ebenezer and the copious amounts of bright red blood seemed to emphasise this impression. Oliver moved in closely to try and ascertain the source of the blood. It did not take long to discover it. The baronet's nightshirt was torn just below the left shoulder and pulling the material gently to one side Oliver observed through the ragged gap a vicious wound – probably a knife wound he thought – to the upper chest. As he leaned forward to scrutinise the breach further, something remarkable occurred.

Sir Ebenezer opened his eyes and sighed. The pupils failed to focus on the world before the eyes lids fluttered shut again.

'My God!' cried Oliver. 'He's still alive.' With a violence he never intended he reached down and grabbed the old man's exposed right arm, his fingers testing the wrist for a pulse. It was there. Faint and irregular. But it was there.

'We must get a doctor without delay,' snapped Oliver.

'Yes sir,' responded the butler, his face a mask of shock and confusion. He turned quickly on his heel and left the chamber.

Dr Cornelius Benbow arrived on the scene less than an hour later. He lived in the nearby hamlet and Bulstrode had virtually dragged the medical man from his bed to bring him back to the manor house. Dr Benbow looked and dressed like a scarecrow, appearing in a rough shapeless tweed jacket with patches at the elbows and frayed cuffs, with ill-matching baggy trousers and shabby mud-spattered boots covering his lower-half. He was looked far more agricultural than medical. His thick greying hair exploded from his head in all directions as though it had seen neither brush nor comb in recent times. His face was round and shiny with two distinct rosy cheeks but, Oliver observed, his bright blue eyes radiated a kind of sharp intelligence that was at once both reassuring and comforting.

Without a word, he attended to the patient. 'My, my,' he said to himself. 'This is serious. Very serious. He has lost a great deal of blood.' He turned a stern face to Bulstrode. 'Hot water, please. I must dress the wound first.'

Once again Bulstrode turned quickly on his heel and left the chamber.

As Dr Benbow opened his capacious medical bag and began to remove various items, he cast a glance at Oliver. 'And who might you be, sir?' he enquired.

'I am Oliver Twist, Sir Ebenezer's lawyer.'

'I see. And do you know what has gone on here? How this came about?'

Oliver shook his head. 'I do not, sir. It seems that Sir Ebenezer was attacked in the night.'

Dr Benbow cut away the baronet's night shirt with a small pair of scissors to expose the wound. 'This is very nasty but the knife has missed the heart and any major blood vessels as far as I can ascertain – but it is deep. He really needs one of those experimental blood transfusions I've read about to make up for his loss of blood but I'm just a country practitioner with none of that fancy apparatus or London expertise at my command. I'm afraid his lordship will have to do with my care and attention. Ah, here comes the hot water.'

While the dishevelled medic set about dressing and binding the wound, Oliver turned these dramatic events over in his mind once more. He was trying to see a pattern and an overall picture. Obviously someone had tried to kill Sir Ebenezer – and looking at the pale comatose body in front of him, maybe they would succeed. The old fellow had hung on to life by a thread thus far, but it seemed unlikely that he would escape the embrace of the grim reaper. This raised the two key questions of who and why. Oliver wondered whether the 'why' had something to do with the old man's desire to change his will in favour of his illegitimate son. But who would know of that? As far as he was aware only Jack, himself and the absent secretary Roger Lightwood were privy to that information unless Sir Ebenezer had confided in someone else without telling him. If Sir Ebenezer dies, we may never find out, he mooted.

Murder, Oliver reasoned, is mainly prompted either by hatred or greed – or both. Taking this as a working hypothesis, the ideal culprit would appear to be Jeremiah Throate, the penurious and rejected legitimate offspring of Sir Ebenezer who gave such a dramatic performance in the dining hall last evening. He seemed to possess the reckless spirit for such a rash and dastardly act. But could he, when brought to the point, actually murder his own father? That corrupting elixir of anger and alcohol may well have prompted him to take that fatal action. If not Jeremiah, who else had cause to kill the old man? For the moment, Oliver drew a blank. He was well aware there would be other candidates but he lacked the knowledge to take this consideration further. He needed more information and more facts upon which to build a theory. It would seem logical to assume that the malefactor was someone within the household but that was not necessarily certain. He made a mental note to check later if there were any signs of a forced entry.

He had a private word in Bulstrode's capacious ear. 'I think it would be wise and appropriate to inform Lady Amelia and her son of the tragedy,' he said sotto voce.

Bulstrode's bright eyes flashed and he nodded. 'I have already been to master Jeremiah's room but he was not there. It seems that he has left the house early this morning but I will now go and pass on the sad news to Lady Amelia. She will by now have completed her morning toilet.'

In the same time-honoured, practised fashion, Bulstrode once again turned slowly on his heel and left the chamber.

So Jeremiah has 'left the house', thought Oliver with interest. Certainly the actions of a guilty man. Perhaps the matter was that simple. Son kills father to obtain his inheritance earlier than nature intended. However, if this were the case, surely he would have handled the matter with more finesse. It was all rather too obvious – unless of course the murder was a rash, drink-fuelled spur-of-the-moment decision. Oliver's ruminations were interrupted by a faint groaning sound which penetrated the hush of the room. It came from Sir Ebenezer, whose body was now stirring and his eyelids fluttering like two errant butterflies.

'Praise be,' said Dr Benbow. 'The old goat is a real fighter. The arrogance of the aristocracy often finds unusual channels in which to exhibit itself.' So saying he took a phial of pale green liquid from his bag and applied it to Sir Ebenezer's lips.

'Come on sir, drink it down,' the doctor chimed loudly and slowly poured the liquid into the old man's mouth. Some dribbled down his chin, but most of it was consumed.

Dr Benbow stood back from the bed and gave a short dark

chuckle. 'Well, there is life in the old dog yet. All is not lost.' He threw a brief smile at Oliver who returned it with a nod.

'That is good news,' he said.

'We must now wait for time and nature to take their course. But surely, this…' the doctor indicated the wound… 'is a matter for the police. The savage attack has been made on an exalted person of the realm…'

'The police will not be involved. This is a private matter.' This imperious statement uttered in clear stentorian tones came from Lady Amelia Throate who was standing in the doorway. Like a queen at a state occasion she entered the room and progressed to the bed. Here she gazed down at her husband with no sign of emotion on her fine chiselled features. Oliver knew that the aristocracy considered a demonstration of grief or high emotion of any kind unbecoming and repugnant, but he was surprised that she exhibited no shock, sadness nor sorrow whatsoever at the sight of her blood bespattered husband. Her face was a hard emotionless mask.

'Will he live?' she asked sharply, turning to the doctor.

Benbow, who was obviously used to the cold ways of her ladyship, seemed unruffled by her brusque manner. He gave an animated shrug, his wild hair quivering in response. 'I don't know. He has lost a considerable amount of blood and I would expect him to be dead by now… but remarkably he remains with us. It is possible that he will recover.'

'I see. Well, do what you can, doctor.' With one final glance at the pale unconscious figure lying in the bed she turned to go and then spying Oliver she addressed him.

'Good morning, Mr Twist. I trust I can rely on your discretion in this matter. No details of this unfortunate incident should leave this house.'

Unfortunate incident. Obviously the lady of the house was a mistress of the understatement. He nodded in reluctant acceptance of her request. 'As you wish, mi' lady. But in hiding the truth, you are allowing a villain, a possible murderer, to escape. Whoever has done this deed should be brought to justice.'

'What would be the purpose of that? How will it affect matters here? Not a jot. The capture of such a malefactor will not influence my husband's chances of living or dying. Justice is an overrated concept, I'm afraid, more valued in the theory than in practice. We shall have justice elsewhere in the end. The matter is closed. This unfortunate incident is secret history.'

Without further words she left the chamber leaving behind her an icy blast.

Dr Benbow broke the silence by snapping his capacious medical bag shut. 'Well,' he said stretching, 'my work here is done for the moment. I shall return in the late afternoon to see if there has been any change in the patient. Someone should be in attendance at the bedside at all times.'

'I will arrange for one of the maids to sit with him,' intoned Bulstrode.

'And if there is any change however minor in his condition you must send for me.'

'I understand, sir.'

'In the meantime, Bulstrode, since you dragged me from my slumbers betimes, perhaps you'd be good enough to find me some breakfast. A couple of eggs and a fine rasher of bacon would go down a treat, I can tell you. Like a treat.'

Bulstrode nodded.

'Perhaps my young companion would care to join me also.'

The mention of breakfast made Oliver suddenly realise how hungry he felt. All the drama had sharpened his appetite.

'If that would be convenient,' he said.

Bulstrode nodded. 'If you two gentlemen would make your way down to the dining hall, I will organise the matter.'

'Oh, could you make that three breakfasts,' Oliver said, before Bulstrode departed. 'I will attempt to rouse my clerk Mr Dawkins and encourage him to join us.'

'Certainly, sir.'

Although the hour of ten in the morning was but a few minutes away, Jack Dawkins was still abed and, thought Oliver as he knocked heartily on his door, no doubt dreaming his Dodgerish dreams. It opened moments later and a bleary sleep-absorbed face peered out. 'What is it? A fire?'

'Not quite. But certain dramatic events have been taking place while you have been snoring into your pillow.'

'Don't tell me young Jeremiah killed his father in order to inherit this old pile of bricks.'

'You are not far from the mark.'

'God's bodkin, I thought this lawyering lark was a sedate gentlemanly thing. Come in, my dear Oliver and tell me all while I pull on my clothes.'

Oliver found it useful to present his friend with a recital of the events of the morning for it allowed him to put all the elements in place and present himself with a clear overall picture.

'And to think I slept through the whole thing,' observed Jack, scraping his tangled locks into some semblance of order. 'How does this leave us, Oliver? What do we do now?'

'I'm not entirely sure. We still have a commission – to find Sir Ebenezer's son. The lost child of his youthful affair. There is now more than ever a sense of urgency concerning that task. Who can say how long the old fellow is for this world but I also feel that it is important to discover the identity of the perpetrator of last night's dastardly deed.'

'That shouldn't be too difficult. It's got to be that drunken lunatic who made an exhibition of himself last night in the dining hall. The son, Jeremiah.'

Oliver pulled a face. 'Maybe,' he said.

Jack Dawkins gave a sarcastic chuckle. 'Maybe? You have some other candidate in mind?'

'Not at present but my legal training has taught me to always look beyond the obvious.'

'Anything you say, Master Twist.'

CHAPTER THIRTEEN

Reuben Bechstein's shop in Murray's Court always appeared closed. There was no light in the grimy window to indicate that the establishment was open for business. Indeed it was only the presence of three mildewed brass balls hanging disconsolately over the shabby doorway that gave any evidence that this dismal premises was in fact a business and not just a derelict dwelling waiting with patience for demolition.

Once inside, the prospective customer new to the establishment may well have believed that Bechstein's was a wholesale merchant for fine dust and cobwebs for these seemed to be the principal items on show in his gloomy emporium. Daylight hardly filtered through the bleary panes and the only other source of illumination was a spindly guttering candle which Bechstein kept by him on the counter. He sat motionless with infinite patience not unlike a small squat bald-headed spider waiting for the next customer. He had the facility of sending both his brain and body into a kind of suspended animation in between the sporadic visitation of clients. He felt neither the cold – there was never any warmth on these premises – nor the tedious passage of time.

The many clocks which ticked and tocked noisily on shelves and cabinets that crowded the shop were just making their way towards the prick of noon, when Reuben Bechstein received his first visitation of the day. A tall swarthy man with a hangdog expression and what would have been an ebullient swagger had not alcohol and a certain haunted look undermined it. The shop bell clunked tunelessly to herald his arrival. Despite the sepulchral illumination, the old pawnbroker recognised the customer. It was Jeremiah Throate. A regular.

Bechstein snapped out of his trance, his arms scrabbling over the counter in readiness to examine the article brought for perusal – whatever it was.

'Good day, sir,' he croaked in a voice that was little used and so had grown rusty with the passing of the years. 'What can I do for you?' In essence the words were reversed in his own mind. 'What can you do for me?' is what he really meant.

Throate leaned over the counter and retrieved an item from his coat pocket. He allowed himself a brief smug smile as he laid the pearl necklace on the counter.

'What will you give me for this choice item?' he said smoothly.

Bechstein gazed at the necklace for a moment before clamping a magnifying implement to his eye in order to examine it at close quarters. For some seconds he studied the pearls closely by the flickering light of the candle and then lifting the necklace gently, he weighed the item in his sensitive arachnid fingers. Finally, he placed one of the largest pearls between his rotting teeth and bit gently upon it. With a shake of his head, he replaced the necklace on the counter. He murmured a few incomprehensible words to himself before addressing his customer.

'I hope that you didn't pay too much for this little trinket, my dear sir. It is mere paste. Not worth more than a few guineas, I'm afraid.'

Throate's body stiffened. 'You lie, you rogue.'

Bechstein, who was used to such accusations from irate and greedy customers, merely smiled. 'If that is what you think, take it away. Try elsewhere. Anyone who knows his pearls will tell you the same. Imitation. Cheap paste.'

Throate snatched up the necklace away from Bechstein's spidery clutches but already his spirits were sinking. He knew in his heart that the fellow was telling the truth. He held the pearls close to his face. To his uneducated eye they seemed perfect, although he could now appreciate that they did feel a trifle light in weight.

'As you are one of my regulars, sir, I'm prepared to offer three guineas for the item if that will help.'

If that will help! The words bore a shaft into Throate's heart. Three guineas! When he owed a hundred! He had pinned his hope on the blasted pearls. What was his mother doing with a paste necklace? What had happened to the real one?

Throate nodded dumbly as he handed back the cheap trinket to the pawnbroker. 'Very well,' he said, the words hardly more than a whisper.

Bechstein nodded and smiled. With one deft speedy movement he scooped up the item and placed it in a drawer. From his capacious leather purse which dangled like a fat dead rat from the belt around his waist he withdrew a number of coins and placed them on the counter.

'There we are, sir,' he said graciously. 'Full payment for said article.'

Throate scraped the coins up with a weary grunt and without further intercourse hurried from the shop.

Emerging into the dingy light of the cramped court where sunlight rarely strayed, he suddenly found himself flanked by two strangers. They epitomised the word 'disreputable'. They were swarthy in appearance, unshaven, unkempt and uncouth. Neither had a full set of teeth and their greasy, tattered and ill-fitting clothes would have been rejected by any self-respecting scarecrow. To Throate's surprise and disgust, each man took him by the arm as though they were ready to march him away – which in fact they were.

'Good day to you, Mister Throate,' said one, touching his shabby hat with two even shabbier gloved fingers.

'Or should that be Sir Jeremiah Throate now?' said the other, grinning, exposing what few teeth he had.

Throate's surprise at their approach darkened into something approaching fear when he realised they knew who he was. Who were these verminous creatures and what did they want with him? The two men tightened their grip around his arms and, as if to answer his unspoken thought, one of them said, 'We have come to take you to a friend of yours. He is most anxious to have words with his Lordship. Come along now.'

'The Devil I will,' Throate cried brusquely as he tried to shake the two unsavoury limpets from his arms but without any success. Their grip grew tighter and stronger causing him to wince with pain.

'I think you will,' said the stouter of the two producing a short pointed knife and holding it up to his victim's throat.

'We don't want to do you here, but we will if we have to,' said the other, grinning like a cheerful gargoyle. 'It's up to you.'

Throate made the sensible choice and complied with their demands. The trio shuffled from the court, down an alley and into a waiting carriage. Throate was bundled inside with one of his abductors while the other hauled himself up into the driver's seat.

The blinds were drawn as the carriage set off at some speed.

So many questions were whirling around in Throate's mind now but he had little time to assess them let alone try to answer any as his fellow travellers cudgelled him heartily on the back of his head with the butt of a pistol. A sudden explosion of light accompanied by a sharp searing plain in the head lasted a few seconds before Jeremiah Throate slumped lifeless on to the floor of the rocking carriage. His assailant pulled a doubtful face, his thick ugly lips curving downwards in an expression of dismay. 'I hopes I ain't overdone it,' he said to himself, inspecting the butt of the pistol, now tipped with blood. 'Mr Trench wanted this specimen alive.'

As Fate would have it, he hadn't overdone it and some thirty minutes later, a foggy, groggy consciousness slowly began to creep back into Jeremiah Throate's inert body. At first he heard voices, echoing, it seemed down a dark, smoky corridor and then the sensation of light, hazy and grey, forced itself upon him, enticing him to prise open his eyelids. Everything was a blur at first as though having been immersed in water for some time his head was now thrust above the surface. Everything shimmered indistinctly before him. He also realised that the voices he thought he had heard actually belonged to just one person. A tall thin man dressed in black. As his senses were slowly restored to him, the overwhelming sensation was the dull throbbing pain in his head.

Then he remembered. In short memory bursts he recollected the last few minutes before… before the pain and the darkness.

'Ah, you are with us once more,' said the voice of the tall thin man dressed in black.

Jeremiah Throate raised his head to focus on the speaker. Both actions caused him considerable pain and he grimaced.

'I am afraid that Master Kepple was rather over-zealous in his treatment of you, Sir Jeremiah for which I must apologise.'

Several things became obvious to Throate all at once. He was in a light airy room which was devoid of furniture apart from the chair he was sitting on, his hands were secured behind his back and that the man standing before him was Eugene Trench.

'What is all this? What do you want from me?' Throate asked in what seemed to him to be a strangely disembodied voice.

Trench gave a slight bow but there was no reverence or respect in the gesture. It was a joke, a sneer, a travesty.

'Your Lordship,' he said sarcastically.

Throate frowned. What game were these people playing with him? The gross villains who had captured him had also found humour in addressing him in this manner. What did it all mean?

'I've brought you here,' continued Trench, as he began to stroll around the room, his boots clicking sharply on the bare floorboards, 'not just in order to celebrate your good fortune to make secure arrangements for the payment of your not inconsiderable debt to me.'

With some discomfort, Throate shook his head in bewilderment. 'What good news?'

'No play acting please. It is pointless and insulting to my intelligence.'

'I really do not know what you are talking about.'

There was a passionate earnestness in Throate's response that caused Trench to cease his perambulations and stare at his captive with curiosity.

'I refer to the death of your father and your natural accession to his title.'

'The death of my father…'

Trench rolled his eyes. 'This will not do, Throate. I know very well that your father has been murdered and that I am looking directly at the culprit of the crime now.'

'Murdered. What do you mean? How do you know?'

'I have been informed. A reliable source.'

'Who?'

Trench shook his head. 'It is politic that I preserve the individual's anonymity. Suffice it to say that they were employed in a very minor capacity at Throate Manor and have deserted their post now. I am like Macbeth in Mr Shakespeare's play, there are many houses where I keep 'a servant fee'd'.

'But I was there last night and my father was hale and hearty…'

'And was dead by this morning, stabbed through the heart.'

At this news a flurry of mixed emotions filled Throate's senses. In an instant he was aware of all the various implications his father's death would bring. He had lost the man who had brought him into the world and nurtured him when a youth, but a man from whom had grown distant and indeed, a man who he had started to hate. His death also meant that he would inherit his title and riches and along with his mother become master of Throate Manor and all its lands. If this news were true.

'I cannot believe it,' he said at last.

Trench smirked. 'More Macbeth: 'methinks the lad doth protest too much'. The gossip with the servants is that Master Throate himself is the murderer. He threatened his father in front of witnesses last night at dinner and then carried out the deed in the appropriately named dead of night.'

An image of Jeremiah's father lying prostrate in a pool of blood flashed into his mind and although he was quick to dismiss it, he was surprised how much the vision pleased him.

'I… kill my father. No, no. It is a lie. I would not… I could not… My father… No.'

Trench held up his hand to stop this emotional prevarication. 'It is not my place to judge and besides I care not whether you slaughtered the old man or not. The most important point is that you now have claim to half his wealth and that allows you to pay me the considerable debt you owe me. You have not forgotten those guineas, I trust.'

'Is it really true that my father is dead?'

'You have need to ask me that?'

'Yes, by God, I do. The last time I saw my father he was drunk but alive. I swear it.'

For a fleeting moment a look of uncertainty fluttered across Trench's features. His eyes narrowed and his lips pursed as he surveyed his captive with a keenly.

'And you had no hand in his demise?' Trench asked at length.

Jeremiah Throate shook his head. 'If my father is dead, I was unaware of it.'

Trench smiled or at least his lips curled upwards a little. It was the nearest he got to a show of pleasure or amusement. 'Well, you surprise me, my friend. I felt sure that you had done the old man in to get your greedy fingers on the loot. Now you are asking me to believe that some other kind soul took it into their own hands to do your dirty work, thus propelling you into a position of wealth and position – Sir Jeremiah.'

'I tell you…. if my father is dead – murdered – I swear I have no knowledge or involvement in the deed.'

'Well, it matters little to me whether you knifed the old codger or not. The outcome is the same, you are now in a position to rifle the Throate coffers and come up with the money to settle your debts – with interest, of course.'

'Interest?'

'It is not without considerable trouble that I have had to track you down and bring you here. Time and money, your Lordship. Time and money. I must be recompensed for my trouble. That will add another twenty guineas to your bill.'

Jeremiah Throate opened his mouth to protest, but common sense prevailed and he shut it again. He was in no position to protest, to state terms or to disagree about anything. He was a captive of the cruellest of malefactors – a pipe upon which Trench could play whatever tune he wished.

'You must return to Throate Manor post haste to offer succour to your mother and claim the title and the requisite amount of funds. My trusted companions, Mr Kepple and Mr Joint here will accompany you to make sure your journey is a swift one which does not allow you time to construct various machinations concerning your new fortune that would bring me displeasure and bring your own existence into jeopardy. I am sure you understand.'

Jeremiah Throate understood all too well.

CHAPTER FOURTEEN

The journey back to London was a miserable one for Oliver Twist. He and Jack had been obliged to take the public coach from Dorking which was crowded to bursting and ill-ventilated. The weather was extremely inclement with the wind buffeting the coach and sending fierce errant drafts into the carriage that chilled to the marrow. However, it wasn't only these discomforts that lowered his spirits, it was the circumstances in which he now found himself: that of a young lawyer with a severely wounded client from a murderous attack who had secured a promise from him to discover the whereabouts of his illegitimate son. It was a task he felt ill-suited for and one he had no desire to undertake. But he had given his word. And he knew that his employers would have wished him to. Such an important and long standing client of the firm of Gripwind and Biddle must be indulged at all costs.

While Oliver's brow was creased with worry and discomfort, his companion Jack Dawkins slumbered peacefully by his side, emitting a gentle purr of a snore every fifteen minutes or so. Oliver envied his friend's ability to place the real world at bay at will. Whether asleep or awake, Jack had the great facility to banish worries and concerns from his mind. This, of course, was partly due to him never quite recognising the implications and consequences of challenging situations.

Oliver knew that when they returned to the office, he would have to report to Mr Gripwind, giving him a full account of all that had transpired at Throate Manor during their ill-fated visit. He was also cognisant of the fact that he would have to place upon his head the metaphorical detective's hat and begin his search for the Unknown Throate.

Jack Dawkins gave a gentle snore and snuggled down deeper into his great coat. 'Oh, for such oblivion,' murmured Oliver to himself.

While these thoughts were playing around the young lawyer's brain, he failed to notice three horsemen passing the coach, travelling in the opposite direction. Fate had arranged that major characters in this drama should criss-cross each other at this juncture, for the three riders were none other than Jeremiah Throate and his two grim chaperones, Barney Kepple and Alf Joint. If Oliver had glanced out of the window he would have observed the three men, each stern of face, with Jeremiah Throate's expression by far the sternest.

* * *

The louring clouds and incessant swish of rain against the window pane did not dampen Roger Lightwood's mood of contentment as he attended to his morning ablutions. Outside, the promenade of Brighton was all but deserted apart from a few hardy souls bent like hairpins against the wind and the rain, but in Roger's world it was all sunshine and warmth for he knew that afternoon he would be snatching a few hours of bliss with his beloved. He had been informed that following lunch, Lady Whitestone indulged in a prolonged nap which afforded Felicity Waring some time to herself and so an assignation with Roger had been arranged. It would be brief but delicious. Sadly it would be their last meeting for some time as this was the last day of Roger's vacation. That evening he was to return to Throate Manor and his secretarial duties. Much had to be arranged between the two sweethearts before they were separated by menial responsibilities. Their future had to be discussed and planned for. At the thought of the future wrapped in the warm clouds of connubial bliss, Roger's heart almost exploded with pleasure. His mind had been so absorbed in these beatific contemplations that he had not noticed that he had tied his cravat inside out. On eventually observing this, he smiled broadly at his foolishness. Such was the power of love, he told himself. He was indeed a happy and a very lucky man.

A tap at the door seemed innocuous, but it was about to rob Roger Lightwood of this sense of happiness and luck. A minion appeared on the threshold, a youth of spotty complexion dressed in the clothes of a bell boy which were too large for him. He held in his hand a pale blue envelope.

'Message for Mr R Lightwood,' he intoned in a mechanical fashion, his glassy eyes never quite making contact with the recipient of the missive.

'I am he,' responded Roger and held out his hand for the envelope. For a brief moment, the youth seemed reluctant to relinquish it and then with a shrug of the shoulder he passed it over to Roger and without another word, he turned on his heel and disappeared down the corridor.

Roger sat on the bed and tore open the envelope and read the letter contained within. The first words his eyes fell upon were 'My Dearest Roger,' which prompted a strange tingling feeling to manifest itself up his spine. Quickly, he glanced at the signature and it was as he guessed, as he hoped, that of 'your own Felicity'. After establishing the provenance of the epistle, Roger now devoured the contents, a task that gradually dulled the brightness in his eye and created tenseness about the lips which diminished the attractiveness of his features considerably.

'My Dearest Roger,' he read again before consuming the body of the letter which ran:

'I write in haste. On a sudden whim Lady Whitestone has decided to return home today. She has not enjoyed her stay in Brighton. Too few people have paid court to her. In fact no one has paid court to her and today's inclement weather and cool temperature was the final straw. We are to catch the noon train back

to town. As a result, I will not be able to keep our rendezvous this afternoon and indeed, I have no time to come along to your hotel to bid you adieu. This is so cruel but as a kept lackey I must do as my mistress commands. There is much packing and final preparations to be made for our return journey. For the moment we shall have to keep in contact by letter. The address by which you may reach me is printed overleaf. Please write soon. I long for the day when we shall be reunited.

Your own Felicity.'

Roger stared at the letter for some moments almost as though he was posing for a statue: 'Lovelorn Youth on Receiving Bad News from His Sweetheart'. His spirits sank as did his shoulders. He had not contemplated such an outcome. His life had become like the helter skelter ride on the pier. Last night he had been high, at the top, and now this letter had brought him swiftly whizzing down to the bottom. As if to demonstrate this situation, he sneezed. And then sneezed again. The malady had returned.

* * *

In the bustling noisy damp crowd that thronged the Brighton station that lunchtime, one figure cut a swathe through the multitudinous travellers, her furled parasol held aloft like a military standard. This aged Britannia was none other than Lady Wilhelmina Whitestone who was hurrying, with dogged determination, towards the reserved First Class carriage on the London bound train. Trailing in her wake, like two ferry boats, were her companion, Felicity Waring, burdened by two of her employer's suitcases and a perspiring railway porter pushing a trolley with the remainder of her ladyship's luggage. Batting the odd impertinent soul who had the temerity to get in her way with her parasol, Lady Whitestone reached her appointed carriage some time before the others. She waited imperiously, until the little porter skipped round from his trolley and opened the compartment door.

In the shadows near the bookstall, stood a tall man observing this scene with heightened emotion. His eyes, a little damp, focused on the slight figure of Felicity Waring as she supervised the transference of the luggage on to the train. Once this operation had been carried out, she thanked the porter and passed him a small coin before boarding the train herself, as she did so, she turned for a fleeting moment and gazed out at the platform, little realising that she was being observed by the man in the shadows.

Roger Lightwood placed his palm to his lips and blew a kiss out towards her. 'Farewell, my love,' he muttered.

Felicity Waring unaware of the gesture, disappeared from sight into the gloom of the carriage.

CHAPTER FIFTEEN

Jeremiah Throate strode into the hall of Throate Manor, closely followed by his two companions. The manservant Bulstrode appeared before them, as though manifested out of thin air.

'Where is my mother?' snapped Jeremiah, his swagger returning somewhat now that he was on home territory.

'Good day, Master Jeremy. Lady Amelia is in the morning room.'

Without another word, Jeremiah swept past the butler as did the other two men. On reaching the door of the morning room, he turned to Kepple and Joint. 'You wait here until I determine the lie of the land. Mother can be difficult. Your presence may cause complications.'

The two malefactors exchanged glances. In truth neither knew the best course of action they should take. Should they obey Throate's instructions or should they ignore them. True to form, they took the least line of resistance and both nodded their heads in agreement.

Throate slipped into the morning room. His mother was seated by the window attending to some needlepoint. She glanced up with surprise and then disdain as she recognised the visitor.

'Is it true, mother?' said Jeremiah, approaching her.

'Is what true?'

'About father – that he is dead?'

A thin smile materialised on her ladyship's face and her eyes twinkled with dark amusement. 'It hasn't taken long for one of the vultures to start circling,' she said, laying down her needlework. 'I am sorry to disappoint you, my boy, but your father is not dead. He lives.'

A mixture of emotions invaded Jeremiah Throate's senses. He hadn't wished the irritating, stubborn old fool any harm and was somewhat relieved that he wasn't dead while, at the same time, he had relished the idea of assuming his father's title and the monetary accoutrements that this would bring. He was also conscious that there were dire consequences to his continuing state of penury in the form of the two cut-throats waiting outside the room and their cruel master in the city.

Lady Amelia resumed her needlework. 'I am sure you are dismayed,' she said, her voice calm but brittle, 'that your attempt to kill your father failed. It seems you are incompetent at murder as all else.'

'Kill my father? What on earth do you mean?'

'Please don't play the innocent with me. We both know very well you tried to stab your father to death last evening. You nearly succeeded, but the old devil is made of stern stuff and he survived.'

Jeremiah shook his head vigorously. 'I don't know what you are talking about. I... I would never harm the old boy. Someone stabbed him, you say. Well, it wasn't me. It must have been someone else.'

'Nonsense. Who would want to kill him? What benefit would anyone receive by his demise. Only you.'

'No. No. No!' Jeremiah threw himself down on his knees by his mother's side. 'You have to believe me. I didn't do it. I couldn't do it. I... I am not so base a creature as to kill my own flesh and blood.'

Amelia Throate paused and turned to face her son, her eyes searching his features, apparently searching for the truth in his troubled visage. She sighed heavily.

'In truth, I do not know what to think. I am not fully convinced by your protestations, but as your mother I suppose I have a duty to accept your word.'

'Bless you.' He made to kiss his mother's hand but she withdrew it.

Like a naughty schoolboy summoned to the headmaster's office, he rose to his feet and bowed his head. 'I have a pressing problem, however, which brings me here today.'

'I have no wish to hear of your pressing problems. I have sufficient of my own,' came the terse reply.

'But my life is at stake.'

'It is a well-worn tale. Your life always seems to be at stake. A gambling debt no doubt. As usual.'

'Mother, there are two men in the corridor outside this room, two men who have accompanied me here in order to secure certain monies which I owe them. If they do not get it, they will kill me.'

'Then they had better get on with it. As we established yesterday, you will not receive another penny from me or your father while there is breath left in our bodies. You have preyed upon our monetary kindness and gullibility for the last time.'

At these words, the heat of desperate madness overtook Jeremiah Throate. Wild schemes exploded in his mind, sending searing fragments to every convolution of his cerebral cortex. Should he strangle his mother and tear her necklace and rings from her person and offer them to the thugs waiting without? Should he reach for the paper knife on the nearby table and stab himself to death? Should he rush into the hallway and throw himself on the villains' mercy? Even to his ravaged brain, this last option seemed the weakest. Throate was well aware that those swarthy cut-throats had no concept of the notion of mercy. It was as foreign to them as was soap and water. Then, out of the ether, another solution materialised. With staring eyes, Throate glanced at the window and the garden and sky beyond.

Escape.

That's what he had to do: escape.

With a few bounds, he was by the window and unfastening the hasp. His mother gazed on in astonishment.

'What on earth are you doing?' she cried, jumping to her feet but by the time the words had left her mouth, her errant son had disappeared through the aperture and was racing across the lawn.

Lady Amelia sank back into her chair. 'The world has gone mad,' she muttered to herself, not quite realising that it was about to become a great deal madder.

Some moments later, the door of the morning room crashed open and there stood two sinister and scruffy looking individuals. On observing them, Lady Amelia very swiftly came to the conclusion that if some crazed scientist had attempted to create two beings that were half man and some part rodent, they would look like these creatures that stood before her, adopting what she assumed they believed was a menacing pose.

'Where is he?' said one of them.

Lady Amelia did not reply but just glanced at the open window. The two men rushed forward and leaned out. By now there was no sign of the fleeing Throate.

'The devil. He's escaped.'

'Best get after him. We can't afford to lose the blighter.'

Like clowns at a circus, the two men crashed into each other as they both attempted to climb out of the window at the same time. They tried again, and once more they collided.

'I'll go first,' said one of them, holding the other back.

Eventually both men were out of the room and haring across the lawn. Slowly, almost as though she was in a trance, Lady Amelia Throate rose from her chair once more and slowly crossed to the window and closed it. She shook her head as though attempting to dispel the memory of the last few minutes from her mind. Although it was very early in the day, she felt in need of a glass of brandy which she hoped would help to restore life's equilibrium.

CHAPTER SIXTEEN

Mr Gripwind steepled his fingers before his face and sighed. 'A very unfortunate situation, my dear Oliver. Very unfortunate. And, indeed, unique in my experience. Certainly, as a young solicitor I was instructed to follow one of my client's wives to ascertain as to whether she had a lover and was being unfaithful to said client – but that was not so much detective work as just being a bit of a sneak.'

Oliver was seated opposite Mr Gripwind in his dusty office back at the Inns of Court. Sunlight filtered through the windows dappling the various piles of legal papers that decorated the chamber. He had just recounted the whole of his experiences at Throate Manor including the attempted murder of the old baronet and the task that had been imposed upon him by Sir Ebenezer to find his illegitimate son. He knew that he was going against the baronet's wishes of keeping the matter secret but he believed his obligations to his employer were far more important and essential. How could he carry out the task given him without Mr Gripwind's knowledge?

'Yes, yes,' continued Mr Gripwind, expansively. 'Detective work. Well, you must be about it, Oliver. We can neither deny nor disappoint our venerable client in his demands and obviously your investigations must be carried out with some alacrity. From what you say Sir Ebenezer may not be very long for this life. We must locate this illegitimate heir before the coffin lid is screwed down on the old fellow. Isn't that so?'

'Yes, sir,' agreed Oliver with little enthusiasm or conviction in his voice.

'Good man. Now then, what will be your first manoeuvre? Do you have a plan of action?'

'A very vague one, I suppose.'

'Vague is not encouraging, but at least you do have something up your sleeve, eh?'

It was obvious Mr Gripwind was eager for confirmation of this assumption. Oliver nodded.

'Well, come, come. Pray tell.'

'I intend to visit the orphanage where the child was lodged and see if I can ascertain what happened to him after that. However, I fear that it will be a little like trying to catch soap bubbles in the palm of your hand…'

Mr Gripwind smiled at the young man's conceit. 'It is my experience that if you travel hopefully, it lightens the load of the journey, no matter how disappointing the destination reveals itself to be.'

'I will bear that in mind,' said Oliver.

* * *

Tranton House was a shabby-looking Georgian town house situated south of the river in Battersea. The property looked so careworn that it was difficult to conceive that it had ever seen better days when its paintwork shone, its windows gleamed and the stone was bright and clean and shimmered like burnished gold in the sunlight. Everything about the property now seemed to indicate that it was fading away, turning to dust. Its frontage was blackened with age and traversed here and there by the mummified fingers of dead ivy. Even the weeds in the garden had died away creating an undulating seascape of crusted foliage.

'Crikey,' said Jack Dawkins as he gazed at the building, 'it looks more like a haunted house from those pictures in story books rather than an orphanage.'

Oliver nodded in agreement. 'In many ways an orphanage is a haunted house,' he observed quietly.

Jack pulled a face. 'My, that's deep, Oliver. Very deep. Too deep for me, I reckon. I can't get my head down that far.'

Oliver smiled. 'Take no notice of me. My mind is wandering.'

Indeed it was wandering, wandering back to a time he knew of, but could not remember. A time when he was housed as a baby in a similar establishment. He had been a scrap of mewling humanity with a dead mother, cast upon the world without a living soul who really cared for him. He shuddered at the thought and then with a Herculean shrug thrust it aside. That was the past and thank the Lord, it was dead and gone and it must remain so. As for now - there was business to conduct, a task to be performed, an investigation to carry out. He must be about it.

With a funereal gait, Oliver and Jack walked down the pathway leading to the decrepit door of Tranton House. Raising the large rusty iron ring which served as a knocker, he rapped it twice on the flaking woodwork. He could hear its thunderous reverberations echoing into the far reaches of the building like distant cannon fire.

After a brief interval, the door creaked open a few inches. At first, it seemed to the two men that it had performed this operation of its own volition or had been manipulated by some unseen ghostly hand but then lowering their sights they observed a small child, a ragged urchin peering out at them through the crack. Its scruffy face was smeared with dirt, the hair a tangle of knots and the eyes wild and staring. It was difficult at this stage to judge what sex this creature was and, even when it spoke with a squeaky, high pitched monotone, the conundrum was not solved.

'What d'yer want?' it asked.

'We wish to speak to the person in charge of this orphanage. Mr Sponge.' Oliver had only gleaned that one name in his researches regarding the establishment. He held out his card to the youth, who snatched it from him with a grubby claw.

The child's eyes widened. 'There ain't no Mr Sponge here, just old Ma Sponge. She's the gaffer.'

'Well, we certainly need to see the gaffer, young 'un,' observed Jack cheerily. 'So why not take us to her. It is a matter of the utmost importance.'

The child pursed its lips and the eyes flickered erratically as it digested this suggestion. 'Wait here,' came the reply at length and the door closed.

'An orphanage run by orphans,' observed Oliver wryly.

After a five minute interval, the door opened again. This time an older child appeared in the aperture. This time there was no mistaking the sex. He was a tough looking youth of about eleven or twelve years of age. He was wearing a cheap suit and waistcoat with what had once been a fine silk cravat but now resembled a coloured dish rag. His hair had been plastered down by the application of some pungent oil.

'Afternoon, gents. Am I correct in assumpting that you are a wanting to see her ladyship, Mrs Sponge?' he said grandly.

'Yes,' said Oliver. 'We are here on legal business.'

'What's that then?'

'Private stuff, young 'un. Take us to Mrs Sponge,' said Jack with an edge of aggression in his voice. He was fed up hanging around outside this mausoleum being interrogated by infants.

His outburst did the trick. The youth opened the door wide and bade them enter with a 'Follow me, gents.'

They were led down a series of gloomy corridors past numerous doors behind which could be heard myriad children's voices. Oliver was struck by the fact that while many of these youthful explosions were noisy, none seemed to be filled with a sense of happiness and good humour. There were just shrieks of anger and moans of dismay. While these cries assailed their ears, not one child was observed, save for their comical guide. Oliver was reminded of his visits to the police cells he had visited in the course of his duties.

Eventually, they reached a large door upon which the youth

rapped in a particular staccato fashion which to Oliver sounded very much like a code to provide assurance to occupant of the room of the identity of the visitor.

A loud voice emerged from behind the oak panelling of the door. 'Enter!' it said, with all the imperiousness of Queen Victoria launching a ship.

'In yer go, gents,' said the young man, already retreating into the shadows.

Oliver and Jack entered.

The room was brightly lit and opulent. A fire blazed merrily in the grate and the furnishings, while somewhat gaudy in colour, were of the finest material. A chaise longue was situated by the fireplace and close by was a small table which housed a sherry decanter and glasses and an overflowing fruit bowl that boasted of black and green grapes, a pineapple and a trio of tangerines. It was, thought Oliver, a fur-lined womb within the bleak environs of Tranton House.

The occupant of the room was sitting behind a large desk which was littered with documents and files. It was a woman of ample proportions, bursting out of a silk gown which to Oliver's mind was more suitable for evening wear. For good measure, the lady had added a couple of chins to the one she had originally been given and had attempted to hold back time by the application of heavy make-up which bleached her cheeks and blackened her eyes. She gazed at her visitors through a lorgnette for some moments and then glanced down at Oliver's card.

'I am Madame Camilla Sponge,' she announced grandly. 'Which of you is Mr Twist?' At first hearing, her voice sounded refined and cultured, but it soon became clear to Oliver that this was a performance, an adopted voice which was slipped on as one might an expensive item of clothing to disguise one's penury. There was a slight undertone of roughness and artificiality which marred the perfection of her performance as a lady. This fact placed Oliver on his guard. By contrast, at first at least, Jack seemed taken in by the overt grandeur of Madame Sponge.

'I am Oliver Twist.'

'And the other gentleman...?'

'This is my trusted clerk, Jack Dawkins.'

She turned her attention on Jack, holding the lorgnette closer to her eyes and viewing him as though he were a medical specimen in a lab. She wrinkled her nose in mild distaste.

'Pray take a seat, gentlemen, and state your business. I am a busy woman. This orphanage don't … doesn't run itself. I have many duties, many calls upon my time.'

'We are here in an attempt to trace one of the children you had in your charge twenty five years ago.'

Madame Sponge raised her not inconsiderable eyebrows and chuckled, her chins wobbling in unison. 'My, we are going back some years.'

'This was a time when you were in charge.' Oliver knew this for certain. He had checked the records with diligence.

Madame Sponge hesitated but could see from Oliver's expression that to deny the fact would be a mistake.

'Why yes. Of course, I was a very young girl then myself, you understand. Hardly out of kindergarten.' She gave a high pitched whinny of amusement of which any horse would have been proud.

'You keep records…'

'Of course we keep records. I run a very organised gaff here, I can assure you.'

'So you knows who comes here, where from and then where the little blighters go when they are taken up?' enquired Jack, cutting to the quick as always.

'Indeed.'

'In the summer of 1825, a certain Miss Louise Clerihew left a child, an infant boy, only a few weeks old on your doorstep,' said Oliver. 'My client wishes to know what happened to this child. Who took him, adopted him.'

'And who, may I ask, is your client?'

Oliver shook his head gently. 'I am afraid I am not at liberty to reveal his identity.'

Madame Sponge snorted. 'Hah. Liberty is it? We hear a lot

about liberty in this city. It seems it is the provenance of the wealthy who can do what they like, obtain anything what they want just by asking. They are the ones who take the liberty! Well, Mr Twist, not in this case. You can run back to your nosey-parkering client and tell him that I am not at *liberty* to provide him with the information he requires.' Madame Sponge flounced back in her chair with a self-satisfied smirk registered on her heavily made up face.

Oliver had not expected this response and for some moments was struck dumb, not quite sure what to do next. Jack Dawkins, on the other hand, always ready to dive in at the deep end, did not hesitate to think before speaking.

'You are so right, Mrs Sponge,' he said leaning very close to Oliver as though he was about to whisper something in his ear but at the last moment appearing to think better of it. 'Indeed, indeed,' he continued in his natural jaunty manner. 'We are just the dogsbodies in this matter only carrying out our client's wishes – well not so much wishes more like demands. If we return empty-handed, it will be the worse for us, won't it, Mr Twist?'

Jack did not wait for Oliver to respond to this statement but carried on. 'I am sure that we can come to some… arrangement that suits us both,' he said, lowering his voice and grinning seductively.

'What arrangement is that?' asked Madame Sponge momentarily intrigued.

Like a conjuror, Jack Dawkins held up his right hand and produced a bright shining sovereign. 'We can… purchase the information required.'

Madame Sponge leaned forward, lorgnette clamped to her face, her eyes ogling the golden coin.

'This little beauty has a brother and sister,' continued Jack and with a dextrous swivel of his fingers revealed two more sovereigns.

The sight of all three coins caused Madame Sponge to lean even further forward and lick her lips avariciously.

'All three can be yours if you will vouchsafe the information to us, Madame Sponge. A business deal between business people. What do you say?'

Without hesitation, she rose imperiously from her chair, her demeanour having taken a radical volte face. 'Very well, gentlemen, under the circumstances, it seems your request is a reasonable one. I will see what can be done. If you will wait awhile, I will consult our records.'

With a curt smile she swept from the room, her gown all a rustle and crackle.

After her departure, Jack and Oliver burst out laughing. 'A masterstroke, Jack.'

'I know the type. Pompous and imperious on the surface but would sell their old mother to a body snatcher for sixpence.'

'But tell me, where did you manage to obtain those sovereigns?'

The smile faded from Jack's face and he suddenly assumed a sheepish demeanour. 'Ah, well, perhaps you'll not be too happy about that.'

'What do you mean?'

'They're yours, Oliver. I just dipped you.'

'You dipped me? You mean you picked my pocket?'

Jack nodded dumbly. 'Yeah. When I leaned close to you. I'm very skilled at that sort of thing, as you well know. You see, I knew that the old bird wouldn't tell us what we wanted to know without a bribe. And they want to see the money in the flesh as it were. The flashing gold hypnotises 'em. Now, as you are well aware, I ain't got no cash to call my own, so…'

'So you availed yourself of mine.'

'I had to. Done the trick, though, hasn't' it?'

Oliver had to admit that it had indeed 'done the trick'. And as such he could not be angry with his friend. Indeed he was impressed with his resourcefulness. He just wished that it had not been at his own expense. Three guineas would be hard to replace.

'Let's hope that the information Madame Sponge presents to us is worth it,' he observed.

It wasn't long before the lady herself returned rustling into the room, carrying a small ledger. 'I have here the details which I believe you require, gentlemen,' she announced plonking the ledger on her desk with some force. 'Now, before I divulge the information you require, we have a business transaction to conduct. We are talking cash terms.'

With some reluctance, Jack Dawkins placed the three sovereigns down on the desk. With the speed of a lizard's tongue, they were scooped up by Madame Sponge and slipped into a drawer.

Picking up the ledger, she studied it for a few moments before addressing Oliver and Jack. 'In September in the year of our Lord, 1825, a child of three months of age was left on the doorstep of the orphanage with a note asking that the mite be taken care of. The note was signed by someone called Louise. We took the child in and raised it until he was twelve years of age. I remember the critter well. He was a pale-faced rangy youth, tall for his age and somewhat delicate. We named the boy Tom. And he was eventually sold to an Amos Braggle as an apprentice carpenter in 1837. That, gentlemen, is all the information I have.'

Oliver needed to learn more but he could see from her fierce demeanour that he would not be able to squeeze much more information from the Sponge creature. 'Do you have details of Amos Braggle's premises? What address was given?' he asked tentatively.

Madame Sponge snorted and for a moment Oliver thought that she would demand a further sovereign for this further titbit of information, but after a moment she appeared to relent and consulted the ledger once more.

'Braggle has – or rather had – a workshop in Cheapside: Furnace Alley. Whether it is still there, I cannot say.' She slammed the ledger shut and rose from her chair. 'That, I think, concludes our business and so, gentlemen, I will bid you a good day.' She flicked her hand in a dismissive fashion as though to waft the men out of her office. Oliver and Jack needed no further prompting. They left that instant.

CHAPTER SEVENTEEN

Sir Ebenezer Throate reached out for the light he glimpsed at the far end of the dark tunnel. He knew he must reach it if he was to survive but all his efforts were painful and his progress was infinitely slow. He was also conscious of the fierce pain in his chest. However, there was a dogged determination within the old aristocrat, matured through centuries of breeding, which forced him to carry on. As the light grew somewhat brighter, he began to hear voices, gentle murmuring voices. He was nearly there. Nearly back. He redoubled his efforts and with one final surge, his eyes flickered open. The world was a kaleidoscopic blur beyond the tunnel. It was as though he was seeing things through a frosted pane of glass. He flickered his eyelids like butterfly wings and then slowly, gradually, things grew clearer.

'Great heavens! I think he's awake, sir. Look he's opened his eyes.' It was a female voice. One that he recognised vaguely.

There was a rustling movement and then a dark shadow fell over him and he stared up into a man's face. 'Sir Ebenezer, can you hear me?' it said.

Floating out of the ether he heard the word, 'Yes'. It took him a few moments to realise that it was actually he who had given birth to that baby utterance.

The face came closer. Sir Ebenezer recognised it now, but

couldn't give a name to its owner.

'Who are you?' Again the words seem to materialise in the air rather than emanate from his lips, although he was now fully aware that he was uttering them.

'It's Cornelius, Sir Ebenezer. Doctor Benbow.'

'Benbow. Doctor. Am I ill?'

'You are – but recovering, God be praised.'

The baronet thought for a moment, or at least tried to but the old clockwork mechanism in his brain was proving somewhat recalcitrant. However, the state of his health soon bored him and a more important appetite took precedent.

'I could do with a brandy. A large one.'

Doctor Cornelius Benbow grinned. The old devil really was on the mend. Lady Amelia would be pleased.

* * *

'Draw me a hot bath, Waring.' As usual Lady Whitestone's voice was imperious and brusque without any element of politeness or warmth. It was the tone of an irritable commander ordering the troops to battle. 'After such a tiring journey,' she continued, 'I need a reviving soak before I take to my bed for an early night.'

Felicity did as she was bidden. She and her mistress were now ensconced once more in her ladyship's Chelsea town house after the train journey from Brighton. Since leaving the seaside resort, Felicity's mind had been awhirl with thoughts about her new romance and how sudden and cruel the imposed breach that had been forced upon her by the unexpected early departure. Now dark clouds completely obliterated the happy sunshine on her blissful landscape. She had no idea when she would see her beloved again. They were adrift from each other, separated, imprisoned by their duties, serving those who had power and money which gave them power to control them for solely selfish reasons. As a result she and Roger were robbed of the freedom to be happy. As she watched the water pour from the taps filling up the bath in readiness for her mistress' 'reviving soak', she was overcome with a desire to fling the old harridan into it face down and hold her there until the life ebbed out of her. Felicity's heart raced as a clear vision of this event flashed in her mind and for a brief moment she felt unsteady on her feet as though she might easily tumble forward into the bath herself. Luckily some innate sense of preservation came to her rescue and she managed to dismiss all dramatic images of her mistress floundering and splashing in the lavender scented waters. New thoughts came to her now. She knew that once she had been relieved of her duties for the evening, Felicity wanted to write a long and passionate letter to Roger. The main thrust of this missive, apart from declaring her undying love for him, was to enquire in desperate terms what on earth were they to do in order for them to be united on a permanent basis. It was a desperate dilemma for which she had no solution, but she hoped her darling and clever paramour would have some positive thoughts on the matter.

Later, after leaving Lady Whitestone gently snoring in her bed, she made her way back to her own cramped quarters. As she did so, a figure emerged from the shadows on the landing. The dark silhouette gave Felicity a shock and she gave a brief cry of alarm.

'It's only me,' announced the dark silhouette.

Arthur Wren, the footman. She had not given him a thought since she had been enveloped in the pink cloud of romantic happiness engendered by her liaison with Roger Lightwood.

'I am so pleased to see you back so early, my dear,' he announced in his dark, clipped tones, those tones that she once had considered mellifluous and attractive but now on hearing them again thought them somewhat common and comic.

He stepped out of the shadows, a wide smile on his face which caused his military moustache to twitch erratically. 'I was wondering if you'd like to come down into the kitchen for glass of hot milk and we could… have a little tete-a-tete,' he said, his eyes gleaming mischievously.

She knew what he meant by 'a little tete-a-tete'. It was one of his favourite expressions. It meant her sitting on his lap in a chair by the kitchen grate while he cuddled her, whispered practised sweet nothings in her ear and gave her the occasional peck on the cheek which finally led to a proper goodnight kiss. In the past, this routine had held some attraction for her, particularly after a long frustrating and barren day with her demanding mistress, but now, following her Damascus Road revelations in Brighton with Roger, she viewed the prospect of close contact with Arthur Wren with alarm and distaste. Any notion of an attachment to this stiff, ungainly Romeo had been blown away by the winds of real romance.

'I am so tired after my journey,' she replied, her voice formal and cold. 'I just want to retire for the night.'

'But...' he began to protest gently, the smile fading and his moustache drooping.

'Goodnight, Arthur,' she said, brushing past him and hurrying away, desperate to end this interview.

He was left alone in the gloom of the corridor, puzzled and disappointed. This was not like his Felicity – he had come to think of her in those terms. Something was wrong. He had to discover what.

* * *

In another part of London, much less salubrious than Chelsea, Jeremiah Throate huddled in a dark corner of a dark alley, harbouring dark thoughts. He waited and watched as various late night pedestrians wandered by. He not only had to be cunning, perceptive and bold – qualities that came naturally to him in a card game – but he had to be brutal, vicious and recklessly brave. These latter qualities were strangers to him. He kept running a series of clichés through his mind in preparation for his deed: 'needs must when the Devil drives', 'I must gird up my loins' and 'he who hesitates is lost'. He knew that he had to choose a solitary fellow. Two or more would be too much of a dangerous challenge. Also, it was not worth the effort to tackle anyone who would not, like a fat oyster, reveal a significant pearl as a reward at the end of his endeavours. He had been forced by circumstances down into these grimy realms and so any action he took wearing his newly assumed lowly mantle had to be worth the degradation.

And here he came. Just after some forlorn church bell chimed the hour of eleven, an unsteady fellow waddled down the street. He was of ample girth and, from what dim lighting was available provided by a sickly moon and a feeble gas lamp, he appeared to be wearing clothes of quality.

As he neared the patch of darkness, he had secured for himself, Throate stepped forward, blocking the fellow's way.

'Give me your money and all your valuables,' he croaked, his voice dry and harsh with nerves and tension.

The man, heavy in drink, lifted his gaze to stare at the dark stranger who had blocked his path.

'I am sorry, sir, I am a trifle deaf and I did not hear what you said. If you are requiring directions, I am afraid I cannot help you. I am a stranger in this part of town.' He chuckled lightly. 'If the truth be known, I am rather lost myself.'

Jeremiah thrust the knife he had been grasping hard behind his back in front of the bewildered man's face. A look of horror quickly replaced the one of gentle bewilderment that had resided there.

'Oh, gracious,' cried the man, staggering back. 'Help! Help! Murder!'

'Shut up you old fool and hand me over your purse.'

The man was too frightened and too much in drink to follow this simple instruction. In befuddled panic, he turned awkwardly to make his escape. He managed to take only a few steps before Jeremiah thrust the knife into the back of his neck. The man froze in mid-stride like a grotesque statue, an obscene gurgling sound emanating from his open mouth and then in an instant he collapsed to the ground in a silent heap.

Jeremiah Throate was stunned by what he had just done. His intention had been to frighten the poor devil – frighten him into passing over his valuables. Not to wound him – not to… Oh, Heaven forbid, not to kill him. His stomach churned and he felt the bile rise up in his mouth. Turning away, he crouched down and was violently sick.

He remained in this undignified foetal position for some moments before the sense of self-preservation asserted itself once more. The deed was done. There was no going back. He examined the body. It was already cooling. The man was indeed dead. At this confirmation, the stomach churned once more but he controlled it. With shaking fingers, he rifled the corpse's clothing. He extracted a purse, a pocket watch and relieved the fat fingers of three rings.

Stuffing this loot into his pockets, he stood and gazed down at the body, which now had a fine red pool of blood circling the head like a crimson halo. 'I'm sorry,' Jeremiah said, faintly, addressing the corpse.

In the distance there came the sound of raucous voices, two, three or maybe even more: a merry crew wending their way home. Coming his way. Turning on his heel, Jeremiah Throate ran off into the darkness.

Some hours later, he lay in some damp bed, in cheap lodgings that he had managed to secure with part of the dead man's cash. His body was stiff with fear and self-loathing. He had never considered himself a man with high moral principles. That fact had never bothered him. His own well-being had always been his sole concern. But he had never thought of himself as a bad man. But he was now. A very bad man. He was a murderer.

CHAPTER EIGHTEEN

Lady Amelia Throate's maid tapped gently on her mistress's bedroom door and awaited the usual stentorian order of 'Enter.'

The instruction came as usual, but not with quite the same harshness and arrogant authoritative force. The maid entered to find Lady Amelia sitting up in bed gazing with some distraction at the thin reed of sunlight which was visible through the narrow gap in the curtains.

'Good morning, M'lady. Shall I draw the curtains?'

It was some moments before a reply was given. 'Yes. Then a strong cup of tea.'

The maid swept the drapes asunder flooding the room with bright lemon early morning sunlight before disappearing, hurrying to the kitchen to make the requested 'strong cup of tea.'

Lady Amelia sighed. 'The best laid plans…' she murmured to herself. Oh, how careless she had been. A more deep-seated and ponderous sigh followed this observation. The big question, the very big question which had loomed over her in the dark watches of the night forbidding sleep to visit her, was, 'What was she to do now?' She may well ask this confounded and confounding riddle again, but no sensible answer was forthcoming. The old devil had been so resilient! One thing was certain: she had to be very, very careful indeed. Oh, and there was another thing that was certain: she could not face returning to the status quo. That understood, action had to be taken. And the understanding of this brought her round to the infuriating question again: 'What was she to do now?'

* * *

While Lady Amelia was pondering and cogitating as she waited for her 'strong cup of tea', Roger Lightwood was alighting from the coach which had brought him back to the portals of Throate Manor after his holiday sojourn to Brighton. With a strange absent-minded air, he collected the few items of luggage, paid the driver and made his way to the main entrance of the Manor. At this moment in time he had no notion of the dramatic events that had taken place during his absence and, indeed, contemplation of his duties and responsibilities was the farthest from his mind. His thoughts were focused solely on Felicity Waring, the young lady who had captured both his heart and mind to the exclusion of virtually everything else. Since seeing her depart from Brighton Station, he had not eaten or drunk anything, barely slept and only through a kind of mechanical procedure had he remembered to shave and comb his hair before setting off back to Throate Manor. The irritating cold symptoms had returned but now he was sure that these would be eradicated forever if he could arrange it for he and Felicity to be united in a lifelong union.

He gave one ponderous sniff, before ringing the bell. Bulstrode was overjoyed to see him. His training as a manservant that had straitjacketed any outward show of emotion for decades prevented him from hugging the young man and expressing his delight at seeing someone who was reasonable, decent and lacking aristocratic eccentricities returning to the Manor but he did allow himself the pleasure of extending an extra firm handshake to Lightwood. Even pre-occupied as he was, Roger noticed the more than usual warm and fulsome nature of this gesture.

Once inside the hall, Bulstrode leaned forward, tugging the sleeve of Roger's overcoat and in a conspiratorial manner and whispered softly. 'Things have been amiss since you went away, Mr Lightwood.'

Roger raised an eyebrow. 'Amiss?'

In a hurried and succinct but fairly theatrical fashion, Bulstrode recounted all the events that had occurred at the hall while Roger had been in Brighton: the assault on Sir Ebenezer, the dramatic entrances and exits of Jeremiah Throate and the appearance of the two 'rather soiled and disreputable gentlemen' who came and then left with amazing speed.

'Good gracious,' exclaimed Roger, suddenly dragged into the present by this vibrant recital. 'And how is Sir Ebenezer?'

'On the mend, I believe. As I understand it, he is out of immediate danger but it will be many days before he is his old self again.'

'And you say Lady Amelia forbade the police being brought into the matter?'

Bulstrode nodded. 'No doubt she was fearful of the scandal that would ensue. She maintained that as Sir Ebenezer survived the attack, no real harm was done…'

Roger shook his head. 'Nevertheless, if a murder has been attempted…'

Bulstrode shrugged his ancient shoulders. 'That's how the matter was left. She swore Doctor Benbow to secrecy. You know how her ladyship always gets her own way when she sets her mind to it.'

Roger did. 'Well, if it is convenient, I would like to see his Lordship right away. I am sorry that I was absent when no doubt he had need of me. Is he able to receive visitors?'

Bulstrode allowed himself a little smile. 'I am sure he will be pleased to see you.'

Moments later Roger tapped on Sir Ebenezer's bedroom door and entered. Maisie, one of the kitchen maids, was sitting by the bed on nurse sentry duty. She was roused from her gentle doze by Roger's arrival in the room and jumped up from her chair.

'How is he?' Roger enquired.

'He's… sleeping,' came the awkward reply.

'Give me five minutes alone with him, would you?'

Maisie gave a little curtsey and scurried from the room.

Roger pulled a chair up close to the bed and leaned forward and gazed at the haggard features of his employer which were peeping above the white sheet.

'How are you feeling, sir?' he asked gently.

Sir Ebenezer's eyes flickered at the sound of this new voice and gradually the lids creaked open.

'Good morning, Sir Ebenezer,' Roger said cheerily, relieved to see that there was some kind of life in the old dog yet.

Sir Ebenezer's eyes widened as he gazed upon his visitor and recognition dawned.

'Roger. Is it Roger?' he said, his voice resembling the creak of rusty hinges.

'Yes it is Roger.'

The old man smiled, a trickle of spittle escaping down his chin. 'You are a sight for sore eyes, my boy. I have not been well, you know.'

'Indeed. I am sorry I was absent when you needed me.'

Sir Ebenezer made a valiant effort to shake his head. 'Nonsense. But it is good to have you back again.' For a moment the light faded in his eyes and Roger thought that the baronet was about to slip back into sleep but then suddenly he rallied again, shifting slightly to pull himself up into a semi-sitting position.

'Someone tried to murder me,' he croaked. 'Someone stabbed me.'

Roger nodded. 'So I believe.'

'Who was it, Roger? Who tried to do me in?'

'I don't know, sir.'

'Was it Jeremiah – after my money?'

'I don't know, sir.'

Sir Ebenezer's skeletal hand snaked out from under the bed clothes and clasped his bony fingers around Roger's wrist. 'You must find out, my boy. Find out who tried to murder me. They could... they could well try again.'

Before Roger could respond to this dramatic request, the door of the chamber opened and Lady Amelia Throate sailed in.

'Ah, so you have returned, Mr Lightwood.'

Roger rose from his chair, gently releasing Sir Ebenezer's hand from his wrist, and gave a gentle bow.

'Yes, your ladyship, and to this very sad situation.' He turned and gazed down at Sir Ebenezer who it appeared had resumed his slumbers.

'A most unfortunate incident but one that the family will overcome. Sir Ebenezer is over the worst and he will rally. Fighting spirit is in his blood. We must draw a veil over the affair and move on.'

'But surely…'

'There are no 'but surelys' Mr Lightwood. Both Sir Ebenezer and I are of the same mind that this unpleasant incident must remain private and secret – and I charge you not to discuss the matter with anyone. This is family business and must remain so. Do I make myself clear?'

There were many things Roger Lightwood would like to have said in response to Lady Amelia's declaration but decorum, self-preservation and a keen awareness that it would be pointless to argue with the stony faced mistress of Throate Manor prevented him from doing no more than nod his head gently and mutter the word, 'Yes'.

'Good. Now I suggest that you leave my husband to rest and for you to resume your duties.'

Like a schoolboy admonished for some silly jape, Roger Lightwood departed the chamber, his metaphorical tail clamped between his legs.

CHAPTER NINETEEN

Furnace Alley was narrow and long, the properties at either side leaned outwards, the upper stories were so protuberant it seemed as though they wished to embrace each other. As a result there was little daylight permitted to filter down through the narrow gap. It was a fine sunny day, but on Furnace Alley it appeared to be twilight.

Oliver and Jack had wandered the length of it twice looking for Amos Braggle's establishment without success.

'We've been sold a dud,' announced Jack with some ire. 'That bleedin' woman tricked us for three guineas.'

Oliver was not convinced. 'Well, it was twenty five years ago. It is possible that this Braggle fellow has moved on. Perhaps his business expanded and he needed bigger premises.'

Jack chewed his lip a little. 'You could be right, I suppose. In fact, he could have moved elsewhere.' He pointed skywards, his grubby forefinger aiming at a miniscule patch of blue glimpsed between the drunken chimney pots.

Oliver sighed. 'Indeed. It is possible.'

Jack seeing this as an assurance of fact, crossed himself.

'Let's go back down the alley again, with a slower tread and keener eyes.'

'If you say so.'

At what Jack considered was a snail's pace, they traversed the narrow alleyway again. Halfway down Oliver came to an abrupt halt.

'What is it?' asked Jack puzzled.

'That sign there. It's quite new.'

Jack gazed at the sign, which was attached to the railings outside the shop below a bow window filled with bolts of cloth and a mannequin dressed in the most grotesque costume in a vibrant pink fabric. The sign read 'Samuel Cruncher – Draper and Haberdasher'.

'You're not needing a new set of buttons or another satin waistcoat are you, Oliver?'

'No, no. You are missing my point. Come closer.' He tugged his companion nearer to the shop front and the sign. 'Look more closely.'

Jack almost rubbed his nose along the sign until the point he had been missing became all too clear to him. There was, faintly behind the bright new lettering, the ghostly remnants of the previous sign, the one that had been painted over. Not all the letters or indeed the sense was visible but with one eye closed and an inquisitive mind one could decipher some of the letters that may very well make out the name 'Braggle'.

'This must have been his shop,' cried Oliver.

Jack pursed his lips and, peering closer, nodded. 'Yeah. I guess you're right. And so he has moved on.'

'Indeed, but perhaps the present incumbent has knowledge of his whereabouts.'

Jack gave a theatrical shrug to indicate that he thought that probability was unlikely.

'Let's find out,' replied Oliver, unabashed by his companion's lack of enthusiasm.

On entering Samuel Cruncher's emporium, a trio of tiny bells atop the door trilled noisily announcing their arrival. The bijou establishment was crammed with rolls of cloth of all colours, but most in a vibrant hue. There were baskets of buttons, shelves of filigree lace and a mannequin attired in a wedding gown of the most outre design. From behind this bizarre and risible display, there emerged the figure of an extremely tall, thin man wearing a turquoise silk jacket, a canary yellow waistcoat and cream breeches. Balanced somewhat precariously on his head was a high fronted blonde wig. As he approached them, Oliver could see that the man's face was powdered and his cheeks rouged. He bowed theatrically.

'Good day, gentlemen. I am Samuel Cruncher. Welcome to my establishment. How may I be of service?' The voice was high and sibilant.

'I wonder if you can help us with some information?' said Oliver.

Cruncher threw up his arms in the air and his eyes and mouth opened wide. It was as though he had just been stabbed in the back.

'Information! Information! I sell cloth and material of the finest quality to the gentry. High born ladies clamour for my wedding gowns; gentlemen of note devour me waistcoats. I do not peddle information, I'm afraid. Perhaps you should seek a library.'

'I just wondered if you had any news of Mr Braggle.'

Cruncher's visage darkened. 'Oh, him,' came the sneering response.

'Yes, Amos Braggle, the previous owner of this shop.'

'Oh, I know very well who Amos Braggle is – or rather was. If you are seeking him, I suggest you trot to St Christopher's church round the corner. You'll find him next to that hideous mausoleum housing the remains of some poet or other. He's in the graveyard there.' Cruncher extracted a large silk handkerchief from his pocket and dabbed his nose as though protecting it from a very unpleasant smell.

'He's dead then,' observed Jack.

Cruncher rolled his eyes. 'As he's lying six feet under - one would hope so.' He was about to turn his back on the two men for it was obvious to him they had not come in to buy any of his stock, when Oliver said, 'Do I take it that you and he did not get along?'

'You take it correctly, sir. When he was closing his business down in order to retire, I made an offer for the premises. That was when the trouble started.'

'Oh, dear,' Oliver said sympathetically.

Cruncher gave him a half smile. 'Oh dear is a mild version of my view on the matter.'

'What happened?'

Samuel Cruncher hesitated. Oliver could see that the fellow was undecided whether to tell the two strangers exactly what to do with their curiosity and send them off with giant fleas in their ears or take the opportunity of exercise his ire in full by recounting the Braggle saga in rich detail. In the end he settled for the latter.

'Braggle couldn't make up his mind. He wanted to sell the shop; he didn't want to sell the shop. He was prepared to accept a reasonable price for the premises; he wanted an exorbitant price for the premises. He drove me wild with his vacillations. I ordered stock; I had to cancel stock. I made preparations to move in. Then he changed his mind and I had to run around altering these. This happened several times. The man drove me wild.'

'How very frustrating,' sympathised Oliver.

'I bet you wanted to punch the bloke in the phizzog,' added Jack.

'Indeed, I did. And it was all because of his son.'

'Really,' said Oliver, with some relish. 'What about his son?'

'A very good question.' Cruncher was warming to his tale now. He leaned forward and lowered his voice in conspiratorial fashion. 'From what I could gather, the young lad wasn't really his son. Braggle wasn't married. Well, there was no wife in view anyway. I reckoned he'd taken on the boy at some point with a view to using him as an apprentice in the shop and a kind of relationship had developed. He'd grown fond of the boy. That was part of my problem.'

Oliver raised his eyebrows in query as a prompt for Cruncher to continue.

'I say that he was fond of the boy. He was besotted by him. With no family of his own, he seemed to have placed the brat high on a pedestal. He attended to the lad's every whim. It seemed to me that he wanted to give the boy all the advantages he had lacked as a youth: money, education, privilege.'

'How old was the lad?'

Cruncher shrugged. 'Not yet twenty. I have to admit that he was a bright young fellow. Inoffensive in his own way. He'd been privately educated. Braggle had seen to that and it was mooted that he'd be going to university. The old man wanted that for him, but the boy was uncertain. That was the nub of the old man's dithering. He intended to sell the business, retire and pass on the bulk of his fortune such as it was to the boy. However, the youngster seemed to be content to carry on the business, working in the shop. I suppose that was all that he had known. And so on Monday the shop was being sold. On Tuesday it was withdrawn from sale. And then on Wednesday...' Cruncher was now growing more agitated as he recollected what to him was the very disturbing episode from his past. His hands fluttered erratically like distressed butterflies, the wig trembled dangerously as though it would lose its moorings at any minute and take flight, while his voice moved into an even higher register.

'No consideration was given to the disastrous effect this was having on my nerves. I had a property and a future. I didn't have a property... It was like an emotional see saw. I became a gibbering wreck. My friends feared for my sanity. I can tell you that, gentlemen: they feared for my sanity, they did.'

Oliver and Jack nodded in sympathetic unison.

'In the end, I wanted to strangle them both. Father and son. One afternoon we had a showdown in the shop. I had reached the end of my tether. I just exploded with anger and frustration.'

Cruncher paused and with a flourish of the silk handkerchief he dabbed his eyes which had grown moist with the emotion that his recollections had prompted. 'The whole episode still haunts me, gentlemen.' He paused a moment, his face rippling with emotion. 'And do you know, when I broke down in front of them – here in this very shop – sobbing and begging them to stop their cruel vacillations... do you know they had the temerity, the effrontery, the nerve to appear surprised at my distress. Surprised! I ask you. They claimed they had no idea of the devil's hell they were dragging me through. What kind of insensitive insects were they?'

'Insensitive insects, indeed,' agreed Jack decisively.

'Well, my outburst brought them to their senses. The youth

agreed to fly off to university and the old codger agreed to sell me the shop.'

'All's well that ends well, then?' Jack flashed Cruncher a smile.

'Eventually, I suppose. It is an episode of my life I have no wish to repeat, I can tell you that for sure.'

'Well, Mr Cruncher, you certainly have a splendid emporium here.' Oliver gazed around the premises with a smile. 'I shall certainly recommend it to my friends and colleagues,' said Oliver.

Jack secretly thought he was over-egging the pudding but the effete Mr Cruncher beamed graciously and gave one of his little bows. 'You are too kind, sir.'

'I have a maiden aunt who would look divine in that hue of pink.' Oliver pointed to a swathe of luminous pink cloth that was draped across the counter. 'What shade do you call that?'

Cruncher waltzed over to the material. 'How discerning you are sir. This is the latest fashion, just in from Paris. It is African Dawn. Guaranteed to lift the features and enhance the figure.'

'Charming,' said Oliver, his voice gaining a softer mellifluous tone. 'Well, my friend and I must be on our way, but I thank you for your time, Mr Cruncher. It has been a delight to make your acquaintance.'

By now Oliver's gentle charm had won the day or at least won Samuel Cruncher over. The handkerchief fluttered once more. 'On the contrary, dear sir, the pleasure was all mine. Do give your regards to your aunt. I look forward to making her acquaintance.'

'Indeed,' Oliver seemed to be about to turn on his heel and make his way to the door when he hesitated. 'Do you know what happened to the boy?'

'The boy? Oh, you mean Braggle's lad. In the end I believe that he attended the University College of London to study law. While he was there old Braggle died and the boy came into a modest fortune. What happened to him after that I could not say.'

'That was… how many years ago?'

Cruncher placed a well-manicured finger to his pursed lips. 'I've been here six years… I believe Braggle died four years ago.'

'What was the boy's name?'

'Tom Braggle.'

'Thank you so much, sir.' Giving Jack a tug at the elbow, the two of them were out in the street in a trice.

'Well,' said Oliver rubbing his hands, 'that was most instructive.'

'It certainly was. I never knew you had a maiden aunt who went in for garish clothes.'

The two men laughed.

'I guess I know where we're headed now,' said Jack as they moved down the narrow thoroughfare.

'Indeed. I believe you do,' agreed Oliver with a dry smile.

CHAPTER TWENTY

Lizzie Barnes, the cook/housekeeper at Throate Manor, was surprised to discover her mistress, Lady Amelia walking through the kitchen door. This never happened. On no previous occasion had the grand lady ever deigned to descend those well-worn stone steps into the nether reaches of the manor to visit the vaulted kitchen. This unique event caused Lizzie Barnes' heart to race. She could not conceive of any reason for this. She felt sure that it must presage ill tidings of some kind. It was part of Lizzie Barnes' nature to always think the worst would happen, that every dark cloud had an even darker lining. This negative view stemmed from her unhappy youth and nothing that had happened in her life since had managed to dislodge this dour and nihilistic view of existence – *her* existence at least. She had her secrets and God forbid Lady Amelia should learn of them.

The presence of this imperious wraith in her domain could only mean one thing: something was wrong. Had she somehow displeased her ladyship? Was she about to be sacked? Sent on her way. Thrown out into the world once more without money or a roof over her head. History repeating itself? Suddenly she realised that she was crying. Her eyes had watered and tears began to fall gently down her rosy cheeks in an anticipation of the tragedy that was about happen to her – whatever it was. Lady Amelia observed this but thought no doubt the woman had been peeling onions or leaning too closely over a steaming pan. These menials did this sort of thing. She certainly did not acquaint Lizzie's strained features or moist cheeks with emotion.

'Ah, there you are,' said her ladyship, as though the cook had been hiding behind a mound of vegetables.

'Yes, ma'am,' agreed Lizzie, wobbling slightly giving the impression that she was about to curtsy but had thought better of it.

The surreal conversation continued when Lady Amelia suddenly uttered the word 'Soup!' in exclamatory tones.

'Soup?' queried Lizzie.

'Yes. I gather Doctor Benbow has recommended soup, healthy life-giving soup as a restorative for my ailing husband. Soup that will bring him back to us whole and healthy... well reasonably so.'

'Oh, yes.'

'And you are preparing it now?'

Instinctively, Lizzie Barnes glanced over at the large pan on the oven with its gently undulating contents. 'Yes, yes, I am. Vegetable soup with a sprinkling of ham fragments. That should build the master's strength up.'

Lady Amelia observed the pan and wrinkled her nose in distaste. 'I am sure it will,' she commented without much conviction. 'Let me sample the broth.'

Lizzie raised her eyebrows in surprise. 'You want to taste the soup?'

'Yes. Go fetch me a small dish.'

Somewhat flustered at this request, Lizzie hurried off to the crockery cupboard to carry out this request. All this was very strange to her. Not only had Lady Amelia never set foot in the kitchen before but she had previously refused to partake of anything as lowly as vegetable soup. On returning with a china bowl, she found her mistress standing over the simmering pan and stirring it.

Lizzie ladled out a small portion of soup into a bowl and

presented it with a spoon to Lady Amelia. She took one small sip, her face replicating a medieval gargoyle. 'Needs a little more salt,' she said brusquely, thrusting the dish and spoon into the cook's hand. Without another word, she turned on her heel and swept out of the kitchen, leaving Lizzie Barnes open-mouthed in surprise. 'Now what was that all about,' she muttered to herself as she reached for the jar of salt.

* * *

Eugene Trench tapped the fingers of both hands in a rapid tattoo. 'He's here in London. Somewhere. We must find him.' He gazed up darkly at his two henchmen, Kepple and Joint, who were standing shifting their feet and examining their palms like naughty school boys.

'You were most careless to let Master Throate escape. Most careless.'

The two men shivered. There was real dark menace in the repeated phrase. Kepple mumbled something but Trench ignored it. 'It's your job to find him. Is that understood?'

They nodded dumbly.

'Put the word out. Say there's a five pound reward for letting you know where Throate is. Is that understood?'

Both men acknowledged in gruff whispers that they did indeed understand.

'Then what are you waiting for, you idiots? Be about it.'

In an ungainly scuffle the two men left the chamber.

* * *

'My Dearest Felicity

How long the days and hours seem since we last met, last talked, last held each other close, last kissed. My heart aches to be with you again. Our separation has placed me on the rack. What makes things worse is that I have no notion as to when we shall be united. I had hoped to discuss the matter with my employer, Sir Ebenezer Throate and see if it was possible for him to find you some employment at Throate Manor until we could be married and maybe then we could take a small cottage on the estate. Oh, what a wonderful dream that would be.

Unfortunately, fate has thrown an obstacle in that particular pathway. I returned to discover that my employer is seriously ill and indeed may not recover. The circumstances surrounding his dramatic decline in health are rather complicated and I have been sworn to secrecy concerning the details of the matter. However, should his health fade and he passes away, I am afraid that my own future will be in doubt. I am sure that I would be dismissed from my post for I am well aware that Lady Amelia has no fondness for me and believes I am an unnecessary drain on the family purse. So it would seem that at the moment no definite plans can be made to secure our future happiness. The only bright spark on our dark horizon is the possibility of a brief meeting. If I could get away for a day, I could travel to London and spend a few hours in your company if you could secure a similar escape from your duties. Do let me know, my darling, if this is possible and practical. I shall wait with bated breath and an aching heart until I hear from you.

Believe me to be your most adoring,

Roger.'

Felicity Waring laid the letter down on the coverlet on her bed and smoothed the paper out, allowing her fingers to run gently across the missive with sensuous care. A small tear appeared in the corner of her right eye. Oh cruel world, she thought. Why must we be separated, rather like those lovers in that Shakespeare play, Romeo and Juliet. If only she had money, wealth, the means to allow her independence and personal freedom, she could be with her love. Instead she was shackled to that wrinkled harridan who was, at this moment, snoring grotesquely a few rooms away and who in a very short time would be calling out for her to attend to her morning toilette. And her duties for the day would start and continue until the old crone retired for the night, her face plastered in some unction she believed foolishly would make her look young and beautiful. There was no respite for Felicity in that day long entrapment, apart from an hour or so when her charge took an afternoon nap. What chance had she to secure the time for even the briefest of liaisons with dear Roger. The tear grew bigger and was joined by a fellow in the other eye.

She would have slumped down on the bed in despair but she was frightened of crumpling the letter that laid there. What was she to do? What could she do to extricate herself from this prison cell? Her dark thoughts were interrupted by the stentorian tones of Lady Whitestone calling from her bedroom. She sounded to be in her usual ill-humour. Wiping her eyes, and straightening her dress, Felicity, like a well-trained dog, made her way to her mistress's bedroom, slipping on the heavy chains of duty as she did so.

* * *

Dr Benbow was pleased with his patient's progress. He wasn't quite out of the woods yet, but the path to the lesser brambles and sunshine beyond was now visible. Sir Ebenezer was still sleeping but it was a natural, restful sleep which the medical man hoped would restore the patient's energy and recuperative reserves. Benbow felt for Sir Ebenezer's pulse. It was still faint but regular.

At that moment the servant girl entered the room carrying a tray which contained a bowl of something brown and steaming. 'Some soup for his lordship,' she said shyly.

The doctor nodded. 'Place it on the table by his bed.' She did so, curtsied and made a hurried exit. The doctor stared at the soup, still steaming despite its protracted journey from the kitchen, and then glanced at his slumbering patient. He certainly wasn't going to wake him up to partake of some broth. Sleep would do the old man greater benefit than a few mouthfuls of vegetable stock. However, it did look quite good though. He leaned over the bowl and breathed in the steamy fumes. It smelt good also. It was quite a while since he had partaken of some victuals. As he studied the bowl further, he found his tummy began to rumble gently and pangs of hunger materialised out of nowhere. Goodness, now that soup looked so appetising. Like a rural elixir. There was also a crumbly chunk of bread leaning seductively by the bowl. It would probably be cold and indigestible by the time the old man woke. It would be such a pity to waste it. Surely, it would not be too terrible to take a few mouthfuls.

Somewhat furtively he glanced around the room to ascertain that the servant girl had indeed gone before taking hold of the spoon and dipping it deep into the bowl of soup. He sipped it, feeling the pungent liquid fill his mouth with a warm glow. He took another spoonful. It was interesting rather than delicious. It had a strange piquant taste but, by Jove, it appeased his hunger. Like an alcoholic presented with a full bottle of gin, he could not resist taking yet another taste. And another. And another. Before he knew it the bowl was nearly empty. It was then that he began to feel a little odd. The rumbling in his tummy had stopped and now it began to feel constricted as though someone was tightening his belt in a savage fashion. He began to sweat profusely and his throat felt as though it was on fire. In some distress, with great effort he rose from the chair. This sudden ague that had attacked his constitution was increasing in its vehemence. As he made his way to the door like a stumbling drunkard, his vision began to blur and the room swayed around him, moving in and out of focus. At the back of his tortured mind he realised what had happened to him. It was monstrous and tragic but it could be the only explanation.

His fingers felt for the door knob and eventually they found it.

With a Herculean effort, he wrenched open the door and staggered on to the landing, colliding with Roger Lightwood and collapsing into his arms.

'I've been poisoned,' he croaked, his vocal chords almost giving up the ghost. 'I've been poisoned.' It was at this point that death overtook him.

CHAPTER TWENTY ONE

It was late in the day when Oliver and Jack entered the cramped office at the University of London which bore the legend 'Admissions Record Office'. It was a dingy chamber which seemed to have been taken over by a whole army of box files and book cases groaning with leather bound ledgers. In the midst of this gloomy haven, illuminated by a series of candles, sat a tall, spindly geriatric gentleman with a thatch of straw coloured hair which emerged from his scalp at a variety of acute angles as though they were desperate to escape their moorings. He was seated at a tall desk, scribbling away with a monster quill pen, the feather of which flashed rhythmically to and fro across the fellow's cadaverous face like a fluffy pendulum.

So engrossed in his task was he, that it took him sometime to become cognisant of the fact that two strangers had entered his domain. On eventually realising this, he stopped his activity immediately and rather like a mechanical toy, with stiff precise movements, he placed his quill down on the desk and swivelled on his chair to face them. He had a long thin face with sunken cheeks and a pallor that a ghost would have been proud to own. He peered at his visitors inquisitively over an ancient pair of pince nez.

'Gentlemen,' he said, his voice thin and reedy, 'you do know where you are?'

Oliver nodded. 'We believe we do. This is the Admissions Record Office.'

The man shifted in his chair and nodded his head vigorously, causing his pince-nez to slip down to the end of his long bony nose where they balanced themselves most precariously on the tip. 'Correct, correct. How wonderful. This is something of a red letter day. The last time anyone came in here who was not a known employee of the university was…' He closed his eyes and muttered gently to himself for some thirty seconds, before announcing, 'The tenth of September, the year before last and that was a representative from a scholarly gown company who had lost his way.' He grinned a skeletal grin. 'Are you sure you gentlemen have not lost your way also?'

'I don't believe so,' said Oliver. 'We are seeking information which I believe you can provide for us.'

'Oh, excellent, excellent. I hope the information you seek will be difficult to obtain. I do love a challenge. Simple tasks are so mundane, don't you think?' He ran his hands together with such ferocious glee and relish, Jack thought he may well start a fire. 'My name is Scrope-Mantle: a hyphenated name I inherited from my dear parents who were determined that my mother should not relinquish her maiden name on the occasion of her marriage. Manville Scrope-Mantle at your service.' His head sank on to his chest in a slow deferential movement.

Oliver gave a curt bow in response as it seemed appropriate to do so. He wanted to keep on the good side of this apparently obliging fellow. Jack Dawkins followed suit in a less efficient and decorous manner.

'I am Oliver Twist and this is my assistant, Jack Dawkins. We are representatives of the legal firm Gripwind and Biddle. We are seeking information regarding a past student at the university,' said Oliver.

'Well, we have hundreds of them to choose from.'

'His name is Braggle. Tom or Thomas Braggle.'

'What years did he attend?'

'Ah, that I cannot be sure. Some five or six years ago.'

Scrope-Mantle clapped his hands. 'Excellently vague. A very pleasing challenge. Now gentlemen I suggest you take a seat on the old wooden bench over there because – with a modicum of luck – I shall be quite some time.' Without another word, he hopped off his stool and like a large gentrified stick insect disappeared behind a stack of files into the darker and dustier recesses of the room.

Oliver and Jack exchanged glances and slight shrugs of the shoulders and did as they were bidden. They sat in silence and waited while in the distance, unseen, they heard Scrope-Mantle rustling paper and muttering to himself in a chirpy fashion like a parrot that had discovered a large cache of bird seed.

Time passed, the candles dwindled and evening shadows began to creep into the room. Jack yawned. He was bored and pessimistic. He had held little hope for this exercise in the first place but now he considered it a futile one. He was convinced that the gibbering idiot he could hear in the dusty realm beyond would fail miserably in his mission. Jack was longing for a pint of ale and something warm to munch. On the other hand, Oliver was occupying his time mulling over all the information they had gleaned about the young man they were seeking. Admittedly there were mere fragments of the tapestry that, as yet, could not be woven into a whole, but with each new addition the picture was growing and he had play about with these fragments. Oliver was convinced that imagination as well as facts would help to solve this mystery

'Are you making any progress, sir?' called out Jack Dawkins suddenly with a brusqueness that clearly indicated that his patience was waning.

After a pause came the muffled response. 'Yes, yes. Possibly. Definitely …and yet I'm not sure.'

'Blimey,' muttered Jack, 'we could be here till doomsday – and then we'd be no wiser.'

'Have a little patience, old fellow. A few hours of our time matters not if we obtain the information we seek.'

'*If*. That's a monster if, Oliver.'

Oliver had no response to this, partly because he knew Jack was correct. The pair then lapsed into silence once more, while Scrope-Mantle's chuntering continued.

A further forty minutes passed and then they heard a cry of triumph and moments later, a dusty Scrope-Mantle stumbled into view clasping a tattered sheet of paper. It had yellowed with age and the ink was now a pale cousin of its earlier bold self.

'I have it. I have it,' he cried, panting heavily as though he had just run a marathon or scaled a mountain peak. 'And it is most satisfying,' he added, 'because it presents a mystery. Very satisfying.'

'A mystery?' queried Oliver.

Scrope-Mantle nodded vigorously and laid the sheet of paper down on his desk. 'Come, come, see for yourself.'

Both Oliver and Jack moved to the desk and peered down at the paper. Scrope-Mantle's bony finger traced out the faded handwritten script.

'See, here. October 1850. Thomas Braggle enrols at the University to study law and commerce. The end of year comment from the Dean: 'An excellent student who has consistently worked well'. Then the second year... The comment from the Dean: 'There has been a falling off of effort this semester. The student seems troubled and distracted for some strange reason'. Then, in his third and final year, 'This particular student left summarily without taking his final exams'.'

'What explanation was given for this? It seems a remarkably rash thing to do. Something quite dramatic must have occurred to bring about this state of affairs,' said Oliver with some consternation.

Scrope-Mantle gave a gentle smile of satisfaction. 'There are no reasons given, no explanation provided why Mr Braggle absented himself from the university in such a fashion at this crucial time. It leaves quite a satisfying mystery, don't you think?'

'We have enough mystery to be going on with, thank you,' observed Jack. 'We could do without more being heaped on our load.'

Scrope-Mantle nodded with feigned sympathy. 'The young have many ways of causing us consternation. However, I do have one scrap of information which may well provide some consolation to you.' His finger hovered over the faded script on the tattered page. 'There is a forwarding address to which his possessions should be sent.'

Oliver and Jack leaned forward to scrutinise the faded script. When their eyes focused on the address scribbled on the page they both simultaneously gave a sharp intake of breath.

'Good gracious,' cried Oliver.

'Crikey Moses,' cried Jack.

And they both exchanged shocked, open-mouthed stares.

* * *

'It's a beauty. One of the finest that Bowes and Mandelson ever produced.' Amos Crimper caressed the pistol he had just retrieved from the window of his emporium, 'Amos Crimper, Gunsmith to the Gentry'. Judging by the clothes and demeanour, the fellow who had expressed an interest in the pistol was hardly a member of 'the Gentry' – his clothes were creased and rumpled, his hair unkempt and his chin had obviously not seen a razor for at least two days. However, he was a potential customer – a breed that was somewhat thin on the ground of late. Mister Crimper could not be as fussy as he once had been in choosing who to serve.

'You would find it hard to obtain a more accurate and serviceable weapon than this little beauty,' he was saying, as he continued to stroke at butt and barrel as though it was a new born baby.

Jeremiah Throate held out his hand – a fairly grubby one, Crimper observed, to take hold of the gun. With some reluctance, the gunsmith passed it over. Throate grasped it firmly. He liked the feel of it. The weight of the thing and the comfort of the handle gave him confidence. He took a step back and held his arm out straight, aiming at the glass display case behind Crimper who winced and gave a little whelp of alarm as he did so.

'Do, do be careful, sir,' he cried.

'Is it loaded?' asked Throate.

'I'm not sure. Please put it down and I will check.' Crimper managed to generate a small laugh. 'We wouldn't want any accidents, would we?'

'Oh, I can check myself to see if this little beauty is ready for action.'

Crimper's eyes bulged and his face paled. He really didn't like the tone of this fellow's remark. There was a certain air of danger in his manner.

'Oh, yes. It has ammunition neatly stowed. Very convenient.'

Crimper gave another nervous laugh and held out his hand. 'If you please, sir?'

Throate raised his brow in gentle query. 'What…?'

'If you'll pass the gun back to me.'

'Oh, I can't do that.'

'You… you can't do that? Why… why…why?' Crimper was now beside himself with terror. He was convinced that this ruffian was about to shoot him.

'It's just what I need. Fits my purposes exactly. So I intend to take it.'

'Oh, I see. You wish to purchase the weapon,' grinned the gunsmith, the invisible clutching hand around his heart releasing its tight grip a little.

The man shook his head. 'No. I intend to take it.'

'I'm sorry, I don't understand.'

Throate took a step forward and pressed the point of the pistol against Crimper's chest. 'I intend to take it,' he repeated darkly and then added, in softer tones as though speaking to a child, 'to steal it.'

'Steal…' It seemed that Crimper still did not quite understand Throate's words, although his senses told him to be frightened.

'Take it without paying for it.'

'No, no, sir, you cannot do that.'

'Oh yes I can. In fact I can do it one of two ways. I can just slip it into my belt and walk out of the shop, allowing you to get on with your business and keeping your miserable mouth shut – or if you cause some disturbance I can just shoot you and walk out of the shop anyway.'

Now the fog cleared and the situation became clear to Crimper. 'Oh,' he said.

Throate smiled. 'Which is it to be?'

'I… I would take it as a great favour if… if you would not harm me. I will not cause a disturbance, I assure you.'

'Good man, Master Crimper. It has been a pleasure to do business with you.' Throate slipped the pistol in his belt, to the left side so that it was hidden by his jacket and then gave a swift salute to the quivering gunsmith before quitting his premises. With swift strides, almost breaking into a trot, Throate put as much ground between him and Crimper's shop as he could.

The feeling of the pistol held snugly by his belt gave Jeremiah Throate a boost in confidence and hope. Now he was equipped for the task in hand – the task he had decided to set himself as he tossed and turned on the cramped bed in his shabby lodgings during the watches of the night. In essence, he realised that there really was only one course of action to extricate himself from the life-threatening dilemma in which he was enmeshed. In simple terms, he had to turn the tables and provide a life threatening scenario for his nemesis. More than life threatening, actually: life taking, in fact. He had to kill Eugene Trench. As his hand surreptitiously found its way past the fold of his jacket, clasping the handle of the pistol, he smiled. Now he had the means to carry out the task. And he would enjoy it.

CHAPTER TWENTY TWO

Sir Ebenezer Throate woke with a start. His eyes flickered open and in automatic response to his full consciousness, he sat bolt upright in bed. 'I'm hungry. I want some food. And a brandy!' he cried in a voice that was firm and clear.

The young girl sitting by his bedside gave a cry of alarm. 'Oh, my goodness,' she shrieked as though she had witnessed a return from the dead and gathering up her skirts she ran from the room.

In the hall downstairs, Roger Lightwood was in conversation with a large, full bellied individual dressed in a thick tweed suit and the possessor of two shaggy eyebrows which were in danger of curtaining his eyes from the world. This was Inspector Bottle of the Hatfield Constabulary who had come to Throate Manor to investigate the death – the possible homicide – of Dr Cornelius Benbow.

'We have only the dead man's word that he was poisoned,' he was saying in his expansive and pompous manner that made him the target for mimicry amongst the lowly constables under his command. 'We have to ask ourselves this question: who would want to kill this medical gentleman? What was the motive? In my investigation of crime, which is quite considerable, I can assure you, I have found it imperative that there should always be a motive. There cannot be a crime without motive.'

Roger knew that he could not provide a motive – not at the moment anyway. However, it had seemed to him maybe that Dr Benbow was not the intended victim. That was Sir Ebenezer. After all, one failed attempt had been made on his life. It was quite possible the determined murderer would have another go. Unfortunately, he had been sworn to secrecy about the stabbing of his master – 'a family affair only' he had been told – and so he could not pass on his thoughts on this matter to Inspector Bottle. He had noticed the bowl with a small quantity of soup on Sir Ebenezer's bedside table. It was unlikely that the comatose occupant of the bed had imbibed any of the soup for he had not been conscious for hours. Therefore it seemed to Roger that for some reason – hunger or greed – the doctor had helped himself to the soup. But now, mysteriously, the bowl had disappeared and the remaining contents could not be tested for poison.

'Crime and motive go hand in hand,' Bottle was repeating the notion *ad nauseum*. 'I cannot believe anyone in this house would have just cause to end the life of our own humble and dedicated Doctor Benbow. A man of his age and … comfortable bulk is more likely to be prey to a weak heart and suffer a heart attack. No crime, no motive, just cruel Fate. I know that Lady Amelia is of the same mind.'

Before Roger could respond to Bottle's bluster, the little maid who had been sitting in attendance by Sir Ebenezer's bedside came scuttling down the stairs whimpering as if all the devils in hell were after her.

'What on earth's the matter, Maisie?' asked Roger, grabbling the girl gently and stopping her in her tacks.

Maisie gulped for air, her chest rising and falling in rapid succession. 'It's Sir Ebeb.. Sir Eben… Sir Ebe…'

'Yes, Sir Ebenezer, what about him?'

Maisie's eyes widened. 'He's come back to life.'

'Silly girl. He's never been dead.'

'But he's sitting up in bed asking for food… and a brandy.'

Roger grinned. 'Is he now? The old rascal. He really has come back to us.' He turned swiftly to Inspector Bottle. 'If you'll excuse me, I must attend upon my employer.'

Bottle nodded his head and gave a curt bow. 'Of course,' he said, relieved to be allowed to escape and not be involved in any more nonsense about murder. Huh, he thought, homicide in an ancestral pile like Throate Manor, how ridiculous. 'I have pressing business elsewhere,' Bottle added pompously. 'Farmer Featherstone had some chickens go missing and he's certain that it wasn't a fox this time.' The policeman turned smartly on his heel and almost hurried his way to the main door.

Roger made his way to Sir Ebenezer's bedroom just in time to see the old man attempt to get out of bed.

'No, sir,' he cried, rushing forward to catch his employer before he sank to the floor. 'You're not strong enough yet, sir. It will be a few days before you are able to stroll about.'

Sir Ebenezer pursed his lips. 'You could be right, my boy. I was always one for wanting to run before I could walk.'

Roger helped him back into bed. 'It's so good to see that you are really on the mend. We have been most worried about you.'

'Hah! We Throates are made of stern stuff. Tell you what, my boy, I am dashed hungry. Could do with a piece of well-cooked meat and a flagon of claret to wash it down. That'll help set me up.'

'I'll see to it straight away.'

'Good man. And, oh Roger…'

'Yes, sir.'

'It's good to have you back.' His aged arm snaked gently out from the bedclothes and offered itself to Roger.

Roger beamed as he grabbed the aged palm. 'And it's good to have *you* back, sir,' he said.

* * *

Lady Amelia was distraught. Is there really a God in heaven or a Devil in Hell? Which of these two deities was prepared to help her? She didn't care as long as one of them stepped forward and plucked her from the dreary mire into which she was sinking. Up to now all her brilliant (ah ah!) schemes had failed, stabbings, poison. What the...! She had little time left on this earth. Was she really destined to spend those fading years here in this mausoleum? Surely she would be allowed an opportunity to grasp a little happiness before the curtain descended. She gazed at herself in the dressing table mirror. Oh, that aged face, those drooping brows, the ragged neck. It was the ruin of a visage. Where was the Amelia who sparkled, beguiled, entranced...? How had she turned into this cobwebbed harpy trussed up like a turkey in February with fading flesh and a rotting carcass bound to a dolt like Ebenezer? Perhaps she should end it all now. Slit her wrists, cast herself from the highest balcony on the estate or just splash down into one of the fish ponds in the grounds. At least then it would be over. But no! She didn't want it to be over. She deserved more. She would have more. Somehow.

Somehow.

CHAPTER TWENTY THREE

Eugene Trench was back at his old haunt – The Saracen's Head, leaning on the bar chatting to his old cohort, Hubert Faddle, the landlord.

'I'm looking forward to the game tonight,' he said, sipping his gin and water. 'Not just because we'll fleece another nonce but as a diversion to the worries I've been having.'

'Worries?' said Faddle, his mouth turned down in sympathy. 'I am sorry to hear that. I thought you were swimming along nicely like a trout upstream. What worries are these then?'

Trench twisted his features. 'They're not really serious. It's just that someone that has irritated me greatly, like a raspberry seed in your teeth that you can't get rid of. You lick your tongue round the tooth but the little devil stays put and irritates the hell out of you. That's how it's been with Throate. He owes me money and you know how I feel about debtors. Worse than baby killers they are. They should be disposed of in the harshest fashion.'

Trench grasped his glass so tightly as he expressed these thoughts that Faddle thought he may well crush it. The landlord nodded calmly. 'Throate, that was the fellow we fleeced at the last big game.'

'Yes, we *would* have fleeced him if he hadn't been shorn already.' Trench slammed his drink down, a certain amount of gin splashing over the side of the glass and on to the counter. 'That's one thing I can't stand, a dishonest punter who hasn't got the decency to allow us to squeak him dry. In their arrogant stupidity, they come here thinking they'll do that to us.'

'You'll be dealing with him then?'

'Oh, you can bet your life on that. When I can find the devil! He's gone to ground, but I'll snout him out.'

Faddle gave another shake of the head. It was a non-commital gesture. He well knew that if a man wanted to disappear in this great labyrinthine city, it was an easy task to accomplish. There were boltholes galore. Even the smartest and keenest of bloodhounds could fail in seeking someone out. He knew this and of course Trench knew this and his awareness of this fact was at the root of his incipient anger.

'Why don't you take a rest in your old room before the game tonight? Relax in readiness. We have a really big goat tethered to the post: a member of the judiciary. His purse should go some way to easing your mind.'

Trench smiled and tapped the landlord's arm with affection. 'Thank you, Hubert, as always. I'll finish my drink and then take another up to the room. A rest will do me good.'

* * *

Some two hours later as the sun was setting, a stout fellow in dark clothing entered the inn premises. His three cornered hat was pulled well down over his forehead in order to place his features in shadow. He moved with a stiff awkward gait through the crowd of drinkers by the bar and with an authoritative wave of the hand attracted the attention of the landlord. Hubert Faddle was well aware who this stranger was, although he had never seen him before in his life. They all came in like this: dark anonymous clothing, hat pulled down to disguise their features. Some even wore false whiskers and eye glasses in a belief that they were fooling the world. It was greed, Faddle mused casually, that brought them here – the gentlefolk who were either desirous of increasing their wealth or desperate to gain sufficient funds to extricate them from debt which they had so carelessly incurred. He felt nothing but contempt for them and had no scruples at being involved in the process of tricking them out of all the money they were prepared to risk in a gambling school. The fools.

'Mr Faddle,' whispered the stranger in a hoarse, strangled fashion.

The landlord nodded. 'And you must be Mr Crow.' They were all Mr Crow. That was the *nom de plume* they were instructed to give when arrangements were made for them to attend the game.

Mr Crow glanced nervously around the bar before replying. 'Yes, I am he.'

'Let me get you a drink and then take a seat. The game will not begin for another hour.'

'Another hour! I was told to be here by sunset.'

'Just a precaution, you understand. Just relax, sir. All will be well. Now what is your pleasure?'

Mr Crow hesitated. He wasn't happy with this change of arrangement. As a high court judge, he was used to being in charge and controlling events. Being a pawn was new to him and unsettling.

'Do you have a decent brandy?' he asked stoically.

'Take a seat, I'll bring one over.'

Mr Crow searched for an inconspicuous corner where he could fade into the background until he was beckoned to the game. He was beginning to wish he had never contemplated this venture in the first place.

Hubert Faddle brought over a large glass of brandy and assured him the wait would not be too long. In reality, Faddle knew that it would. Keeping the eager gambler waiting was part of the plan; it unnerved them and introduced a pleasing uncertainty into the proceedings, which, along with the free flowing alcohol, made it easier for Trench to carry out his magical sleights of hand and empty the victim's purse.

Mr Crow pulled his hat further down over his eyes and leant forward, staring at his drink. All the anticipated pleasure of a covert card game had disappeared in a matter of moments. After taking a large gulp of the brandy, he placed his brain into neutral, a facility he had developed when involved in a long, boring drawn-out trial. The eyes were sharp and appeared alert, but the mind was in absentia.

It was because of this self-induced trance that Mr Crow did not notice the two men who entered the bar some five minutes later. They made their way to the bar. A few of the customers cast suspicious glances at the duo. They were not regulars and their dress and manner, especially that of the fair-haired one, clearly indicated that they were away from their usual territory and slumming it to enter this particular establishment.

Hubert Faddle didn't like the look of them either. Strangers appearing in his public house on the night of a big card game made him nervous. They could easily be representatives of the law or agents of a rival gang wanting to disrupt proceedings. His barmaid, Annie made a beeline to serve the strangers but he intercepted her. 'I'll deal with them,' he whispered in her ear before stepping ahead of her to the bar counter. 'What's it to be, gentlemen?' he said with a half-smile on his podgy face and a reasonably pleasant manner – not too pleasant as to make this couple feel particularly welcome.

Oliver was about to launch the enquiry which had brought them to the premises, but Jack nudged his friend out of the way. 'Two tankards of your finest ale, landlord,' he said cheerily. 'I've heard it's the best beer in these parts.'

'Have you now?' returned Faddle, a little non-plussed at this response. As he set about obtaining the beer, Jack leaned over and observed, sotto voce, 'It's best not to jump straight in with questions in a place like this, Oliver. We stick out like two Christians in a lion's den. I know these people. Be too eager and they'll either clam up or worse still, eject us with certain hurts about our body.'

Oliver nodded. 'I bow to your greater wisdom in this matter,' he said, with the ghost of a twinkle in the eye.

'We'll take our drinks, sit a while and then I'll order a couple more and drop the name into the conversation. Can I suggest you leave it to me?'

'Very well, but do not give the real reason why we seek the fellow.'

'I don't have a pudding for a head, Master Twist,' snapped Jack as he collected the tankards Faddle had placed on the counter. 'Now, be a good chap and pay the man.'

Oliver did as he was told and they retired to an empty table near the fire.

'Mmm, it is good ale,' said Jack after downing a third of his tankard in one gulp which left him with a frothy moustache adorning the top of his lip. 'This is just the sort of establishment that Fagin used to frequent when the old skinflint felt like a little intoxication.'

'Indeed, it is,' agreed Oliver.

'Do you ever think about the old devil?'

'He pops into my head from time to time. Unbidden and unwelcome, I have to say, but there he is.'

'Yeah, I know what you mean. Unlike you, Oliver, I don't see those days as all bad. We did have some laughs didn't we?'

'I suppose we did,' agreed Oliver reluctantly, but he felt uncomfortable admitting it. Indeed, there were laughs but a greater supply of tears and bruises.

'I still get a giggle when I think about that dodging move that Fagin taught us when he we had to distract a gent who'd caught one of us dipping. We called it Fagin's Diversion. FD for short. D'you remember?'

'Heaven's,' said Oliver, 'I haven't thought about that for years. FD, yes.'

Jack grinned. 'It was quite like a military manoeuvre. We both approached the fellow head on and then you swung sharply to the right and I dodged to the left. Our target was so confused by all this that we managed to slip by him in a trice.' The thought of this prompted a prolonged chuckle from Jack.

Oliver smiled gently. He had other thoughts on his mind. He was staring at the dark coated fellow he observed in the shadows at the far side of the room. He was sitting for the most part with his head forward over the table and his hat pulled well down over his forehead, but on the occasion that he took a drink, he was forced to raise his head slightly and most of his features were revealed.

'Good Gracious. Judge Carabine.'

'What?' Jack Dawkin's forehead creased like a concertina's bellows.

'That fellow over there. The one with the tri-corn hat.'

'What about him?'

'I'm sure it's Judge Carabine.'

'And who's he when he's at home?'

'He's the sternest judge in the Old Bailey, the criminal court adjacent to Newgate.'

Jack shivered at the mention of Newgate. 'There's very few who escape the rope who come up before Judge Jeffrey Carabine.'

'What the hell is he doing in this dump?'

Oliver shrugged. 'Well, you may ask. Certainly the way he's behaving he certainly doesn't want anyone to know who he is.'

Jack giggled heartily. 'Let's pop over and say hello. How you doing, your Lordship? Sent anyone to the gallows recently?'

'Not a good idea. If he sees me, he could make my life very difficult. He wields great power.'

'He just looks like a sad, lonely old bloke.'

'With a heart of ice and a vindictive nature. Heaven knows what he is doing here but he must not see me or my career will be over.'

Jack shook his head in bewilderment. 'Why? We're doing him no harm.'

'A respectable member of the judiciary does not frequent a lowly tavern like this in a shrouded disguise unless his purpose – how shall I phrase this – is not quite… kosher, as Fagin might say. It is a secret visitation.'

'For what purpose?'

'I have no idea. Perhaps to meet a woman, although I would have thought his wenching days were over. It must have disreputable connotations. And I am sure that if he becomes aware that I know of his presence here, I'm convinced he will do his utmost to silence me, to destroy me, to propel me into the darkness.'

'What a way you have with words, Oliver. A veritable Shakespeare you are.'

'I am afraid that we must postpone our mission tonight. I want to wake up with a career and prospects tomorrow.'

Jack emptied his tankard and ran his sleeve across his mouth. 'And I want you to wake up to tomorrow with a career and prospects as well. I depend on you.'

Exchanging grim smiles the two friends slunk out of The Saracen's Head.

CHAPTER TWENTY FOUR

Felicity had just finished writing a passionate, wordy and completely effusive love letter to Roger Lightwood when there was a knock at her door. It was sharp and imperative. She was surprised that effect of flesh on wood could create such an intimidating sound, but it did. At first she could not imagine who the visitor to her room could be. It certainly was not Lady Whitestone. Felicity had left her grumbling in her sleep some forty minutes ago. The fact that she wouldn't allow consciousness to visit her until dawn was well and truly established.

Felicity moved to the door and leaning her face forward she called out: 'Who is it?'

'It's me. Arthur. I have to see you,' came the muffled reply.

Felicity gave a silent groan. He had never approached her room before which unnerved her. She really didn't want to see Arthur or become entangled in a conversation with him. No doubt he would want to talk about their relationship, their blossoming romance - but to her it had withered and died. There was a faint strand of guilt wrapped up in her emotions. She knew she was being unreasonable and cruel in rejecting Arthur in such a sudden and abrupt fashion, but at the same time she was well aware that it would be very wrong to pretend there was a rose tinted romantic future for them. There was only one man who could hold a place in her heart: Roger Lightwood. Compared to him, Arthur Wren was a mere insubstantial shadow. While Felicity was pondering how to respond, the insistent knock came again.

'Let me in, Felicity. I need to see you.'

The rough aggressive note in his voice startled her. 'No, no,' she cried. 'It is not appropriate now. I am ready for bed. Please go away.'

'I must see you.' The voice was louder now and had a threatening edge to it. He rattled the doorknob and shook the door as though he was attempting to break it down to gain entry.

Felicity gave a small shriek of fear and stepped back from door. 'Go away. You are frightening me,' she cried, wrapping her arms around her slender frame for comfort.

'I need to see you. I... I love you.' The voice was more conciliatory now but it still remained insistent.

'No, no. You must leave me alone. Go away,' was all that she could muster.

There was a silence and then a thunderous bang as he thumped his fist hard against the door in anger and frustration. 'You strumpet!' he cried. 'You have duped me. Led me on. You will pay for this. Mark my words, my fine lady: You will pay for this.' He thumped the door once again and then she heard his retreating footsteps down the corridor.

Felicity threw herself on the bed and burst into tears. She felt frightened, alone and terribly vulnerable. What was going to happen to her? Would she ever find happiness? As the bleak answer reared itself up in her mind's eye, she buried her head in the pillow, sobbing her heart out.

* * *

Mr Crow, as he was referred to in the game of cards in the upper room of The Saracen's Head, was feeling very sorry for himself. Not only was he a little lightheaded, thanks to the never empty brandy glass at his side, but devastated at the current state of his finances. After a very encouraging start, when he had hauled in quite a considerable amount of cash, he had now fallen on hard times and the money was slipping through his fingers like water from a tap. Initially there had been four players round the table but two had dropped out and he was left playing a fellow called Trench who certainly knew his way around a deck of cards. Crow felt like a rank amateur in his presence.

'I am so low in cash now,' said Crow with rare humility, 'that I had better finish before I become bankrupt.'

'Oh, no. One more game. We must have one more game,' said Trench with icy smoothness. It was an order not a suggestion.

'But I have so little cash left.'

Trench beamed. 'Never mind, put in what you have, along with that pearl neck pin and your silver snuff box. They can be your collateral.'

The Judge was certainly not happy about this arrangement. He really wanted to leave while he still had a few coins left to call his own. As for the pin – a present from his wife – and the snuff box – it had belonged to his father – held for him, an unsentimental man, emotional connections which he did not want to lose. However, as a high court judge of long-standing, he had developed a keen appreciation of mood and circumstance and was well aware of the eyes that peered at him through the candle-flickering gloom of that stuffy room - eyes that he was quite sure posed a physical threat to his person if he did not fall in with Trench's suggestion. In other words, he was trapped. He cursed himself for allowing himself to become involved in such a situation as he placed these treasured personal items, along with his few remaining coins, in the centre of the table. He knew he would never see them again. These were not games of intelligence and cunning. His opponent was a cheat. A master of prestidigitation and the sleight of hand – a cheat nonetheless. The rogue deserved to hang… And if he had his way.

But he did not have his way.

Some thirty minutes later, he shuffled from the darkened tavern

– the drinkers had long gone – almost relieved that he still had a coat on his back. Well, he told himself with great chagrin, he had learned his lesson. No more would he go seeking out illicit card games in dubious gambling haunts. In future he would restrict himself to a few rounds of poker with his genteel colleagues at his club. The excitement would be tepid, but at least he would retain both his dignity and his family heirlooms.

As Judge Crow (as we must think of him) made his way towards the main thoroughfare on his long journey home, he passed by a narrow alley less than a hundred yards from The Saracen's Head. As he did so, he failed to observe a dark figure hiding there in the shadows. Hiding and waiting.

* * *

'What do we do next?' asked Jack Dawkins as he and Oliver Twist sat around the sitting room fire late that night.

Oliver didn't know but was loathe to admit it. 'Well,' he said slowly, dragging the word out almost to the crack of doom. 'Well,' he said again in the same manner, while he cudgelled his brains to come up with a pertinent reply. He knew that Jack saw him as a fount of wisdom and a sharp thinker and he didn't want to let the fellow down. 'Well,' came the third, strangulated utterance, 'we have made considerable progress today. We now know where Sir Ebenezer's illegitimate offspring was taken from the orphanage and who brought him up.'

'Brought up as Tom Braggle, an apprentice carpenter who started at university…' added Jack.

'And then he left under some kind of cloud. And his forwarding address was The Saracen's Head, Houndsditch.'

'And bad company was mentioned.'

'Yes, well, I reckon we were in the midst of bad company tonight in that very tavern. But in response to your query regarding what we do next, I'm afraid the answer is as plain as the nose on your face.

Tomorrow, I'm afraid we shall have to revisit to the Saracen's Head and make a further attempt to discover if Tom Braggle is still known there.'

Jack nodded glumly. 'So be it. Let's hope there ain't no members of the judiciary in attendance this time.'

'I trust so.'

'And on that note I think I will take myself off to dreamland.'

'Good night, old fellow.'

Left alone, Oliver stared at the dying embers of the fire and pondered further. Where on earth was all this business leading? By some trick of fate, he had wandered into a weird landscape. He was a lawyer – that was his calling - but now it seemed he had turned into some kind of enquiry agent and adventurer. A glowing coal sank to the lower regions of the grate with a gentle hiss emitting a final spurt of orange flame. This seemed to place a new thought in his mind. Perhaps this was his life's lot. He was never to be settled. He had started life as a workhouse brat, became a pickpocket under the control of a crooked pied piper and then was transformed into a pampered foundling before maturing and … And now, here he was seeking the illegitimate son of a rich aristocratic client in the lowest drinking houses in London. Life's rich tapestry? If so, oh how he wished for a bland piece of plain material with no surprising pattern instead. With a sigh, Oliver doused the lights and made his way upstairs.

* * *

Jeremiah Throate consulted his watch. It was just after one in the morning. Perhaps he had misjudged things. Was it possible that his mortal enemy – he really thought of him in that clichéd fashion – was staying the night in The Saracen's Head? He never used to. He had observed the last gambler leave nearly an hour ago: a slouching wretch in dark clothing and a tri-corn hat worn low. He recognised the gait and demeanour of a serious loser. A duped loser. After all, he had been one himself. It was likely that Trench and that worm of a landlord were dividing the spoils over a final drink of the night, but how long did that take? Throate was beginning to shiver and to have thoughts about abandoning his vigil. After all, he could kill Trench another day. A few more hours would not make that much difference, although he was eager to send the devil to kingdom come. Such an act would, he felt, bring a kind of serenity to his troubled soul.

As these thoughts drifted around his tired mind, he heard the sound of a door being unlatched and opening on its creaking hinges. This was accompanied by the sound of muffled voices. Someone was leaving the tavern at last. Edging his way to the corner of the alley, he peered around the corner. He could see two figures in the narrow shaft of pale light emanating from the door way. Two figures whom he recognised; Hubert Faddle and Eugene Trench. Throate felt his heart begin to race. The moment had come. He now could carry out his plan. The thought of it caused him to shiver with a mixture of fear and excitement. The door of the tavern closed with a groan and Trench set off walking briskly.

Throate dug his hand into his jacket and dragged the pistol from its resting place. By this time, Trench who was walking briskly had passed the alley and was being devoured by the shadows further up the street.

Throate stepped out of the alley and, holding the pistol at arm's length, aimed it at the back of the disappearing silhouette which was his 'mortal enemy' Eugene Trench.

He pulled the trigger.

It did not move. Nothing happened.

He pulled the trigger again. It resisted the pressure of his finger. It was jammed. A third attempt also ended in failure. He stared in disbelief at the useless weapon. He opened his mouth but no utterance emerged. He was lost for words.

He glanced up the street. His mortal enemy had been swallowed up by the darkness.

CHAPTER TWENTY FIVE

'Great Heavens girl, take more care. You're brushing my hair, not pulling out weeds in a cabbage patch,' Wilhelmina Whitestone snapped angrily at Felicity Waring as she carried out the morning's hair brushing duties with far more vigour than usual. 'I don't know what's got into you today. You seem to be in some sort of dream. Pull yourself out of it at once or it will be the worse for you, my girl!'

'I'm sorry, Lady Wilhelmina,' muttered Felicity in response to this brittle tirade. It was true, she was in some sort of dream this morning: a bad dream. She couldn't eradicate the words of Arthur Wren from her mind and the vicious way they had been expressed: 'You strumpet! You have duped me. Led me on. You will pay for this. Mark my words, my fine lady. You will pay for this'. They had echoed in her head from the moment they had been uttered. She hardly slept a wink that night, worrying that Arthur would break down her bedroom door and act out his revenge. She shuddered again at the thought of it. She did feel a pang of guilt for rejecting him after she had been so warm to the fellow in the past, but now her heart and affections were held by another, it would be so wrong to carry on any kind of intimate relationship with another man.

'Come on, come on. Attend to your duties instead of gawping there like an indolent statue.' Her mistress's fierce tones shook her from her reverie. 'I'm sorry, Lady Wilhelmina,' she repeated.

'You know that I particularly wish to look my best today when I go to Lady Twemlow's luncheon party. She is always ferocious in her scrutiny of her guests' appearance. I want to make sure I outshine her in glamour and beauty. I have a reputation to uphold.'

'I am sure you will do that easily,' said Felicity mechanically, as she began brushing her mistress's hair with more care.

'So am I,' came the brusque reply, 'provided that my hair is treated with gentleness and sensitivity.'

As Felicity brushed the thin grey locks, attempting to tease some body into them, her mind was elsewhere. Once more, a small knot of fear was beginning to grow inside her as she realised that while her mistress was away from the house attending this pompous luncheon party given by the grotesque harridan Lady Twemlow – out of the same self-deluded and arrogant stable as Wilhelmina Whitestone herself – she would be alone on the premises with Arthur Wren. What on earth was she to do? If only Roger Lightwood were here to protect her.

* * *

It was mid-morning when Oliver and Jack approached The Saracen's Head again. This time the door was shut and there was no sign of activity.

'It's my understanding that landlords sleep late, Oliver.'

'I am sure you are correct, but it is only just over an hour before noon when thirsty men desire their ale. Surely Mr Faddle will have completed his morning ablutions by now.'

Jack said nothing, but his expression indicated that he thought this concept was unlikely.

Undaunted, Oliver rapped loudly on the door. When, after a minute there was no response, he repeated the action, knocking louder and longer than before. A window above them creaked open and a tousled head poked out.

'Come back at noon. We're shut now,' cried the apparition.

'Ah, Mr Faddle. It is not drink I require, but a conversation with you concerning a legal matter.'

The landlord frowned. 'Legal matter. What legal matter?'

Oliver could tell he had hooked his fish. 'If I could take some ten minutes of your time, I could explain. I cannot do so openly in the street.'

'A legal matter, you say?'

'Indeed, I am a representative of Messrs Gripwind and Biddle, a legal firm in the city.'

'Are you now. Very well. Wait there while I get dressed and come down for you.' With that Hubert Faddle disappeared and the window banged shut.

Oliver and Jack exchanged amused glances and then waited. Some ten minutes later the door of The Saracen's Head creaked open and the landlord bid them enter. The bar parlour was gloomy and rich in the stench of sour ale and pipe tobacco. So unpleasantly pungent was the atmosphere that Oliver could feel his breakfast stirring unpleasantly in his gut.

'Sit yerself down gentlemen.' Faddle indicated a table by the curtained window. 'Now I fancy my morning tankard of ale. Can I get one for you two?'

Oliver shook his head vigorously. The thought of cold ale at this time of day, especially when the pungent atmosphere was making his breakfast rebel would lead to an emetic disaster. On the other hand, Jack nodded vigorously. 'A pint of ale would slip down very nicely, thank you.' He flashed a smile at Oliver.

Faddle produced the drinks and sat down, passing a tankard to Jack. 'That'll be two pence, young sir,' he said with a grin.

Jack's jaw dropped. He had assumed that the ale would be on the house. He glanced over at Oliver, his eyes wide in surprise, but his friend just smirked. With flustered reluctance, Jack rummaged in his pockets and produced the two pence.

'Thank you,' said Faddle scooping the money up in a well-practised fashion. 'Now then, legal business. What legal business?'

'We are trying to trace someone who we believe lodged on these premises some two or three years ago.'

Faddle's face fell. He had been harbouring a fancy notion that some unknown benefactor had died and left him a sum of money. That was the sort of 'legal business' he was interested in.

'Oh, yes,' was his guarded response.

Jack slurped his ale and wiped the froth away with the sleeve of his coat.

'The man in question is Thomas Braggle.'

'Oh, him.'

'You know this man then.'

'Yes, I know him. Long streak of water.' He gave a mouth twisting sneer before taking a gulp of ale.

'What can you tell me about him?'

'Well now, this is legal business ain't it? That's what you said.'

Oliver nodded apprehensively.

'Legal business is fees and costs and such like. Fees have to be paid. Information comes at a price. You being legal gentlemen will know that.'

'How much?' said Jack, cutting to the quick but failing to keep the anger from his voice.

Faddle pursed his lips. 'I'm not a greedy man, gentlemen. I reckon a couple of sovereigns would fit the bill.'

'I am sure that can be arranged, Mr Faddle, providing you have real information about Thomas Braggle.'

'Oh, that I can confirm. No problem there, I assure you.'

Oliver reached inside his purse and withdrew two sovereigns and placed them on the table. 'Let us hear what you have to tell us, Mr Faddle, and then the sovereigns can be yours.'

The landlord nodded and smiled. 'We occasionally had the odd card school in one of the upper rooms in this establishment. It is a friendly social event. Perhaps you'd like to join us some time. We're having a game tonight.' He rubbed his hands together avariciously.

Oliver shook his head. 'We're not ones for gambling are we,

Mister Dawkins?'

Jack opened his mouth to speak, to contradict this assertion but he observed the warning in his friend's glance and he just nodded in agreement.

'Pray continue with your narrative, Mr Faddle,' prompted Oliver.

'Very well. Young Master Braggle became a regular here when he was a student a learning things. Sadly, he was reckless in his dealings with cards. Betting large sums and losing. We tried to warn him, tried to keep him on the straight and narrow but he was a hot-headed young fellow and took no heed of us. As a result he fell into debt and borrowed to excavate himself out of his hole, only to end up deeper than ever down the pit. In the end he was forced to give up his learning, sell what chattels he had and come to live here. I felt sorry for the lad and gave him a job, as barman and cellar man. A menial role you might say, way below his capabilities, but he was grateful and settled in here quite nicely.'

Faddle took another gulp of ale.

Oliver waited for the rest of the tale. He was well experienced dealing with devious characters to know that he wasn't being told the full details of Braggle's story. This was a censored and sanitised version, but at least there were some details which would be of use.

'There's not much more to tell, gentlemen. One day Mr Braggle just upped and left. He never told us why or where he was going. He paid all his dues though.'

'Are you sure he didn't say where he was going?' asked Jack, his eyes narrowing with suspicion. 'Surely there was more to his leaving than what you've just said.'

Faddle seemed surprised and a little taken back by this interjection – an interjection from the monkey rather than the organ grinder. Oliver reacted quickly to this subtle change by slipping his hand over the two sovereigns.

'It does seem an abrupt end to your story, Mr Faddle,' he said judiciously. 'I think my friend and I are of one mind that there is a little more to tell. We certainly do not want to leave here with half a tale…' - his hand now picked up the sovereigns and jingled them '…

you will appreciate our concern.'

Faddle's eyes flickered nervously. He knew that he was in danger of losing his reward and it was clear he was wondering just how much he could reveal to these to 'legal gentlemen'. After a moment's pause, he gave a hearty chuckle but it was unconvincing merriment and both Oliver and Jack knew it.

'Well,' said Faddle, 'there is really not much I can add… but apparently our young friend encountered a gentleman in the city – under what circumstances I honestly do not know – and this gentleman, a rich cove, offered Braggle a proper job.'

'What kind of job?' asked Jack.

Faddle shrugged. 'I really have no idea. Truly. But Braggle was pleased as punch about it. It was to be a new life for him and that was why he was determined to cut himself from all ties at The Saracen's Head, despite the fact we had been very kind to him.' Suddenly Faddle's face darkened and he leaned forward in a conspiratorial fashion. 'But I can tell you this,' he said in a hushed voice, 'young Master Braggle left here in a coach which bore a coat of arms on its side.' He sat back with a flourish as though he had produced the crown jewels out of a top hat.

'Did you recognise the coat of arms?' asked Oliver.

Faddle shook his head. 'No, I did not. I have no knowledge of such things. The aristocracy is a closed book to me. I am but a humble inn keeper.'

A little more than that, thought Jack, but on this rare occasion kept his thoughts to himself. He had encountered the breed before: fingers in many pies, most of them unsavoury and not to be trusted with the truth.

'Can you provide any details of this coat of arms?' asked Oliver. 'Think man.' He chinked the coins again as bait.

Faddle screwed up his face in an act of desperate recollection. 'Well, there were… a boar's head… with nasty tusks. I remember that. And an oak tree. Well, I think it was an oak tree. One tree looks like another to me.'

Oliver and Jack exchanged glances, the latter's mouth gaping as he did so. Oliver gave a brief negative shake of the head to indicate that his friend should not say a thing.

'That's all. I only glimpsed the coach briefly. Braggle was anxious to be away,' concluded Faddle.

Oliver passed the two sovereigns to the landlord of The Saracen's Head, bid him good morning, and with Jack in tow, he left the premises.

CHAPTER TWENTY SIX

Jeremiah Throate sat in a gloomy tavern feeling very sorry for himself. Not only had the assassination of his deadly enemy failed miserably because of a faulty pistol – which he had consigned to a watery grave at the bottom of the Thames in a fit of anger – but his supply of cash was running out. The trinkets that he had filched from the man he had robbed (and killed) had realised little by the time the pawn merchant had taken his cut and the few notes from his wallet had gone on lodgings, food and alcohol. He saw a pattern begin to emerge. He would have to do it again: tackle some lonely devil in some benighted alley and relieve him of his cash and valuables, taking as much trouble as he could not to kill the blighter this time, in order that he could survive a few more days in the city. The situation was farcical, horrendous. Whoever controlled the Fates was having an enormous laugh at his expense. Here he was, the son of a baronet, disowned by his parents and unable to return to the family seat in case the thugs employed by his debtor caught him and killed him. As he contemplated this unhappy situation, he sighed, his body shuddering with emotion. There must, there really must be some escape, some solution to his dilemma.

He raised his tankard to his lips and drained it. He decided to move on to a more felicitous drinking hole. Why not? While he still had a few shillings in his pocket he would live the life he was meant to, not the one he was forced to.

* * *

Felicity removed the lustrous diamond necklace from its velvet casket and carefully draped it around Lady Whitestone's neck.

'This will certainly outshine anything that the decrepit Dorothea Twemlow can conjure up from her jewellery box,' observed her ladyship with an acid grin.

'Indeed, it is magnificent,' said Felicity with genuine feeling.

'A family heirloom. And I can tell you, my girl, it is worth a fortune. An absolute fortune.'

* * *

Jeremiah Throate passed through the foyer of the Hotel Rialto and into the smart bar area beyond. He was aware that his clothes were now somewhat shabby for this establishment but he assumed that his bearing and arrogant swagger would carry the day. And they seemed to.

The bar salon was empty apart from two men, smart city types, sitting at a small table by the fire. They looked like father and son. Jeremiah ordered a gin and water and sat close by them. The younger of the men was wearing a very smart morning suit and rested a smart shiny top hat on his knee and was flourishing a gilt edged card in his right hand.

'This is an invitation to Lady Twemlow's Luncheon Party,' he was saying. 'Ghastly event. I'm only going as a favour to my aunt. I have to keep the old dear sweet. It's an investment for when she shuffles off upstairs. I'm hoping there'll be a happy parcel for me in her will when she goes. But, I do so hate these sort of functions. All small sandwiches and empty-headed chatter. It's mainly a female affair with lots of ladies of advanced faces parading around in their dated finery exhibiting the family jewels, attempting to outshine each other.' He spoke in a lively manner, his observations were only slightly seasoned with sarcasm.

His companion, an older fellow more sedately dressed, with a rubicund complexion and the possessor of a curved nose that a goshawk would envy, chuckled at his friend's conversation. 'So no young pretties to soothe the eye then?' he said.

The young man shook his head. 'Just a crew of desiccated dames, bejewelled up to the eyebrows, all believing that the shining diadems brought them back their youth.'

'Poor boy.'

Jeremiah was fascinated by this conversation, especially the mention of 'family jewels' and 'shining diadems'. These phrases made him lick his lips. As he savoured his gin and water, he studied the younger man, the one with the frock coat and top hat. As he did so an idea began to form in his brain. It was a shocking, reckless idea but as it took shape he began to grow excited. It was daring, it was risky, well, it was outrageous but it could be the answer to his current dilemma.

'Indeed, Auberon, my dear fellow, the youngest filly there will no doubt be approaching fifty but looking a decade older.'

Auberon chuckled. 'The only thing for it, Cyril, my dear boy, is to ingratiate yourself to one of the old dears, snatch her tiara and hightail back to your club.'

'It is an idea. And after a few glasses of champagne – if I can secure them – I may well be enticed into doing just that.' Cyril grinned before consulting his pocket watch. 'Ah, I had better be on my way. My aunt is a stickler for time keeping. I am meeting her there at the Twemlow residence in Chelsea.'

The older man raised his glass. 'Bon voyage,' he grinned.

The young man rose, gave a theatrical bow and left the room.

He was swiftly followed by Jeremiah Throate.

Out in the quiet street, the young man began searching for a carriage for hire. He hurried along the pavement and down a narrow alley which would lead him to a major thoroughfare, but he was destined not to reach it. Half way down the alley, he felt a hand on the scruff of his neck, a hand that then swivelled him round so that he came face to face with a tall, dark saturnine figure.

'What the…' He managed to cry before he was punched hard in the face. He heard his nose break just before he lost consciousness and slumped to the floor. Minutes later, the tall saturnine figure emerged from the far side of the alley. He was wearing an impressive frock coat, albeit a little small for his frame, and with a shiny top hat perched precariously on his head.

* * *

Oliver and Jack were seated in Samson's Chop House devouring a pair of lamb cutlets with mashed potatoes and peas. As usual, Jack's method of eating was to fill his mouth to full capacity so that his cheeks bulged before he began the process of chewing and swallowing. As a result, while dining, he had little capacity for conversation, or at least conversation that was decipherable. He had just made a lengthy observation which was completely unintelligible but Oliver could guess what the gist of it was. They had exchanged few words since leaving the Saracen's Head, each of their minds filled with the information they had gleaned and the possible implications. Oliver, in particular, tried hard to fit this part of the puzzle into the whole so that it began to make sense. It seemed to him that the more they learned, the more tangled the mystery became.

He squashed a group of peas with his fork and brought them to his mouth and then hesitated. 'All the indications are that the heart of this conundrum lies back at Throate Manor.'

Jack nodded and added a muffled comment in agreement.

'The coach in which Braggle left the The Saracen's Head was obviously the one owned by Sir Ebenezer Throate: the boar's heads with tusks and the spreading oak tree, part of his family crest, clearly indicate that.'

Jack nodded his head and dabbed his mouth with a napkin. 'So what was he doing at Throate Manor and why didn't Sir Ebenezer tell us?'

Oliver popped the peas in his mouth. 'I don't know. I can't believe he is taking us for a pair of fools, sending us out to look for his lost offspring when the fellow was conveyed there in his coach a few years ago. It is all so confusing.'

'And blooming irritating.'

'I concur on that point.'

'What we gonna do, Oliver?'

'I believe there is only one thing we can do now and that is to convey the information we have gleaned to Sir Ebenezer and see what light he can throw upon the matter. To that end, we shall once more travel down to Throate Manor first thing in the morning.'

'Very well. But I tell you one thing, my friend.'

'What is that?'

'This meat is rather tough.'

* * *

When Lady Whitestone had departed for the Lady Twemlow's luncheon party in all her finery, Felicity had swiftly returned to her room and locked the door. She had not seen Arthur Wren that day, but she knew that he was in the building somewhere and no doubt he was aware of her ladyship's absence. It was an ideal time for him to make another attempt to get her in his clutches – for whatever purpose she shuddered to think. Was he still angry? Would he hurt her or beg her to be his? All such scenarios were abhorrent to her. She just did not want to see him again in private. It would be bad enough during her duties in the company of others. She had made her position clear to him regarding her affections, he should, he must accept them. She prayed that he would.

She lay on her bed with the first volume of a novel and tried to read but the words just danced before her, fluttering in and out of focus, refusing to make sense in her head. She was too tense, too apprehensive to allow herself to be caught up in the life of some fictional characters of no consequence. There was too much drama in her own life for her to concentrate. She dropped the book on the floor by her bed and laid back and closed her eyes, hoping that she could fall asleep. An afternoon nap was a luxury she rarely had the opportunity to indulge in and she had slept very badly the night before.

Despite her qualms, she soon found her body relaxing as her tiredness carried her away into a deep sleep. Her chest rose with a gentle regularity and the tightness of her forehead and the lines around her mouth eased as slumber helped to knit up that ravelled sleeve of care, as the Bard has it.

She was not aware of the turning of the doorknob and the pressure against the door as someone sought entry without success. With a muttered oath, this someone gave up and went away.

Eventually Felicity was roused from her slumbers by the sound of a bell, a small bell that rattled rather than rang. It was Lady Whitestone's bell, the one that summoned Felicity to her mistress's boudoir for some chore or other. It took Felicity some moments to throw off the web of deep sleep and bring herself round and to realise what was happening. She pulled herself on to the side of the bed and brushed down her dress. The bell sounded again. It was insistent. It always was insistent. Had she been asleep so long that Lady Whitestone had returned from the luncheon party and now required assistance to disrobe? She really must have stayed at the function for only a short time. Long enough no doubt to parade around the room showing off the diamond necklace as though it were some grand decoration bestowed on her by royalty. Felicity allowed herself a brief smile at the thought before checking her appearance in the mirror. Satisfied that she looked acceptable, she unlocked her door and hurried along to her mistress's boudoir.

She knocked gently and entered. At first she was surprised to find the room empty. There was no sign of her ladyship. With some hesitation, Felicity called out her name. There was no reply. Then she heard the door close behind her and standing in the shadow was Arthur Wren. His face was pale and damp with sweat and he wore a strange alien expression. His lips parted in a demonic grin.

* * *

Jeremiah Throate passed through the portals of the Twemlow mansion with ease. The flunkey on the door took his invitation without a glance at him. Throate slipped into the throng of the rich and privileged, of whom he had once been a full member himself before his parents had become recalcitrant and boorish. He snatched a glass of champagne from a passing flunkey and downed it in one gulp and then sought out another. The air was filled with empty chatter and the whole scene reminded Throate of a farm yard filled with clucking chickens milling around aimlessly not really taking any notice of each other. The ensemble was predominantly female, mainly ladies of an age when beauty and sweetness had deserted them to be replaced by outrageously expensive and garish gowns adorned with rich sparkling trinkets. Throate was fascinated and delighted as he patrolled the room eyeing these gewgaws with the eye of an eager poacher. Which particular item was to be his? In particular, which would fetch the biggest financial reward? He circled the room numerous times, slowly studying the goods on show while availing himself of further glasses of champagne – the alcohol fuelling not only his greed but his confidence and bravado. After much contemplation, he honed in on one grotesque old crone, a woman with a shrill monotone of a voice and face the texture of a wrinkled sheet. She was also the possessor of a magnificent pearl necklace. This was an ideal piece to take for each of the pearls could be sold separately over a period, keeping him in comparative comfort for some time.

Grabbing a passing waiter, he asked him who the 'stately lady in the blue and gold dress was.'

'That's Lady Whitestone, sir. A great friend of my mistress.'

Throate gave a curt nod and released the fellow.

Now he was ready to put his hazy plan into operation. Slipping back into the hallway, he checked that it was now empty.

Excellent.

All the guests had arrived and the flunkey who had met him at the door had disappeared. He also noticed a charming pewter ornament in the shape of a Grecian urn situated on a shelf nearby. Throate took it from its perch and ran his fingers over it. It was, he thought, quite beautiful, but for him its beauty resided in its weight and sturdiness rather that its shape.

Replacing the ornament back on the shelf, with a satisfied smirk he returned to the room where the guests were still mingling and chatting in a stultified fashion and headed straight for Lady Whitestone who was in conversation with a fat dumpy little woman in an orange gown that somehow matched her complexion. As he drew near to the two, he saw that in fact they were not actually in conversation. The dumpy woman was being talked at in a hectoring fashion by her companion.

Throate strode up to the pair and gave a delicate cough. 'Lady Whitestone,' he said in sonorous tones as though he was about to start delivering a eulogy.

The lady in question, froze mid-sentence and turned her gorgon gaze on this stranger who had had the temerity to interrupt her. Before she could respond, Throate continued. 'I am so sorry to disturb you, your ladyship, but there is a gentleman in the hallway who is desirous to speak to you on a very urgent matter. Apparently some catastrophe has occurred at your house.'

Lady Whitestone's skeletal hand flew up to her face. 'Gracious,' she said, the word escaping hoarsely like a jet of steam. 'Is it Wren? A tall fellow with a preposterous moustache?'

Throate nodded. 'Most likely. He didn't give his name. He seemed greatly distressed and urged me to take you to him.'

'Very well. Take me to him,' snapped the dragon.

Without another word, Throate led Lady Whitestone through the throng and into the hallway – the empty hallway.

'Well, where is the fellow?' crowed her ladyship shifting her gaze rapidly up and down.

In a swift and nimble action, Throate picked up the Grecian urn and brought it down with some force on the back of Lady Whitestone's head. He reckoned that he would need such power in order for the weapon to make sufficient impact hindered as it was by the strange, elaborate concoction the woman wore on her head. For such a voluble creature, Lady Whitestone's reaction to the blow was brief and succinct. A mere soft 'Oh' and she collapsed to the floor.

Throate wasted no time in relieving the prone woman of his prize: the diamond necklace. Stuffing it in his coat pocket, he gave a satisfied chuckle and made for the door. Within minutes he was on the street heading as fast as his legs would carry him from the town house of Lady Twemlow. He was smiling. And why not? In the last few hours he had availed himself of a fine new set of clothes and a precious pearl necklace. There was every reason to smile, wasn't there?

* * *

'Here we are. Just the two of us. In the boudoir.'

Once upon a time Felicity Waring had thought that Arthur Wren was quite good looking. He was tall and slim and had a soldier's bearing with neat features and large blue eyes and there was that rather impressive moustache; but looking at him now in the pale light of Lady Whitestone's bedchamber, he resembled some kind of demon. His flesh was damp and sickly white, while those usually placid blue eyes now bulged in a ferocious mad fashion, as though they were in danger of leaving their sockets. The moustache was damp with sweat and the lips seemed stuck in a maniacal rictus smile. He was the living representation of a drawing from a Penny Dreadful. At first she didn't know what to say, how to respond to this man of whom she had once thought fondly but was now a dark threatening stranger. She edged her way backwards and found herself bumping into the bed.

'That's right, my dear,' Wren gurgled. 'Time to get ready for bed.' He took a step forward. 'Take off your clothes my dear. It is time that we became better acquainted.'

Felicity let out a little scream as the implication of Wren's words became clear to her. She made a desperate attempt to skirt round the bed but he bounded forth, grabbed her arms and with a growl threw her down on to the mattress. Now the little scream grew into a full bloated bellow. In truth it was a mixture of fear and rage. Felicity realised that she was going to have to fight for her life and a flame of anger began to flicker and grow within her tiny frame. Pulling her arms free, she curved her fingers into a claw and struck out at her attacker's face. Her nails made contact with his flesh and she dragged them down his face leaving bloody score lines on each cheek.

Wren gave a whelp of pain and staggered back, losing his footing. He dropped to the floor. This gave Felicity the opportunity to jump from the bed and make an attempt to head for the door, but Wren was on his feet again in an instance and grabbed her once more, thrusting her to him in a clumsy embrace. His face, now bloodied and scarred, appeared like some cruel demon from folklore. He pushed this frightful visage forward in an attempt to kiss her. This time, she seemed to succumb to his advances, but when their lips were almost touching, she jerked her head upwards and bit Wren on the nose. She bit him with the force and tenacity of a terrier. She held on for some moments. So strong was her purchase on the nose that she thought she may well tear the end of it off.

Wren was now mewling with pain and he released his hold of Felicity, his hands flying up to his damaged bloody face. Felicity ran from the room, but she had only reached the landing when she felt a hand tugging at the back of her gown. It was her attacker again. With a roar of fury he swung her round, but in doing so he loosened his grip and she managed to pull away once more. She reached the top of the stairs before he grabbed her again. He shook her hard, blood from his facial wounds flying wildly and spotting dress and face. Instinctively she relaxed her body, going almost limp in Wren's arms and then as he also relaxed his grasp, with a burst of desperate energy she thrust him from her. Surprised by this ferocious action, Wren stumbled backwards and then as he realised he had reached the very edge of the top step, he gave a cry of alarm. Rather like a marionette whose puppeteer has lost control of the strings, his body jangled wildly, arms flailing, head twisting and feet dancing. It was to no avail. He had lost his balance and the inevitable happened. His mouth opened in horror but no sound emerged and in a strange silent motion he fell backwards – into space. He did eventually cry out in pain when his body came into contact with the staircase. His legs flew high in the air causing his carcass to perform a complete somersault before continuing its tortuous journey down the stairs to the bottom. Here it landed in the hallway with a muffled thud and lay still.

For some moments Felicity remained rooted to the spot, shocked into inaction by the speed and terror of the events of the last few minutes. Her mind fought off the image of Arthur Wren's damp blood-stained face pressing close to her. She closed her eyes, took a deep breath and then moved to the bannister rail and gazed down at the body sprawled on the floor in the hallway. The sight made her shudder with emotion – a mixture of horror and relief. It looked like the man was dead.

Like a somnambulist, Felicity made her way down the stairs, treating every step with apprehension. Her eyes were trained on the unmoving body of Arthur Wren lying face down on the hall floor. On reaching him, she knelt down and felt for a pulse. There was none. She shook him gently but there was no response. Then she noticed the unnatural angle of his head in relation to his body. It was as though it had been twisted round by an invisible hand. Twisted until it had snapped.

Great heavens, she thought, standing up and stifling a cry of anguish with her hand, the poor devil has broken his neck. He really is dead. With the acceptance of this fact, she could contain her emotions no longer and burst into tears. What exactly was at the heart of her wretched misery at that moment, she would have been hard pressed to explain. Was she bereft at the death of a man who, until a short time ago, had treated her kindly, with affection? Was she feeling sorry for herself after undergoing a terrible ordeal at the hands of the same man? Or was it the realisation that she was responsible for his ugly death? Whatever the cause and most likely it was a mixture of all three, she dropped to her knees and sobbed her heart out.

What was she to do now?

* * *

At Throate Manor, in the kitchen, Lizzie Barnes had extracted her secret jug of gin and poured herself a generous measure into a stone mug and then added a splash of water. She needed a drink. She needed a mental softener to take away the hard corners and realities of life. Yet again. It seemed that all her plans, all her efforts had come to nought. After all those barren years, she had thought that her dream was about to come true – but not now. She took a long drink of the gin. It burned her throat and made her gag, but she was glad it did. She deserved the discomfort. She deserved the pain.

CHAPTER TWENTY SEVEN

It was one of Lady Twemlow's flunkeys who discovered the body of Lady Whitestone in the hall and in a discrete fashion raised the alarm. Her body was carried into a private sitting room and medical help was summoned. Lady Twemlow was more upset by the disturbance to her party than the condition of her guest. As she gazed down at her unconscious friend, and sneered. 'Wilhomina was always wont to be the centre of attention,' she observed coldly.

The Twemlow family physician by the name of Quelp attended to the patient and was most concerned to see the wound on Lady Whitestone's head. 'The lady had been brutally attacked from behind. There has been a vicious criminal assault. The police should be called.'

'Great heavens, I cannot have great burly policemen tramping about my house during my party. What would the guests think? Please just attend to the lady's hurts and we'll deal with the matter later. The woman's not dead is she? Or dying?'

Quelp was used to Lady Twemlow's curt and imperious manner and was not at all surprised by her dismissive attitude. 'I think she will recover,' he said, cautiously. 'Her breathing is fairly regular but I have no notion of any damage that the concussion may have caused.'

'Bring her round as swiftly as you can and then we will arrange a carriage to take her back to her home where she can be nursed by her own people. Now I must go. I have guests to attend to.'

Without another word she swept from the room like an arctic breeze.

Quelp sighed. If it wasn't for his fee, he would depart these premises immediately. But there was the fee.

He felt his patient's pulse. It was regular and reasonably strong which was a good sign. He attended to the gash on her head, bathing it, applying an astringent antiseptic which caused Lady Whitestone's features to twitch with discomfort, which was another good sign. Quelp then bandaged the head, satisfied that he had done all he could to the surface wound but realising that only time would reveal any affect the blow had on the brain of the lady.

Extracting a small phial of smelling salts, he held it under the nose of his patient. After a few moments, it wrinkled briskly and she gave a dry guttural cough while the eyelids flickered gently but as yet showed no signs of opening completely.

'Can you hear me, your ladyship?' Quelp said softly close to her ear, while he still continued waving the phial under her nose. A moment later, she coughed again and then spluttered and then gasped for air. It was an action which finally propelled her eyes open.

'Welcome back,' grinned Quelp, still holding the restorative phial under her nose.

Lady Whitestone heard the voice as thought it was a whisper on a summer breeze and at the moment all she could see was a kaleidoscopic array of soft shapes and colours.

'Don't try to move just yet,' came the voice again, 'but do try to stay awake.'

'Yes, of course,' said a faint voice.

Quelp felt a sense of relief. No matter what unfortunate incident had brought this lady to her current situation, at least she was alive and would recover in time. His work was almost done.

'A restorative nip of brandy will help to clear the cobwebs,' said Quelp, moving to the door. 'I will arrange it.'

'Thank you so much,' came the gentle reply.

Before obtaining the brandy, Quelp sought out Lady Twemlow

who was still touring the room, interfering with her guests and taking control of their conversation and informed her that Lady W had regained consciousness and that it seemed most likely she would make a full recovery.

Lady Twemlow beamed at this news. 'Excellent. I will pass a message on to her coachman who is in the kitchen with the others. Do you think she will be fit enough to drive home in half an hour?'

Before Quelp could reply – a reply that would have been in the negative – Lady Twemlow continued. 'The sooner she is out of my house and away, she is no longer my responsibility. She must be invalided at home – not here. Make sure she is ready to travel in half an hour.' Without another word she turned and honed in on another group of guests, interrupting their chatter.

And so it was that some thirty minutes later, a frail and somewhat befuddled Lady Wilhelmina Whitestone was seen off the premises by Dr Quelp and bundled into her carriage. The coachman had been told a vague story about his mistress having a fall and banging her head. 'Her own physician should be informed as soon as possible.'

The coachman nodded. 'I'll inform her ladyship's companion, Miss Waring. She will arrange matters,' he said before gently urging the horse to set forth at a gentle trot.

On arriving back at her ladyship's town house, the coachman ran into the house for assistance to help Lady Whitestone inside. To his surprise he encountered her ladyship's physician Dr Sloper in the hallway along with Miss Felicity Waring. His surprise transcended into shock when he observed the body of Arthur Wren lying on the floor at the bottom of the stairs.

'There's been a terrible accident,' said Felicity in a strained voice that was not quite hers.

'A fatal one, I'm afraid,' added Sloper in funeral tones. 'The poor fellow's taken a fatal tumble down the stairs. Broken his neck.'

'Gracious me.' The coachman removed his hat in respect of the corpse. 'That makes two terrible accidents in one day. Her ladyship has hurt her head at the party. She needs medical attention I'm afraid. She's very weak.'

'Where is she?' asked Felicity.

Outside in the carriage. I can't manage to bring her in on me own. She's all of a doodah.'

'I'd better go and take a look at her,' said Sloper. 'In the meantime, it would be best to cover up Mr Wren's body with a blanket.'

'I'll see to it,' said Felicity, relieved at the prospect of hiding the evidence of her deed from view. The sooner the body was out of the house, the better.

* * *

Oliver Twist sat back in his armchair by his own fireside and slowly munched an apple, savouring its juice and texture while he allowed his mind to roam freely over the events of the last few days, conjuring up images and recalling conversations. He was desperately trying to make some sense of the strange puzzle that had been dropped in his lap. Rather than answers and solutions, his cogitations just threw up more questions, which now rattled around his brain. Did Sir Ebenezer know more about the identity and whereabouts of his illegitimate son than he had confided to them and, if so, why was he keeping anything back if he wanted the boy to be found? Who had tried to kill Sir Ebenezer and why? Where was Thomas Braggle now and where had he travelled to in the Throate coach? This last conundrum threw up a remarkable theory that was both fantastic and reasonable in its concept. It was highly improbable, but nevertheless… The more Oliver pondered on it, the more excited he became. Was it really as simple and as farcical as all that?

Oliver's brain began to hurt as these questions and others crowded his brain. He hoped that his visit to the ancestral seat of the Throate family and an audience with Sir Ebenezer the following day would help to clear the mud from these dark waters. With a sigh, he threw the apple core into the grate and watched it sizzle and burn.

* * *

In another location in London, in less salubrious surroundings, Eugene Trench was also musing. His cogitations were aided by a large glass of brandy. He swilled it around the balloon glass until it spun like a small whirlpool and he stared at it closely, drawing inspiration from the sight and the fumes of it. At the centre of his thoughts was Jeremiah Throate. It wasn't just the large sum of money that this oily rascal owed him, that caused Trench to be annoyed, it was the fact that he had managed to slip though his clutches on several occasions. It hurt his overweening pride. This was not a scenario that ever occurred or had never occurred until now. When Eugene Trench wanted to nail a man, he nailed him with ease.

He found his grasp of the brandy glass tightening with frustration. Throate was still a free man, hiding somewhere in London. A needle in a bloody haystack. Although Kepple and Joint were out there searching, Trench had little faith in their prowess in this particular mission. They were effective and fairly efficient where thuggery was concerned but sophisticated thinking, or indeed thinking of any kind, was not their forte. Trench took a sip of brandy and accepted the fact that he would have to do the job himself. But how? He needed some means of luring Jeremiah Throate out into the open, into his clutches. He closed his eyes and thought and thought. Then it came to him. Out of nowhere, it seemed, he conceived of a fully-fledged notion. His eyes flashed open and he took a gulp of the heart-warming liquor. The idea was good and he smiled his vulpine smile. With the death of his father, Sir Ebenezer, Jeremiah would return to Throate Manor to claim his inheritance which would, of course, provide him with the funds to pay for the debt he owed Trench. However this simple transaction would not satisfy Trench now. The young Throate needed to be punished for the inconvenience he had caused and punished severely. The lesson would be harsh one, a warning to others who thought they could get the better of Eugene Trench. There was no doubt about it, the bastard Throate would not live long enough to enjoy his new found wealth.

The vulpine smile broadened, the thin lips parting to allow a glimpse of a row of thin brown teeth. He was pleased with his cogitations. So, it was settled in his mind: he would travel to Throate Manor on the morrow and by some means bring about the death of Sir Ebenezer Throate.

* * *

When Lady Whitestone regained consciousness, she found she was in bed. She did not recognise it as her own bed and indeed she did not recognise her own bedroom as, with a great effort, she pulled herself up into a sitting position. She was able to discern that it was night time for although the shades were drawn she could see a thin strip of dark sky down one side. The room was illuminated by two candles which bathed the room in a faint amber glow. She sighed heavily, hoping vaguely that this action might clear her mind and help her to understand where she was and why she was here.

As she studied her surroundings, she noticed a little bell on the bedside table. That no doubt had been placed there in order for me to summon assistance, her foggy brain told her. She reached out for the bell but it was some moments before she was able to grasp it firmly, her outstretched fingers at first being wide of the mark.

She rang the bell. And kept on ringing it as though she was caught in a spasm and could not stop. There was pleasure in the action. The tinkling filled the air with a kind of manic ferocity for which the bell had not been designed.

Eventually, the door opened and a tall young woman entered.

'Oh, your ladyship, you are awake. Thank heavens,' she said.

'And who are you?'

The young woman hesitated, a look of confusion on her face. 'I am Felicity, your companion. Felicity Waring.'

'Oh,' came the muted reply, which held no meaning that Felicity could determine.

'Can I get you something? Some tea or a glass of water. Would you like a little food?'

Lady Whitestone did not know and the rapidity of the questions defeated her.

'Come sit down by me on the bed and hold my hand,' she said, beckoning the young woman.

With some trepidation. Felicity did as she was bidden and felt the cold clammy claw-like fingers of her mistress take hold of hers.

'You are a good girl, aren't you?'

Felicity was surprised by the question and an image of Arthur Wren flying from her down the staircase flashed into her mind. 'I try to be,' she said, banishing the image.

'I thought so. I do believe I am a good judge of character.' Lady Whitestone smiled and patted Felicity's hand. 'I've had an accident, haven't I?'

The young woman nodded. 'You have hurt your head. You have been concussed, but the doctor said that all will be well but it may take a while before you feel yourself again.'

'Well, that's good, isn't it. Feeling myself again. That would be good.' There was a pause and then she added, 'Who am I?'

* * *

Sir Ebenezer Throate had been awake for some time but had felt no impetus to get out of bed. He felt that his body was not quite ready for such an exertion and was happy to remain beneath the covers for a little while longer. He was reassured that his mind was restored to its normal functioning mode after that passage down into the dark cobwebbed and frightening realm of painful semi-consciousness where nothing seemed real or tangible. Now his task was to piece together the events of the last few days – those that he was able to recall with any reliability – and work out what on earth was going on. The gentle throb in his shoulder was evidence that he had been wounded – wounded by some incompetent malefactor whose intention had been to kill him. Who could that be? Was it the phantom creature who had been haunting his midnight hours these last few weeks? Or was it his despicable son, eager to get his lazy hands on the Throate fortune? If not either of these – who else wanted him dead? It seemed likely there had been a second attempt on his life which had resulted in the demise of Dr Benbow. This thought brought a furrow to his brow. Would there be a third attempt and would this be a successful one? His body stiffened as he contemplated this dark possibility – or was it a probability – or a certainty?

He sat up in bed, fully roused now by these chilling thoughts. It was then that he became conscious of another presence in the room. He glimpsed a dark shape hovering in the shadows.

'Who... who is it?' he called, full of dreaded apprehension, his voice creaky and faint with lack of use.

'It is I,' came the reply as the figure moved slowly to the end of the bed and into the light.

The baronet hooded his eyes and peered at the creature. 'Why, it's Cook,' he said in surprise. 'Lizzie, isn't it?'

'Lizzie Barnes, yes sir,' she said.

'What are you doing here? You should be down in the kitchen. These are my private quarters.'

Lizzie gave a wry smile. 'Oh, I know that.'

Sir Ebenezer didn't like the confidence and the strange note of sarcasm in her voice.

'So... be off with you,' he snapped.

Lizzie gave him a wan smile. 'You are very good at dismissing folk, aren't you, Ebenezer? When they are no longer any use to you, you send them off – to the kitchen or out into the wide cruel world.'

Sir Ebenezer did not like the way this conversation was going, nor the confident stance of this woman who should be servile in his presence, not answering back with a menacing undertone.

'You never really notice the servants, do you Ebenezer? They are not really humans, individuals to you. They're just automatons employed to bring you food and wine and see to all your needs. Like I do and I did. Twenty five years ago I certainly saw to your needs.'

'What are you talking about, woman? You're speaking in riddles.'

'Look at me now. Look at me!'

Sir Ebenezer did as he was bidden as Lizzie Barnes slowly removed her mop cap and shook her long hair free until it fell about her face and almost down to her shoulders.

'Recognise me now?' she said.

The baronet's heart skipped a beat. Could it be? Could it really be?

The name crept to his lips, a memory of long ago. 'Louise,' he said softly like a gentle prayer. And then repeated it. 'Louise.'

She nodded. 'So you do remember.'

Tears welled at the old man's eyes. 'Of course I do. Of course… I have carried the burden of guilt all these years.'

'Hah! Carried it in the lap of luxury. What about the burden I've had to carry, eh?'

The words wounded him to the heart. Sir Ebenezer hung his head in shame. 'I am… so very sorry.'

'Yes. I believe you. That's why I thought you would do something to find our child – to give him some of the warmth, comfort and security that is due to him. It has eaten away at me over the years. I felt helpless and then I lit upon this idea. That's why I came here to work as your skivvy in the kitchen to try and persuade you – force you – to find our boy.'

'My God!' Sir Ebenezer's mouth dropped open as the lightning bolt struck. So, she was his midnight visitor. The woman who had been working in his kitchen, a woman who he had barely noticed was in fact the dark creature that crept into his bedroom at the dead of night and reawakened his guilt and his sentiments for the child he had fathered all those years ago. Her child. He gazed more closely at her. Now that the hair was framing the face he could see the resemblance to the lovely servant girl he had taken advantage of a quarter of a century before. Her face was plumper and lined not only with the passage of time, but the trials and tribulations wrought upon a woman's features when they are out in the world alone, struggling to keep body and soul together. It struck him for the first time that his treatment of Louise, as he knew her then, had damaged two lives: that of his son and the boy's mother. He moaned gently with the ache of grief.

'Well, have you done anything to find our boy?' she asked, her voice firm and challenging.

Sir Ebenezer nodded. 'Yes. Yes. I set two men from legal representatives to work on the case. I pray they will be successful – but… I am not sanguine. It is a long time ago and the trail will be very cold.'

The woman knew he was right. 'If there is a God in Heaven, He will see that things will turn out right. Granted - you and I are sinners, but that boy had nothing to do with our transgressions.'

'The fault lies with me. You were young and innocent and I had power over you.'

'We were both at fault but recriminations now are futile. All I ask is that you keep my secret, as I have kept yours, and keep me informed regarding any progress that is made in the search for our son. Once he has been found…' She paused and crossed herself. 'Once he has been found, I will happily disappear once more, content in the knowledge that you will do the right thing by him and accept him as your own.'

'I will, madam. Believe me, I will,' Sir Ebenezer assured her, his voice trembling with emotion. 'I wish… I wish.' His voice faltered and he got no further. He knew that the sentiment he was about to express was a foolish one. Deeds cannot be undone. Mistakes cannot be eradicated, only remedied to a certain extent. After all the crying, the spilt milk still remains. 'I believe that I shall hear some news – good news I hope – from the young legal gentlemen in the next few days. Whatever information they convey, have no fear, I will pass on to you.'

'Thank you.' The woman replaced her mob cap, pushing her hair under it, and then moved towards the door. As she placed her hand on the handle, she turned once more to face the baronet. 'One more thing, Ebenezer, look to her ladyship. I believe she means to do you ill.' With these chilling words, she left the room.

CHAPTER TWENTY EIGHT

As dawn breaks over London, it can look like a fairy tale capital, filled with glistening beauty and shadows, or it can appear like a dark and miserable annexe of hell. It all depends on the lighting and weather. Huge dark grey clouds shifting across a leaden sunless sky, while rain drenches the earth below, turn the city into a bleak funereal engraving, oozing misery and despair. By contrast, with a young bright yellow sun cheerfully beaming down from a pale blue cloudless sky, the lightest of breezes just managing to rustle the trees, causing the leaves to shimmer in a sprightly dance and the mellow stone of the newer buildings glowing in the early sunshine, good old London Town sparkles like a wedding cake.

On this morning, it was this latter treatment that greeted the inhabitants as they threw off their bedclothes with varying degrees of enthusiasm and prepared to face another day of toil, pleasure or indolence. In room 301 of the Hotel Splendide, just off the Strand, thin fingers of sunlight filtered into the room, playing gently on the face of the dozing incumbent. Curled up in bed in a tight foetal ball was Jeremiah Throate, luxuriating in soft cotton sheets and plump feather pillows. He was still not fully awake, having enjoyed a night of deep satisfying slumber and was reluctant to emerge into full consciousness. It had not taken him long to extract one of the precious stones from the necklace and obtain sufficient funds to allow him to book into this prestigious hotel and indulge in a sumptuous supper in the dining room.

It seemed to him now that he had perhaps begun a new phase of his life. The mixed blessing of being the son of a baronet with a fortune kept forever out of his reach was fading and in his view he had moved pragmatically on to a new path in his life's journey. He had become a thief, a felon, a snatcher of other folks' rich trifles. If he couldn't take what was rightfully his at present, while he waited for the old boy, his father, to die he would fund a pleasant lifestyle by taking what was not rightfully his. This dark conceit brought a thin smile to his sleepy features.

* * *

At Throate Manor, the sun also presented a pleasant scene, although the thick walls and dense timbers failed to allow any warmth to penetrate the building. Roger Lightwood was up early, partly because he had slept badly, his mind awhirl with matters concerning his duties and his misery at being apart from the woman he loved and the related problem of how he was going to resolve this separation. This morning, however, he was determined to see Sir Ebenezer. Since his return from holiday, after the brief initial interview, he had been prevented from visiting his employer by Lady Amelia who had claimed that he was too weak and not sufficiently *compos mentis* to receive visitors yet. He did not believe her.

He knew that Lady Amelia was a late riser which gave him an opportunity of visiting the old man's chamber before she had a chance to stop him. Slipping out of his room, he made his way stealthily through the gloomy labyrinthine corridors to Sir Ebenezer's bedroom.

He knocked gently on the door and entered. The baronet was sitting up in bed with a blank expression on his face, but on seeing Roger approach him he gave a gurgle of pleasure, a broad smile animating his features.

'Roger, by all that's wonderful. Do come in, my dear boy.'

'How are you feeling, sir?'

'Well, as you know I have been in the wars, but it was a little skirmish, that's all. I am on the mend.'

'I am delighted to hear it. I have only been told the lightest of details, what happened?'

Sir Ebenezer shook his head. 'I don't really want to talk about it, my boy. Not today at least. I am trying to wipe it from my memory. To recall the details, when they are so fresh, would disturb me too much. Maybe after some time has elapsed.'

Roger was disappointed at this news but nodded his head to indicate that he understood.

'My main aim now,' said Sir Ebenezer, 'is to get back to normal. To recover the status quo, as it were. With this in mind, I would like to leave this bed and get dressed and take some air. Your visit is very fortuitous because you can help me in this endeavour. My spirit is very willing but I fear that the flesh may be a little hesitant. I'm very creaky and a helping hand would be most useful.'

'Why certainly. I am happy to be of assistance – if you are sure you are up to it.'

'Of course I'm not up to it – but if I wait until I'm up to it, I might be dead. Besides I've got to get out this bed and into my clothes before that harridan swans in here and forbids it. At the moment I don't think I have enough strength to defy her.'

Roger was well aware 'that harridan' referred to Sir Ebenezer's wife. It was a description with which the young man concurred.

'Pull out my smartest suit and matching apparel from the wardrobe over there and lay them out on the bed. In the meantime, I'll attempt to scrape a cold blade across my face to get rid of this awful stubble. Can't risk sending for hot water, that might arouse the dragon from her den.'

While the baronet tottered over to a table near the window which contained a jug of water and a large porcelain bowl Roger investigated the capacious oak wardrobe crammed with clothes.

'Has there been any message from those legal chaps from

Gripwind and Biddle – Mr Twist and his crony?' asked Sir Ebenezer as he poured water into the bowl and began dabbing his face with the water.

'No, not as yet,' Roger replied as he examined a dark grey suit, one he knew was a favourite if his employer. 'What is their brief? I don't believe you informed me regarding this business.'

'God, this razor is blunt or my chin is like a porcupine's rump,' said Sir Ebenezer, ignoring Lightwood's enquiry. 'Still it wakens one up. And that is what I really need now, Roger, my boy: I need waking up.'

* * *

Oliver and Jack were later in reaching the coaching inn than Oliver had planned. This was due to the inordinate time his companion had taken to complete his morning ablutions. It had been Oliver's task to waken his friend, who seemed determined with a Herculean effort to cling on to the remnants of sleep, like a man hanging from a cliff edge by his fingernails, despite being shaken, shouted at and having the bed covers pulled from him with a sudden, swift movement. Once vertical at last, Jack took forever to wash, shave and then arrange his hair into a shape and fashion which suited him. He spent some time in front of the mirror adjusting his thatch first this way and then that. To Oliver, the final result looked very much like the wild rough and tumble look his companion had exhibited when he had been dragged from his bed. Then came the performance of choosing his outfit for the day from his very limited wardrobe. After much consideration, Jack stepped into the very same clothes he had worn the day before.

Oliver was a patient man with a very even temper, but this was wearing both down to snapping point. As usual Jack was blithely unaware of the tensions and irritations he was creating (was he ever?) and as he strode to the front door with a cry of 'Come on, Oliver, let's be off,' he failed to notice his companions fierce look and exasperated exclamation.

The courtyard of the coaching inn was a scene of chaos. There were three coaches in attendance, one of which seemed to be inhabited by a tribe of screaming and mewling children. One scruffy youth was clambering about on the roof of the cab, howling like a wolf and refusing to come down. In charge of the brood was a fat red-faced woman who bellowed incessantly at them to no avail.

'I hope to heaven that is not our coach,' observed Oliver.

'It will not be, I can guarantee you,' responded Jack, 'for I would not set foot on it if it was. I'd rather walk.'

As fate would have it, this highly animated nursery wagon was not their coach. After consulting an official, they were directed to the correct conveyance. They were only just in time for there were only two seats left and the coach was ready to depart. The other passengers glowered at them as they entered, realising that they would now have less room on the journey. Oliver and Jack squeezed themselves into the available spaces, facing each other like stiff bookends.

'Better'n that a load of squawking brats,' observed Jack leaning forward and mothing the words not quite sotto voce, prompting a few disgruntled glances from the other passengers.

Oliver just nodded in response.

With a violent lurch and a loud inarticulate cry from the driver, the coach rocketed forth into motion. It was as though some giant invisible hand had taken hold of the vehicle and shaken it. A shower of parcels and small pieces of hand luggage cascaded down from the rack. One thin fellow in a clerical collar lost his seat altogether and landed on the floor with a yelp. Jack leaned forward to help the poor devil back into his seat.

'There you are, your reverence,' said Jack

'Thank you so much,' replied the man, adjusting his pince-nez.

'That's all right. You can do the same for me next time we're jolted about like corks all at sea.'

The man responded with an embarrassed grin.

For a time, the coach rattled through the streets of London and then shuddered to a halt in a thick stream of traffic. There followed a tedious half hour where the coach inched its way along through a throng of vehicles that crowded and clogged the thoroughfares of the city.

During this tortuous time, Oliver studied the other passengers. Apart from himself and Jack there were four fellow travellers. There was the clerical gentleman, a stern looking lady who was the epitome of a strict governess or matron with pinched features and a mouth that probably never approached a smile; a plump fellow in a tight fitting tweed suit who was reading some sporting periodical and a fourth individual who interested Oliver the most. This fellow was sitting at the furthest corner of carriage on the opposite window seat to Oliver. He was a tall man, dressed in a long leather coat with a high collar, above which appeared a thin skeletal face with bright beady eyes that suggested their owner was a shrewd and difficult customer. There was a definite touch of cruelty about his features that strangely unnerved Oliver. It was a face he thought he had seen before but he was not sure where. Maybe in the dock? The fellow's coat was buttoned, but as Oliver scrutinised it, he suspected that the slight bulge on the right side around the level of the man's waist indicated that he was carrying a pistol.

At length the coach escaped the confines of the city and reached the open road. The horses sped along the rural highway, the carriage now maintaining a regular rocking rhythm.

Jack leaned forward towards his friend. 'What time d'you reckon we'll get to Throate Manor? I'm starving.' He spoke in a husky whisper, but Mr Dawkins' husky whisper had a volume that was stronger than most people's normal speaking voice.

'Not until late afternoon. But fear not, you should be able to grab a morsel or two when we change horses at the Green Dragon en route,' came the reply.

Jack nodded. 'That's good 'cause I didn't want my rumbling tum to disturb the other passengers.' He sat back with a grin, amused by his own observation.

Oliver had noticed that the eyes of sinister cove in the corner had flickered with dark interest and his body had stiffened when he had heard Jack mention the words 'Throate Manor'.

As the journey continued, he found his eyes constantly drawn to examining this dark stranger. If only he could remember where he had seen him before.

In just over an hour after leaving London, the coach pulled into the courtyard of the Green Dragon where fresh horses were to be secured. 'This will be a 'alf 'our hinterlude,' the coachman informed them. With great relief the passengers tumbled out of their confinement, like convicts on parole, stretching their limbs and breathing in the fresh air of freedom. In an instant Jack Dawkins made a beeline for the inn in search of a tankard of ale and some vitals. Oliver was content to forego this pleasure; he had taken the precaution of breakfasting well before setting out that morning and so was content to remain outside enjoying the sunshine and indulging in a gentle stroll. As he took pleasure in exercising his limbs after the cramped conditions inside the coach, he was aware that he was being followed. He turned around suddenly and came face to face with the thin skeletal faced passenger who had attracted his attention. The man doffed his cap in a theatrical manner.

'Pardon me for interrupting your quiet contemplations, sir,' he said in a smooth and what Oliver considered was a palpably false polite manner, 'but I could not help overhearing you and your companion mention Throate Manor.'

Oliver did not respond. He merely raised his eyebrows in gentle enquiry. His lawyer's training had taught him that silence was often the greatest lure, it seduced more information than the witness intended to impart.

'I, er just wondered if you knew the old gentleman who resides there: Sir Ebenezer?'

'What is the purpose of your enquiry, sir? asked Oliver in a not unfriendly fashion.

The man shrugged. 'I was just interested to hear news of the gentleman's welfare. I gather that he has not been in the best of health recently.'

'You know him then?'

The fellow's eyes narrowed and he gave Oliver a shifty look, which told him that a lie was on its way. 'I have encountered the gentleman on occasion, but I am particularly friendly with his son Jeremiah, a fine upstanding fellow. You will have met him, no doubt.'

Again Oliver gave a non-committal smile. 'You are on your way to Throate Manor yourself, Mr...?'

'Trench, Eugene Trench.' The words came out too quickly and the man's face soured as he realised his mistake. What a fool he was to give his real name. 'No, no,' he carried on hurriedly, 'not yet at least. I have business in the village but, who knows, if time allows, I may take a trip up the house and pass on my compliments.'

Oliver flashed him a brief enigmatic smile. 'And what *is* your business, sir?' he asked, snatching the opportunity to turn the tables in this interview. There was something about this fellow he did not like: he was duplicitous, dangerous and his interest in Sir Ebenezer and Throate Manor could bode nothing but ill for the house and its inhabitants.

'Property,' Trench replied airily. 'I deal in property. Other people's property.'

'Houses?'

'Yes, houses, carriages, jewellery et cetera. All kinds of property. If you have something of value to dispose of, I am your man.'

'That must keep you busy.'

'Indeed. A worker ant am I. I enjoy the activity and the rewards it brings. You look like a fine set up young gentleman – what's your game?'

'My game? Oh, I'm not quite sure I've settled on the game yet. I'm still at the inquisitive stage. Ah, I see my companion is returning after taking his fill inside the inn. If you will excuse me.' With a gentle bow, Oliver Twist turned his back on Eugene Trench and walked towards Jack Dawkins who had emerged from the doorway of the inn, running his coat sleeve across his mouth, an habitual gesture of his which indicated that he had just partaken of food and drink and was removing the evidence.

'They have some very tasty pies in there, Oliver. I rather made a glutton of myself by wolfing down two with a nice tankard of cold beer.'

Oliver smiled, patting his friend on his arm in an affectionate paternal fashion. Sometimes he almost regarded Jack like a child for he had all the enthusiasm and mannerisms of an innocent in the world achieving enjoyment from simple pleasures, and lacking the steely discipline of responsibility.

'I trust then that you will be sufficiently fuelled to keep you going for some hours now.'

'Maybe. You know me, Oliver. I likes my grub.'

Oliver chuckled. 'Indeed, I do know you.'

'What were you nattering about with that fellow Trench just now?'

'You know him?'

'Know of him. He's got a bit of a reputation for being a slithery snake. When I was on the game, dipping and that, I heard his name mentioned as a man not to fall foul of. A gambling cheat I gather. He's a bit dangerous. I saw him once with two of his henchmen giving some poor fellow a hard time.'

'What constitutes a hard time?'

'Don't be naïve, my friend.'

Oliver shook his head woefully. 'I don't like it, not one little bit.'

'Don't like what?'

In a swift and a concise manner, Oliver relayed the substance of the conversation he had had with Trench. Then it was Jack's turn to shake his head woefully.

'Blimey, that is creepy. 'He glanced over to where Trench was leaning against the wall of the inn. 'What does he want with Sir Ebenezer? And where does young Master Jeremiah come in?'

'Those are the very questions I asked myself. I am not sure if Trench impinges on our mission, but I do believe we have to watch out for him.'

'And watch our backs.'

Oliver thought for a moment and then grabbed hold of Jack's

sleeve. 'Listen, when we reach the village of Denbigh, as before I'll engage a carriage to take me up to the Manor as arranged, but you stay behind in the village and keep an eye on our friend over there. Follow him in a discreet manner and see what he gets up to.'

Jack Dawkins beamed. 'Like the old days when I shadowed some old geezer ready to snatch his handkerchief – those silken lovelies. I was top of my class in that department. They didn't call me the Artful Dodger for nothin'.'

'Let's hope you haven't gone rusty.'

'Not me.'

'If there is any danger, you'll have to get word to me up at the hall.'

'No problem. Don't worry your head about that.'

'Book a room at the local inn for the night and we'll rendezvous there in the morning unless…'

'Unless something untoward crops up, eh?'

* * *

Morning had also reached Lady Whitestone's London house. Despite the invading sunbeams, the atmosphere was sombre. Dr Sloper had called early to see his patient and Felicity waited outside her employer's bedroom while he ministered to her. He emerged, after twenty minutes, his face a neutral mask.

'How is her ladyship?' enquired Felicity gently.

Sloper gave a shrug of the shoulders. He paused for a moment before replying assembling his thoughts. He knew that he had to be accurate in relaying his verdict so that no recriminations could be aimed in his direction.

'Well,' he said at length, measuring his words carefully, 'physically she is on the mend. She's still a little weak and her head aches but that is to be expected and is quite normal. However, her mental state is quite a puzzle. She seems to have very little grasp of who she is. I have known her ladyship for some years and I have always found her to be, how shall I put it, very forthright in her views. She does not suffer fools gladly.'

Or any one, thought Felicity but remained silent.

'At the moment it would seem the blow to her head has softened her nature somewhat. She seems remarkably meek and amenable which is not the Lady Amelia Whitestone I know. It is probably the result of the concussion and she will, no doubt, return to her usual self in due course. In the meantime treat her kindly, as I'm sure you always do, and answer her every request and whim, as I'm sure you also always do. There must be no tension or resistance to her desires in her life at the moment. Any kind of stress may well retard her recovery. I am sure I am leaving her in safe hands.'

With these words Dr Sloper made a swift departure leaving the house strangely silent. There was now only Maggie the young maid and Sarah the cook, a recluse in the kitchen, on the premises now that Arthur was no longer present. At the thought of him, Felicity felt a pang in her heart. It was guilt, remorse and a certain sadness. She had treated the fellow badly but he had revealed himself to be a monster and in many ways she had escaped a terrible fate.

Slowly she made her way up the stairs once more and, after tapping gently on Lady Whitestone's bedroom door, she entered. The occupant was sitting up in bed gently humming. On seeing Felicity, her eyes widened with delight and she smiled broadly. 'Oh, my dear, how lovely to see you,' she cooed, patting the bed by her side. 'Do come and sit here.'

Felicity hesitated. This kind of familiarity from her employer was alien to her. 'I just came to see if you would like a cup of tea and maybe a boiled egg.'

'What an angel you are. So kind. Tea and an egg with some lovely bread and butter would be most agreeable, but first I'd like you to come and sit by me, my dear Felicity.'

My dear Felicity! The old woman had surely lost her mind. She had never been 'my dear Felicity' in all the time she had been in the harridan's employ.

'Come. Come, come, sit.'

Felicity remembered Dr Sloper's injunction that there should be no resistance to her ladyship's desires which would cause her distress and restrict her recovery. Felicity sat on the bed and Lady Whitestone took hold of her hand. 'You are so good to me, my dear. So very kind. You've been like a daughter to me.'

At these words Felicity's mouth dropped open as though she was struck dumb by the sentiment. Obviously the old lady was delirious. It was as though she had become another woman, as though the fairies had replaced the frosty old witch in the night with this soft-hearted and befuddled one.

'I try to do my job as best I can,' she found herself muttering at length.

'Oh, I think our relationship is much greater than that of employer and employee, don't you think, my dear?'

'Well…'

'I have grown very fond of you and I do believe that you have some affection for me also.'

'Well…'

'Of course my dear. I don't wish to embarrass you. Enough said.' Lady Whitestone squeezed Felicity's hand and gave her a broad smile. 'Now before you arrange for my tea and that lovely egg, I want you to send a note around to my lawyer, old Percy Boffin asking him to come round to see me urgently and for him to bring with him a copy of my will.'

'But are you sure you are well enough to be receiving visitors?'

'Great heaven's yes. I feel fine and I'm sure that with the tea and egg inside me, I'll be wanting to get dressed. Now, my darling girl, be off and carry out my wishes like you always do.'

Despite being bewildered by Lady Whitestone's behaviour and request, as always Felicity carried out her employers wishes.

CHAPTER TWENTY NINE

She saw them!

Amelia Throate had just emerged from her boudoir and was making her stately way to her husband's room to ascertain how the old goat was this morning when she spied him, accompanied by that irritating fellow Lightwood, descending the main staircase. Their progress was slow: Ebenezer was shuffling, uncertain on his feet after many days in bed, and Lightwood was having to support and guide him every step of the way. What on earth were they up to? The old fool shouldn't be out of bed. He wasn't well enough. Such vigorous activity could be too much for him; it could bring on a relapse. This latter thought brought a sly smile to her lips and prevented her from crying out in order bring them to a halt. Instead, she determined to keep watch on them unseen to observe exactly what they were doing.

On reaching the bottom of the staircase, they turned left down the corridor that led towards the rear of the house. They are going to the private garden, thought Amelia Throate. Her husband often liked to walk about there in the morning on his own, enjoying the solitude. 'His escape from me!' she hissed quietly with some passion.

Suddenly, a plan, a daring, vicious, exciting and great problem-solving plan rushed into Lady Amelia Throate's head fully formed.

It was delicious and could work. With care she would make it work. With a chuckle she turned on her heel and made her way up to the top floor of the house, leaving her husband and Lightwood to make their slow progress to the garden.

Within minutes she was on the roof of Throate Manor, making her way along the little wooden boardwalk that ran around the perimeter of the building. The sky was a cloudless blue with a faint chilling breeze but Amelia Throate did not notice it. She was warmed by the thrill of her venture. She moved with great care along the narrow footway, passing at interval the large classic statues perched on the edge of the roof gazing down at the grounds below. Eventually she reached the rear of the building, at the spot overlooking the private garden. It was here that the statues of the three graces were situated. She placed herself between Aglaia and Euphroyne and gazed down. She was disappointed to observe that the garden was empty. Had she been wrong? Had her dratted husband and that equally dratted secretary man gone elsewhere? Her spirits which had been soaring and inflamed by her outrageous plan now began to falter. The scheme that had sprung so perfectly formed to her mind from nowhere seemed to be in danger of crumbling. And then... and then she heard the mutter of voices.

She leaned over further and to her delight she saw her husband and the Lightfoot fellow emerge on to the lawn below. Sir Ebenezer threw his arms wide to embrace the fresh air like an old friend he had not encountered in a long time. He even shook himself free of Lightwood's support and began to stroll about the lawn in an childlike manner – a stiff, slow and awkward childlike manner.

Where would he settle? He would have to settle at some point. She knew her husband's energy levels wouldn't allow him to carry on tottering about in this jerky somnambulistic fashion. Which of the graces did he favour? Would it be Aglaia who represented brightness and light or Thalia the grace of all things blooming. Personally Amelia favoured Euphrosyne who represented joy. How fitting if Euphrosyne were the one who helped her carry out the deed for it would certainly bring her great joy.

At length, her husband returned from his perambulations to join Lightwood, who had stayed on the edge of the lawn keeping a keen eye on his charge.

The two men now engaged in quiet casual conversation, the nature of which Amelia could not determine, placed as she was far above them on the roof. As the two men talked, they moved gently, first this way and then that but frustratingly never stopping still for any length of time. Then Ebenezer spotted a flower in the edge of the lawn. To Amelia's eyes it looked like a butter cup. She saw him move forward, reach down and pluck it and hold it to his nose. He's like an imbecilic child, she thought. He always had that naïve trait even when he was younger. Now, in his weak dotage, it had grown stronger. But nevertheless this naïve appreciation of the little yellow flower had placed him just where she wanted him. Sadly it was not under Euphrosyne's watchful eye. It was Aglaia who was the chosen one. So be it. Now she could be rid of the old devil and be free to live the life she wanted in the time left to her. London society, theatres, gown shops and jewellers beckoned.

Energised by this thought, she moved with stealth to the statue, checked that her husband stood directly in its trajectory and then she heaved against the granite edifice with all her might. At first nothing happened. It didn't move. This surprised her. She assumed that these weathered icons, which had been at the mercy of all the elements for centuries – the heat of the sun, the cold of the ice and snow and the corrosive drenching of the rain would have made them very vulnerable and susceptible to movement by force. Grim determination drove her on; she pushed harder. Eventually, her efforts were rewarded: there came a gentle grating sound of stone shifting on stone. The thing trembled and then moved. With all her might, she leant heavily against the statue of Euphrosyne. It groaned gently and started to tilt. Lady Amelia Throate gave a grunt of exultant pleasure, wrapping her arms around the statue for one final push. Then suddenly with remarkable speed it left its moorings and began its journey. So swift was its descent that she had not time to release her hold on the granite missile and, with a cry of terrified wonder, she and the statue plunged earthwards.

Below, Sir Ebenzer heard the cry of alarm and gazed skywards, as did Roger Littlewood. Both were amazed and shocked to see two dark objects hurtling towards them. With the speed of a lizard, Lightwood grabbed the arm of his employer and dragged him backwards out of harm's way. Just in time as it happened, for a second later the two flying missiles landed where he had been standing.

'What in Heaven …?' Sir Ebenezer managed, before shock robbed him temporarily of further dialogue. Both men gazed in amazement at the two shapes on the lawn. Roger could see that one was a stone edifice, severed in two by the fall, but the other was a human. A woman. She was lying face downwards but he was fairly certain he knew her identity. As did Sir Ebenezer.

Slowly, Roger bent forward and gently turned the body over. It was indeed Lady Amelia Throate, her face caked in mud, traversed with thin rivulets of blood. The glassy eyes were open, but there was no doubt that she was dead.

Roger looked up at Sir Ebenezer and saw that he had grasped that fact also. 'What on earth was the old girl doing up there?' he asked, shaking his head.

I think she was trying to kill you, thought Roger, as he gazed down at the decapitated statue embedded in the damp grass of the lawn. She meant you to be under that thing, his thought continued, but remained unspoken. Taking the old man's arm, he led him towards the French windows. 'Let's go inside,' he said. 'There's nothing we can do now. I'll get Bulstrode to deal with things.'

* * *

Percival Boffin, Lady Whitestone's lawyer, closed his client's bedroom door and stood for some moment as though caught in a trance. He shook his head in bewilderment. Was the woman with whom he had just been in conference the real Lady Whitestone? Where were those gorgon eyes, that guillotine of a voice, that brusque and aggressive demeanour? They had, it would seem, evaporated, and been replaced by a warm glance, a gentle smile, a kindly nature and a reasonableness of nature that he had not experienced before.

With a sigh and shake of the head, he brought himself round from his silent cogitations and, tucking his briefcase under his arm, he made his way down the curving staircase to the hallway below where he found Felicity Waring, her ladyship's companion waiting, an apprehensive frown on her brow.

'Well, young lady, this is a portentous day for you,' he observed.

'Really, sir?'

'Indeed. Indeed. Do you not know why your mistress sent for me?'

Felicity shook her head.

The old lawyer pursed his lips. Should he tell the girl or should he allow her to find out for herself? No doubt Lady Whitestone would pass on the news now that the business was concluded. However, it was so surprising that he could not resist the urge to tell the girl. He was bursting to pass on the information to someone and who more appropriate than Miss Felicity Waring herself. It was totally unprofessional, but he could not help himself.

'Well,' he said slowly, 'I am sure your mistress will make you cognisant of the arrangement but perhaps it is as well that I give you the basic details now so that you will not be shocked when she tells you.'

'Tells me what?'

'Lady Whitestone has settled a considerable amount of her fortune on you. She says that your diligence and kindness to her has touched her heart and she has come to regard you as a daughter that she never had. When she dies, you will be a very rich woman.'

Felicity stared open-mouthed at the old legal gentleman and her body shivered at the startling nature of the words he had just uttered. Was she dreaming? Was this all real? How could the old curmudgeon who had treated her in so ill and a cruel cavalier fashion for over two years now perform a *volte face* and reward her as though she were 'a daughter that she never had'. The world had gone mad. At least, her world had. She suddenly felt faint and weak at the knees. Boffin observing the effect his words had on the young lady guided her to a chair and patted her hand.

'I did not realise that you would be so affected by this news,' he said kindly.

'It is not a jest then?'

Boffin shook his head. 'No, no. That is not my nature. What I told you is the truth. You will inherit the bulk of Lady Whitestone's fortune when she passes on. That is good news, is it not?'

It was sometime later when she was alone that Felicity Waring mused that if as Boffin had asserted, Lady Whitestone now regarded her as a daughter, this was purely as a result of a blow to her head, which had directed the old lady's mind down a kinder more humane path. Her personality had transformed; she had become a different woman. It was as though the wicked fairy had metamorphosed into the benevolent good fairy. It was a fantastic concept, proving that life was a great deal stranger than fairy stories.

*　*　*

'That is the plan, then.' Jack Dawkins tapped the side of his head. 'I shadow Master Trench and sees that he gets up to no good regarding old man Throate, while you engage a carriage and trip off up to the Manor.'

Oliver nodded. 'If nothing ill transpires, I will meet you here at the inn this evening or by the morning at the latest.'

'And if something … er, transpires?'

'Get a message to me as soon as possible up at the Manor.'

Jack gave a mock salute.

They were standing in the courtyard of The Farmer's Boy in Denbigh just having alighted, stiff and tired, from the coach. As they conversed they kept an eagle eye on Eugene Trench who was in conversation with the coach driver.

'Don't fret, Oliver. This line of work is more up my street than sitting on a hard stool in a dusty office. Trust me.'

The two men shook hands and Oliver departed.

Jack made his way to the door of the inn and lurked there in the shadows watching Trench. At length the villain moved away and, clasping a canvas bag that he had retrieved from the luggage rack on the back of the coach, made his way into the village.

Within seconds, Jack had engaged the coach driver in conversation.

'That thin fellow you was gassing with just now, what was he talking about?'

The coachman screwed up his face into a suspicious scowl. 'What's hit to do with you?' he growled aggressively.

Jack drew a short-bladed knife from his belt and held it up before the coachman's face. 'You could say I'm a nosey blighter. A dangerous, nosey blighter. A bit unstable in my ways as well. So, it's not going to hurt you to tell me, is it? Or, it's likely a refusal may hurt you.' He lowered the knife with the blade pointing at the man's stomach.

Immediately the demeanour of the coach driver changed, his lips forming a nervous smile. 'T'were nothin' himportant, sir,' he said.

'I'll be the judge of that,' said Jack.

'Well, he just was a wantin' to 'ire an horse and was asking where there was a farrier in these parts. That's hall.'

'And where is this farrier?'

'At Bell Cross. Left down the road awhile and turn right by the old watermill. You'll see the smithy some hundred yards down the track. Tom Cuff be his name.'

Jack Dawkins slipped the knife back in his belt and tapped the coach driver on the arm.

'I'm much obliged to you,' he said and then made his way out of the courtyard on to the highway.

As he walked briskly, catching sight of Trench in the far distance, he reasoned that if Trench were after a horse, he must have it in mind to ride to the Manor in order to commit some mischief or other up there. Some mischief that he needed to prevent.

* * *

Meanwhile Oliver was being driven in a stately fashion in an old growler hired from *Ethelred Grenson and Sons, Transportation for the Gentry*, who were based and had been founded in Denbigh village in 1790. In fact the driver was old man Grenson himself. Oliver was experiencing a rapid sea change of emotions as he sat back in the carriage gazing out at the lush scenery passing by. He thought that perhaps – maybe – possibly – he had solved the mystery of Sir Ebenezer's son. Well, there was a vague, slender chance he was right; if he wasn't, he had no idea what to do next. However this wasn't his only concern. The image of Eugene Trench loomed up in his imagination. On this point he was quite certain, this scaramouche presented a direct threat to his client. However, the problem was that he had no idea what form or nature this threat might take. He hoped to heaven that Jack would be able prevent any catastrophe. Sadly, he wasn't sure his old friend was up to the demands of the task. Only time would tell.

Oliver grew conscious that the coach was slowing down and yet they were some miles away from Throate Manor. He pulled down the window of the carriage and gazed out. The road they were travelling on was narrow and he observed that there was a horse drawn vehicle approaching in the other direction. As it drew nearer, he saw to his heart stopping consternation that it was a hearse with the top hatted driver dressed in suitable funereal livery.

As the two carriages drew up side by side, the drivers exchanged pleasantries. Oliver could not quite hear the conversation but he judged that the hearse driver was informing old man Grenson about his cargo. Obviously these were two old business men from Denbigh who knew each other well and were on good terms. Eventually, they afforded each other a hearty wave and continued their separate journeys. Oliver lifted the flap at the back of the carriage which allowed him to communicate with the driver.

'What was that all about?' he asked, trying to keep the urgency out of his voice.

'Oh, terrible, young sir,' came the reply. 'There has been a tragedy up at the Manor.'

Oliver's heart sank. 'Sir Ebenezer…' he said.

'No, no. It's her ladyship. A fearful accident. She fell from the roof of the Manor. She be as dead as a doornail. Fell all the way down. What a tragedy. Awful. Awful.'

Oliver closed the flap. Awful, awful indeed. What on earth was he to make of this dark development?

CHAPTER THIRTY

There is an ancient adage that runs: 'old habits die hard'. Like all such adages, it holds the firm gem of a universal truth and could easily be applied to Jeremiah Throate. Indeed his old habits became the great undoing of him. Despite his recent acquisition of wealth, albeit by nefarious ways, and his temporary comfortable quarters in the Hotel Splendide, his natural leanings were not to the glistening shops, theatres and bars of London's West End which the well to do frequent when in town, but his penchant was for the lower drinking houses down by the river where not only could he buy a cheap glass of gin but maybe pick up a game. It is true that his fingers itched and his hands shook if he was away from a gambling ambience for more than a few days. It wasn't the financial rewards that stimulated and thrilled him, but the simple power of winning. The scooping of the cash to his side of the table while staring at the downfallen loser on the other side. It was like vitals and wine to him.

And so, rising late from his bed, only a little before noon, Jeremiah Throate set forth to a little drinking house in Upper-Swandam Lane, the north side of the river to the east of London Bridge, called The Toilers Arms where he hoped that he might muscle in on some little game of chance. He entered the dank and foul smelling establishment and made his way through a throng of shadowy characters to the bar and ordered a gin and water.

The fat barman was less than monosyllabic. Grunts, it appeared was his native language, but nevertheless after paying for his drink, he attempted to engage the fellow in some sort of communication. He slipped a pack of cards from his pocket – he always had one about his person - and used them as a visual aid. 'Is there a game?' he enunciated slowly, fanning the pack. 'Cards,' he added for good measure.

The barman grunted again and mouthed something Jeremiah could not interpret but the fellow's piggy eye glanced in the direction of the end of the bar where a stout individual with a dark straggly beard, smoking a clay pipe stood, idly running his finger through a shallow pool of spilt ale.

Jeremiah assumed that this was the man to give him more information as long as he had mastered the art of talking. Picking up his drink he moved down to the end of the bar and nodded to the man in a friendly fashion. 'I gather you might know if there's a game going on. Cards. Dice maybe?'

The man lifted his grimy features, blew a thick coil of smoke from the corner of his mouth and stared at Jeremiah for a long while without saying a word. Eventually, he spoke. 'Why?' he said and repeated the action with the coil of smoke.

'I'd be interested. I'd like to sit in.'

There was another long interval before the man replied. 'Be here at nine tonight.' With these few words, the conversation was over. He turned his back on Jeremiah, preventing any further intercourse between them. Nevertheless, Jeremiah was satisfied. There was the chance of a game that evening. That pleased him. It would be good to sit around a table once more with a group of greedy men whom he could impoverish with a flash of a full house. While he was smiling at this thought and sipping his gin, he had no notion that he was being observed by two characters sitting far away from the bar in the deepest and dankest section of the inn. They were grinning too for they could not believe their luck. After all their efforts pounding the streets in search of the devil, here was the very prey they were after.

He had just walked into their lair, their sticky web. And they were determined that he would never get out of it.

This was Barney Kepple and Alf Joint, Eugene Trench's redoubtable henchmen. They were small of brain but full of brawn and vile of nature. Without a word, they clinked their mugs of ale in celebration and grinned. They took a gulp of ale and waited.

Eventually, Jeremiah Throate placed his glass down on the counter with a decisive deliberate motion and made his way to the door. Within seconds Kepple and Joint were on their feet and heading in the same direction.

After two gins, Jeremiah felt like returning to his wonderful hotel bed for an afternoon nap before he returned to The Toilers for his game of cards. He wandered down the empty street towards the river as yet still innocent of the silhouetted figures who, with increasing speed, were dogging his footsteps. As he reached the thoroughfare that ran along the murky, sluggish Thames, some instinct caused him to turn round and gaze behind him.

And then he saw them. Although they were in shadow he recognised them straight away. How could he not? He had encountered them before. Close up. They were like familiar sketches by George Cruikshank come to life; grotesque sketch-like creatures, creations of some dark comic imagination. Fearsome and risible at the same time. He turned quickly and increased his pace. They did better than that: they began to run. And as they did so, they extracted their weapons. Kepple had a stout cosh and Joint a savage looking knife.

Jeremiah Throate was now very frightened. In panic, he scrambled over the parapet and dropped down on to the muddy shore of the Thames. He landed unsteadily on his feet but then dropped to his knees which sank into the soggy gritty wetness. He glanced over his shoulder and saw that his pursuers were glaring at him from the parapet, uttering inarticulate Neanderthal cries. Then they began to clamber over the wall. Squelching to his feet, Throate began running again along the sodden shore. He could tell by the sound of threatening yells behind him that they were gaining on him. His heart began to thump against his chest and his eyes watered as he exerted himself to attain a faster pace, but it was difficult on this wet and shifting surface. He stumbled once more and this time fell full length on to the sand. By the time he had managed to stagger to his feet, Kepple and Joint were on him.

* * *

Sir Ebenezer Throate had returned to his bed. He lay awake gazing at the ceiling. He was strangely drained of emotion given that he had just witnessed the death of his wife of some thirty five years. They hadn't been the most idyllic thirty-five years but they had survived them as opposing armies do having moments of conflict and the occasional periods of truce. He had loved Amelia when they got married and the magic had lasted a few years before they… well he had to admit it … before they both grew selfish and only became concerned about themselves and their own individual well-being. This had festered and mutated from dislike to hatred on both their sides. He had mourned the loss of the pretty young maiden long ago and so he wasn't going to do it now. He wasn't heartless enough to feel glad that his wife had died but he could not summon up sufficient sadness within his breast to bring a tear to the eye. She was gone now and it was a pity, but it did bring him a sense of relief and, indeed, a sense of release. With this thought firmly set in his mind, he slipped into peaceful untroubled slumber.

* * *

The horse that Eugene Trench had hired from farrier Tom Cuff was, he thought, a reasonable mount but he had paid a king's ransom for the privilege of borrowing it for the day. He'd also had to cough up a few coins for information regarding the layout of the Throate estate. Cuff knew it well and regarded his knowledge as a commodity to be purchased. In this instance, Trench was content enough to pay; it was an investment which, if all worked out, would pay great dividends.

On Cuff's advice, he had left the main track to the house and was making his way through Cowper's Copse, a straggle of dense woodland that skirted the main grounds of the house.

'When you get to the little wooden bridge by the stream, it is best to leave your horse there and make the rest of the way on foot. There is only a narrow footpath leading up from the lower meadow which will take you up to the rear of the property. The horse would find this very hard going.'

Trench thanked him for his information, suggesting, while never actually confirming, that he was a relative of Sir Ebenezer who was making a surprise visit. He came at last to the wooden bridge, dismounted and tethered the house to one of its struts. Snatching up his carpet bag, which he'd hung from the pommel of the saddle, he made his way across the stream and out into the open countryside. A green meadow stretched out before him with long grass waving in the stiff breeze. It rose up like a rippling green carpet to a plateau beyond on which was perched a strangely shaped building: Throate Manor.

It took him some moments to locate the faint pathway which meandered its way through the waist high stalks towards his goal. With a will, grasping the carpet bag to his chest, he set forth.

* * *

Roger Lightwood sat in his office with a cup of tea and gazed across at the dark suited gentleman opposite him. It was Bulstrode, the Throate's manservant. His ancient features were dappled with tears and his eyes were red from crying.

'I am sorry, Master Lightwood to behave in this fashion. I don't know what has happened to me,' he blubbed, his chest heaving with emotion.

'Grief, my dear Bulstrode. Grief is what has happened to you.'

The old servant nodded soberly. 'I suppose you are right, sir. I have served in this house man and boy for fifty years. I attended to Sir Ebenezer's father, before him. I know it's a foolish thing to say, but I felt part of the family. And now there is this terrible day.'

Lightwood smiled kindly. 'You *are* part of the family. This household wouldn't function without your input. You are part of the substance of the building, its foundations, its furniture, its life. I can see that and I've only been here a short time.'

'Thank you for that, sir. You are very kind. I know that Sir Ebenezer and Lady Amelia have never been what you might say fulsome in their praise and were rarely warm to me personally, but I believe they trusted me, relied on me, and counted on me for support and assurance.'

'Of course they did... do.'

The tears started again. 'And now her ladyship's gone. Cut down so cruelly, well before her allotted time. Poor Lady Amelia. She will be greatly missed.' Bulstrode buried his face in an enormous blue handkerchief.

At this point, Roger was lost for words. He sympathised with the old fellow, and understood his distress but he had no words to counteract these very strong emotions. He was aware that any death was a tragedy, but he could not summon up any real feelings of loss for Lady Amelia. She had treated him with disdain ever since he arrived and was dismissive of his duties. Her treatment of her husband was cruel and harsh. So, he remained silent, allowing the ancient retainer to expunge them from his body in tears and sighs.

Lightwood himself felt drained. The events of the past few weeks had ravaged his sensibilities and wearied him more than he realised. His sudden romantic attachment to Felicity and then the ensuing separation from his beloved, not quite knowing when he would see her again, had affected him greatly. Then there was the murderous attack on his employer which he had been forced to hide from the authorities which was followed by the mysterious death of Dr Benbow, an event that further added to his stress. And now there was the tragic demise of Lady Amelia. It seemed that he was living through a waking nightmare. The fact that he had a sobbing manservant in his room did not help him catch a firm hold on reality. He almost felt like shedding some tears himself.

His miserable contemplations were interrupted by a harsh ringing sound. It was the great doorbell. It jangled vigorously, the clapper striking the large bell chamber with force so that the tintinnabulation could be heard throughout the house. The sound brought a sudden cessation to Bulstrode's sobs. He stiffened, wiped his face vigorously with the now squelchy handkerchief. 'We have a visitor,' he said, rising stiffly, his sense of duty to the Throate family manfully trying to override his emotions. 'I must go and answer the door,' he said.

Lightwood gently returned the man to his seat. 'You are in no fit state at the moment to perform such a duty. I too am a servant of this household. I'll see to the visitor on this occasion. You stay here and regain your composure.'

Moments later, Roger Lightwood pulled open the door of Throate Manor to find a tall young man on the threshold. He had keen eyes, an intelligent face which was framed by blonde hair. He bowed his head in greeting.

'I am Oliver Twist from the firm of Gripwind and Biddle, acting for Sir Ebenezer Throate. I am here to see Sir Ebenezer privately on a matter of great delicacy.'

CHAPTER THIRTY ONE

Barney Kepple and Alf Joint gazed down at the bloody body on the shore of the Thames. It was that of Jeremiah Throate. He lay face down in the mud and he was not moving. Worse than that: he was not breathing. The two men wore expressions of grim dismay.

'We've gone and done it now, Alf,' said Barney. 'This wasn't supposed to happen.'

Alf nodded vigorously. 'I know. I know. We just got carried away.'

Barney gave a self-deprecating sneer. 'Well, that's one way of putting it. We were only supposed to hurt him and then take him back to the gaff – not… not kill the blighter. He's no good dead.'

Alf groaned. 'We're as good as dead 'uns ourselves now. Trench will have our spleens for watch chains.'

'If only you hadn't clubbed him with your stick so hard on the back of his head.'

'What d'yer mean? If only you hadn't stuck your knife in his chest.'

They fell silent for a moment.

'Well, what's done is done. He's dead and that's it,' observed Barney at length.

'What do we do now?'

'We have no option. We make ourselves scarce, I reckon. We disappear. We have to. This little fandango brings our relationship with Trench to a close. We need to get out of London. Away from his clutches.'

'Clutches… yes,' mumbled Alf, his brain hurting.

'Come on, let's get away from here.'

The two men turned and began running, leaving the corpse sprawled out, face down on the wet mud on the shore of the gently flowing Thames. If they had only searched his body before departing, they would have discovered a precious pearl necklace in his inside pocket. However, at high tide both the necklace and Jeremiah Throate's body were swept out into the murky waters of the river.

* * *

Tom Cuff thought it very odd that in less than half an hour he had another stranger on his doorstep requesting a mount and details of the layout of the Throate estate. However, it did not give him too much pause when he knew there was more money to be made out of the situation.

'I'm sorry young fellow,' he said, slipping the coins into the pocket of his leather apron, 'I ain't got a horse I can let you have at the moment. But I do have a pony. She's small and stout but surefooted and will certainly get you where you're going.' He avoided adding the word 'eventually' in case it may prompt a refusal.

Jack Dawkins knew he had no choice in the matter. 'Beggars can't be choosers,' he muttered to himself, as Tom Cuff led him through his smithy to where the beast was tethered. Well, the farrier had been honest: the pony was small and she was stout. He had omitted to mention that she was also rather grizzled with age.

Cuff saddled her up and Jack clambered aboard. Once seated in the saddle, he found his legs almost touched the ground. He was well aware that he made a very comical, indeed farcical sight as he trotted from the yard on to the track that would lead him to Throate Manor. Thank the Lord, he thought, none of my friends can see me now – I look like an act from the circus.

Despite his encouragement to the pony, who was named Flora, the nag seemed intent on taking the journey at a comfortable pace. Pressing his legs vigorously against its flanks, shaking the reins and crying 'Come on Flora, let's fly' had no effect on the pony whatsoever. Jack was beginning to think that it might have been better to go on foot. He dreaded to think how far ahead Eugene Trench was now and what mischief he was up to.

They entered the wood, pony and man, and then remarkably, as though somewhat spooked by the gloom and the low overhanging branches, Flora picked up speed and achieved a reasonable jogging pace. The surroundings were so alien to a city bred boy and bordering on the fairytale fantastical with the spider tracery of interlocking branches above him, split at intervals with pale needle beams of light and strange rustlings and weird squeaks in the darkness. To Jack it resembled the landscape of some strange dream.

He thought back to his Fagin days. They were hard and demanding but there was a kind of rough camaraderie then and no real sense of danger and worry about the future. The old devil had been a hard task master and could not be trusted, but nevertheless Jack had felt a strange kind of security under his regime. Here he was now, wrapped in a world of uncertainty with no indication of how things would end. And he was on his own: a solo agent. The thought made him shiver.

Eventually he reached the wooden bridge as he had been told he would by Tom Cuff. And there was a horse tethered there. Trench's mount no doubt.

'Here's company for you, Flora,' Jack said, dismounting and tying up the pony to one of the struts on the bridge.

Within minutes he was trekking across the meadow of tall grass in pursuit of Eugene Trench. Oh, how he wished he was seated in the snug of a London ale house with a foaming tankard before him.

* * *

Roger Lightwood had led Oliver to one of the sitting rooms in Throate Manor and bid him take a seat. 'Sir Ebenezer is resting now,' he said, standing awkwardly by the fireplace. 'As you know he is not in the best of health and today he has had a tremendous shock. I regret to say that this morning Lady Amelia met with a terrible accident and died.'

Oliver nodded respectfully. This is only confirmed what the coachman had told him. 'I am very sorry to hear that,' he said softly. 'It is a sad state of affairs indeed.'

'As you will know I am responsible for all Sir Ebenezer's private and business matters and so regarding his rather fragile state at the moment, I can assure you whatever information you have to impart to him can be vouchsafed to me.'

'I am not sure that would be quite appropriate, Mr Braggle,' said Oliver.

'I do not see…' Roger Lightwood halted mid-sentence, his face suddenly drained of colour and an expression of horror freezing his features.

'You are Thomas Braggle are you not? You were raised by Amos Braggle of Murray Court.'

It was some moments before Lightwood could reply, his eyes flickering wildly as though he was desperately seeking the words to use in response to this man's statement.

'What nonsense is this?'

'Come now, sir. There is no need for prevarication. Your reaction to my statement clearly reveals that it is correct. There is no shame in the matter and indeed there is much to be gained by admitting the fact that your given name was Thomas Braggle.'

Lightwood turned his back on Oliver and rested his head on the mantelpiece and groaned. 'What do you want of me?'

'Firstly a simple statement admitting that you are who I say you are.'

There was a long tense silence and then Lightwood turned around slowly. Oliver could see that his eyes were moist with tears.

'Very well, I am... I was Thomas Braggle. But I have made a new, brighter life for myself.'

Oliver smiled. 'Much brighter than you realise, sir. I believe I know the outline of your story but I would be obliged if you would recount, in general terms, what happened to you after the death of the man who brought you up and regarded you as his son.'

'Why on earth should you wish to know all that? What is the purpose?'

'Trust me, sir. I mean you no discredit. It is important not only to me and my services to Sir Ebenezer but vital to your future well-being and happiness.'

After a long pause, Lightwood gave a deep sigh. 'Very well,' he said, wearily. 'You seem to know most of my story anyway. I don't suppose dotting the I's and crossing the T's can do me further harm. With what inheritance I gained from my father, Mr Braggle, I enrolled at the University of London to study law and commerce. I call him my father for so I regarded him although I was not of his flesh. I was born an orphan, spending my early years in the poor house.'

Oliver knew all about such circumstances and indicated as much with a nod of the head.

'It was during my second year there, I fell by the wayside. I had lived somewhat extravagantly, I'm afraid. I was not used to handling my own finances and I turned into the prodigal son, spending money lavishly, carelessly I suppose, and inevitably I drifted into debt. In a desperate attempt to extricate myself from the dire situation, I foolishly resorted to gambling as a means of getting my hands on further funds. Of course I failed. It is an idiot's pursuit. I sank deeper into the mire and my studies suffered greatly. Eventually, the whole focus of my life became gambling – the desperate attempt get hold of funds. In the end, I gave up my life at university and took a lowly position in a tavern where regular games of chance were held.'

'The Saracen's Head.'

Lightwood's eyes widened with surprise.

'Why yes... How did you know?'

'Later. Pray continue.'

Lightwood hesitated a moment as though he was about to press Oliver for more detail and then thought better of it and continued his narrative.

'At this time I had reached the bottom of the well. I really thought I would sink beneath the surface of the murky waters. I even contemplated doing away with myself… and then good fortune came to my rescue. I was traversing one of the narrow streets in the city of London – it was an aimless perambulation – when I saw a distinguished old gentleman being set upon by a couple of footpads. They were only youngsters, less than twenty, chancing their arm no doubt, but they had managed to bring their victim to the ground. I roared out a warning as I rushed towards them. For a moment they gazed up at me in surprise, this tall fellow racing towards them, shaking his fists. One of the boys high-tailed it immediately, but the other was more reticent to go and he made a move to reach into the gentleman's coat pocket just as I was upon him. I gave him a swift and heavy clout around the ears and with a sharp cry, one of pain mixed with indignation, he too ran off.

'I helped the gentleman to his feet. He was shaken but unharmed and most profuse in his thanks for 'my gallant actions' as he referred to them. I walked him to a nearby tavern where I plied him with a large brandy which did much to revive his spirits. He introduced himself as Sir Ebenezer Throate who was making one of his rare visits up to town from the country. I remember him saying they would grow even rarer after the unpleasant experience he had just endured. And then, once more, he expressed his unbounded gratitude to me for my actions. We stayed in that tavern for over an hour and chatted most amiably. I told him a little of my history but I cut out the disreputable segments. He just knew me as an ex-university student who had fallen on hard times. He asked me to join him that evening at his hotel to take dinner with him. It was an invitation I was more than happy to accept.'

Oliver could tell from Lightwood's expression and brightness of his eyes that he was actually enjoying relating this part of his history; it allowed him to experience again in a vicarious manner this fortuitous moment from his life.

'That evening my life changed forever. Sir Ebenezer was still full of praise and gratitude for what he regarded as my 'gallant actions' but which in fact were just my natural instincts to go to the aid of a man in trouble. I certainly had not thought I was doing anything out of the ordinary. We chatted and enjoyed each other's company. I sensed that Sir Ebenezer was a lonely man who was delighted in being in amiable company. By the end of the evening he had invited me to come and work for him, to be his secretary, as 'my right hand man' he termed it. He offered me lodgings at the Manor house and an excellent salary. How could I refuse?' Lightwood laughed suddenly. 'I didn't refuse. And so now I am here, serving my master.'

Oliver sat back in his chair. 'Thank you for your frankness and the details you have vouchsafed me. Now I think it is only fair that I give you my story.'

* * *

Trench, somewhat out of breath, had reached the rear of Throate Manor. He leaned against the wall of the old pile, waiting for his breathing to return to its regular rhythm. He was not used to so much physical exertion or the potency of country air which, it seemed to him, had almost as much power of intoxication as bathtub gin. He opened his carpet bag and checked the contents: a pistol, a short rifle and a long knife with a savage serrated blade. It was an assassin's kit, although Trench did not regard himself as an assassin. Although he had been responsible for a number of deaths, he had only actually killed one person himself. But now that was about to change. He was here 'to do in old man Throate' as he conceived the mission in order to flush out his son Jeremiah. On Sir Ebenezer's death, the young man would emerge from hiding to claim the family fortune and that's when Trench would have him – would have him to bleed him of his fortune before bleeding him to death. This thought brought a broad grin to his thin perspiring features. If only he had known that this was now a fool's errand: Jeremiah Throate was dead and thus his plan was futile, but Fate had contrived to make him ignorant of this dark irony.

Fastening up the bag, he began to make his way along the rear of the building in search of an entry to the premises, some insignificant aperture – a door or a window – which would allow him access to the lower reaches of the building so that he then could make his way in a surreptitious fashion to Sir Ebenezer's quarters, wherever they may be. He was confident he could find them and the man himself without too much difficulty.

He soon came across what he was seeking: both a door and a window situated by a small flagged area which had some washing hanging on a line strung between two poles. Creeping up to the window, he gazed through the grimy pane. He saw that the room beyond was the kitchen, a large chamber with all the paraphernalia for cooking including a large oven. Standing at a large rough table in the middle of the room was a plump middle-aged woman, stirring something in a very large bowl. Obviously she was the cook. She was alone and therefore vulnerable. Very vulnerable. Things were going his way very nicely.

He tried the door. It opened easily with a slight creak. The woman, so intent on her stirring duties did not hear him enter and was not aware that there was anyone in the room until a shadow fell across the table. With a little gasp of surprise she turned and looked up to see a tall thin man of grimy aspect holding a pistol. She fell back with a cry of alarm.

'Not another sound, lady, or it will be your last,' the strange man sneered.

Lizzie Barnes' stomach did a somersault and for a few moments she thought she was going to be sick.

'If you do as you're told, I won't harm you,' said the man, waving the pistol at her.

She nodded vigorously, incapable of speech.

'Good girl. Now then I need you to provide me with some information. I want to know something of the layout of this house and in particular where I will find Sir Ebenezer Throate this fine day.'

* * *

Lady Whitestone lay back against the pillow and sighed. 'I cannot eat any more, my dear. I have had sufficient.' Felicity gazed down at the plate that lay on her ladyship's lap. The food - a simple concoction of mashed potatoes and thinly sliced chicken – had hardly been touched.

'Are you sure you cannot manage a few more mouthfuls?'

Lady Whitestone shook her head. 'Sufficient unto the day. I am quite satisfied. Don't fret my dear, I do so hate to see that lovely brow of yours furrowed with concern.'

'Well, we must build up your strength,' Felicity replied.

'It will be restored in due course, I am sure.' Suddenly, she reached out and grabbed Felicity's hand. 'Don't you worry about me, you little darling. Whatever happens to me, I know I've reached the peak of my happiness having you by my side. I am so fond of you.'

A lump lodged itself inside Felicity's throat and she began to weep. In her heart she knew that these sentiments and indeed the whole of Lady Whitestone's recent behaviour was the result of her accident and not the emotions and sentiments of the real person that she had served for over two years, but it touched her to see the woman whom she had hated and reviled behave in such a kind and loving fashion towards her. She wondered how long this beatific transformation would last. Would her mistress fall asleep one evening and wake up the next day as her old self? The thought horrified her, but she realised that it was one she would have to live with.

'Leave me now, my dear,' Lady Whitestone was saying. 'I am still very tired and I would like to sleep.'

'Of course,' said Felicity, taking up the tray from the bed and then on impulse leaning over the old woman, she kissed her on the cheek. 'Good night.'

Lady Whitestone smiled and her eyes shone brightly with pleasure. 'Thank you, my dear. God bless.' And then she slipped very quickly into deep slumber.

* * *

'My commission from Sir Ebenezer was to try and track down a certain individual,' began Oliver in a faltering manner. He had not quite thought out how he would explain matters – very delicate matters – to Roger Lightwood/Thomas Braggle/Bastard Throate.

Lightwood, now his recital was over, had taken a seat opposite, his features indicating that he was all attention which added to Oliver's awkwardness. With a gruff embarrassed cough, Oliver resumed his narrative. 'Sir Ebenezer confided in me – along with my associate Mr Dawkins – that some twenty five years ago he formed a liason with a young lady servant here in Throate Manor. The result of this amorous relationship was that the young woman fell pregnant – was with child. Much to his shame, to avoid a scandal, he sent the girl away with some money and never saw her again. She gave birth in a London poor house and then gave her infant over to a baby farm, where…'

Oliver paused at this juncture for Roger Lightwood emitted a strange gargling sound, half way between a moan and a roar of indignation, and his whole body shook as though suddenly taken by the palsy. 'You're not saying…' he managed to gasp a few moments later, 'you're not. My God, this can't be real.' With another strange cry, he slumped back in his chair, his eyes rolling wildly in their sockets.

'I am sorry to break it to you like this but, it would appear that in fact you are that child. You are Sir Ebenezer's illegitimate son. He set me upon the task of finding you because he wanted to enfold you in his bosom and make reparations for the injustice he wrought upon you.'

'I cannot believe it,' said Lightwood, after a long pause, the words floating out from his mouth as the merest whisper.

'There is a dark irony in this affair, I grant you. It seems that Fate anticipated your father's desires and brought you two together in the strangest of ways.'

'Sir Ebenezer… my father.'

Oliver nodded. 'The trail I have followed from Madame Camila Sponge's establishment to Amos Braggle's old shop where you served your apprenticeship and was brought up by Amos Braggle who gave you his name.'

'A name I disgraced by my profligate ways. That's why I changed it. But is it true? Is Sir Ebenezer really my father…?'

'Yes, sir. The facts speak for themselves.'

'This is… amazing,' Littlewood croaked, running his fingers through his hair. 'I am bewildered and astounded…' Suddenly he paused, his body stiffening. ' But who, then, is my mother?'

'She was a maid servant here at Throate Manor. Her name was Louise Clerihew, but I am afraid I have no notion where she is now or even if she is alive.'

Littlewood began to weep. The dramatic revelations of the last few minutes had hit him hard and his emotions were like a small vessel tossed on a turbulent sea. 'And Sir Ebenezer has no knowledge of her whereabouts?'

Oliver shook his head. 'I'm afraid not. He lost touch with her within weeks of her confessing to him that she was with child. He sent her out into the world with a small amount of money… an act he now feels great guilt about.'

'And so he should – the devil,' snarled Lightwood, wiping the tears away.

'This guilt has eaten away at him over the years and it is only recently with intimations of his own mortality that he wanted to try and right part of his wrong by bringing you into the family household.'

'Part of his wrong! I was left an orphan and my mother… abandoned. How can he right those wrongs?'

'We all make mistakes. You must learn to forgive him.'

Lightwood shook his head. 'I'm …I'm not sure I can…'

Oliver had no response to this. Instead he placed a comforting hand on the young man's shoulder. The two men, drained of conversation formed a dark silent tableau in the gloomy chamber.

* * *

Jack Dawkins had reached the perimeter of Throate Manor and searched the area but there was no sign of Eugene Trench. Jack had been wracking his brains to determine exactly what kind of mischief Trench was up to. Was he planning a robbery, taking some valuable item from the house, or was his mission darker? Was he intending to hurt someone? To kill someone? What he knew of the fellow, Jack was aware that he was quite capable of such a terrible act. But in truth, after much contemplation pondering the matter, he was really no wiser. All he knew was that unless Trench had magical powers to make himself invisible, he must have entered the Manor in some way. If that was really the case, he had little time in which to act. A feeling of panic began to invade Jack's mind and he realised there was only one sensible course of action. He sprinted around the building towards the front and approached the large oaken front door. Taking a deep breath he knocked hard against the wood and tugged vigorously on the bell pull. And continued to ring it until it swung open and to his surprise he found himself face to face with Oliver Twist.

Each man stared at the other for some moments temporarily struck dumb by the vision before him. It was Jack who broke the silence. 'He's in the house. I think he's in the house. Trench!'

As he garbled these words, another figure appeared in the shadows behind Oliver. 'Who is this?' the man enquired in a tired, bewildered voice.

Oliver turned to Roger Lightwood. 'It is my assistant. He has information that an enemy of the Throate family may well be on the premises. A dangerous fellow called Trench. No doubt his intentions are nefarious.'

'Sir Ebenezer,' cried Lightwood.

No further words were necessary. Lightwood turned and headed for the staircase. Oliver followed, along with Jack.

'He's resting in his bedroom,' cried Lightwood as they reached the landing. 'Pray God, he is safe.'

Moments later the three men burst into Sir Ebenezer's bedroom and froze at the sight that met their gaze. Sir Ebenezer was sitting on the bottom of the bed, his eyes wide with bewilderment and fear. Standing by his side with a knife at his neck was a grotesque figure who wore a tight fitting leather mask over his head which concealed all his features.

Both Oliver and Jack knew it was Trench but it would have been difficult to prove it in a court of law.

'Stay put,' the figure growled. 'One move and the execution will take place earlier than planned.'

'Let Sir Ebenezer go,' said Oliver, his voice, much to his surprise, steady and commanding. 'There is nothing to be gained by hurting the gentleman.'

'Isn't there?'

'No there isn't,' cried Jack, aching to move but having the sense to stay still. 'You can't hope to escape from this room. There's three of us here ready to stop you.'

The figure laughed. 'You ain't going to stop me. I come prepared.' While keeping the knife just breaking the skin of the baronet's neck, Trench leaned forward towards a canvas bag on the bed and extracted a pistol. 'This has six chambers. Two bullets apiece, if you don't behave yourselves.' He gurgled with dark merriment before laying the pistol down on the bed within easy grasp.

'Now', he announced grandly, 'I am going to deal with this old goat and then you are going to step aside and allow me to make my grand exit. Don't think you can follow me because I have the key to the room and I'll be locking you in. If you decide to play hero, by damn, I'll shoot you. And I can tell you, gentlemen, that would be give me great pleasure.'

'You villain,' cried Roger Littlewood, his features pale and drawn. He had suddenly been dragged into a nightmare in which a man he had recently been told was his father was going to have his throat cut before his eyes and yet he knew he couldn't do anything about it.

Behind his mask, Trench smiled. 'A villain who has the upper hand. A villain who has been far too clever for the lot of you.'

As he was addressing Lightwood with relish, Oliver tapped Jack's sleeve to gain his attention. 'FD,' he said.

Jack's eyes flashed with excitement and he nodded vigorously. 'FD... now!'

At this signal, both men made a loud weird howling sound, with Oliver feinting to the right and Jack to the left in a pincer movement towards Trench. So sudden and shocking was this dramatic movement that momentarily Trench was paralysed with surprise and before he could regain his composure the two friends were on him. Oliver punched him hard in his masked face while Jack dragged his arm from Sir Ebenezer's neck and twisting his wrist sharply made him drop the knife.

Sir Ebenezer staggered forward away from harm's way and fell into Lightwood's arms. Oliver hit Trench again, knocking him unconscious. He slumped to the floor like a rag doll. Jack snatched two of the curtain cords and bound the villain tightly, before Oliver dragged the leather mask from his head.

'Trench,' cried Roger, staring down at the sweaty twisted face. 'Eugene Trench.'

'The same,' grinned Jack, grabbing hold of Oliver's hand and shaking it vigorously. 'What a team, eh, Oliver. Just like the old days. The FD, eh? Fagin's Diversion. Worked a treat. We learned something useful from the old rascal after all.'

Oliver smiled wryly.

* * *

Dusk was falling as Dr Sloper closed the door of Lady Whitestone's room and made his way like an elusive shadow down the staircase to the sitting room where Felicity was sitting in the growing gloom with only one lamp to illuminate the chamber. She sat forward in her chair in a posture that suggested that she was about to leave it. Leave it with some urgency. She had not been able to relax, eat or function in any practical sense all day. The remarkable change of circumstances in the last twenty fours had completely baffled her mind. It was, she thought, as though she had entered some strange dreamlike state where nothing was real or sensible.

Sloper gave a brief cough to announce his appearance in the room. Felicity stiffened even more and turned her head in a jerky fashion in his direction.

'Oh, Dr Sloper,' she said. And then after a pause, when she had collected her thoughts which were strewn hither and thither about her brain, added, 'And how is the patient this evening?'

Sloper shook his head sadly in a practised manner. It was the shake he always used when he had to pass on grim tidings to family members. 'She is serene and resigned. She knows the end is near and is ready for the journey.'

'The journey… You mean…?'

'I am afraid so, my dear. It is a just a matter of hours now. She is not fighting the inevitable. It is as though she is welcoming it with open arms. You ought to go up to her and say your last fond farewell before she crosses the Rubicon.'

Felicity suddenly found she was sobbing, her body wracked with heaving sighs and the tears gushing down her face. This, for a woman who had been nothing but a torment and a tyrant to her for two years and then in the last few days had treated her with kindness, love and generosity as though she was her daughter.

She found her mistress asleep, breathing lightly, the face, sans powder and paint, aged and wrinkled and yet exuding an aura of tranquility and contentment. Felicity sat beside the bed and took Lady Whitestone's hand in hers and squeezed it gently. The old lady feeling the warmth and the pressure of the hold, smiled and opened her eyes briefly.

'Good night, my dear,' she said, her voice a merest whisper. 'Sweet dreams.' The eyes closed again and she drifted off into that permanent long sleep that awaits us all.

* * *

It was Bulstode, returned to his normal stoical self, who discovered Lizzie Barnes in the kitchen trussed up like a Christmas turkey. As he untied her bonds, he informed her of the dramatic incidents that had occurred at Throate Manor in the last few hours.

'And would you believe it,' he said with excitement as he helped Lizzie to her feet, 'it turns out that Mr Lightwood is really Sir Ebenezer's son.'

Lizzie Barnes gave a shriek, her legs giving way and she collapsed to the ground again.

'My Lord,' cried Bulstrode, 'I had no idea that piece of news would affect you so.'

'Is it true? Is it really true? Roger is…' muttered Lizzie, her mind awhirl as she desperately attempted to come to terms with the news.

'Yes, yes. Sir Ebenezer has said so. That young lawyer from London sorted it all out.'

'The Lord be praised,' grinned Lizzie, as the tears began to fall.

* * *

Sir Ebenezer Throate was seated in his favourite chair in the orangery, clasping a glass of brandy as the evening shadows began to fall. Gathered around him were Oliver Twist, Roger Lightwood and Jack Dawkins. The police had just departed the building with the body of Eugene Trench and a written statement of the incident penned by Oliver and signed by the others.

'I seemed to have lived through a lifetime of events in one day,' Sir Ebenezer observed wryly, before taking a large gulp of the warming liquor. 'I have lost and gained in a most dramatic fashion. Poor Amelia has gone to her maker and I have regained a son. My emotions are all at sea.' Then he turned his tired features towards Lightwood and smiled, 'But Mr Twist you have brought me the greatest gift any man could wish for – his son. His fine, upstanding son.' He reached forward and clasped Lightwood's arm, his eyes moistening. 'Welcome home, my boy. I hope you can forgive me.'

Lightwood knelt down by his father and gave him a gentle kiss on the cheek. 'It would be so very wrong of me not to. God bless you, sir,' he said.

Jack gave a nervous cough, thoroughly embarrassed by this sentimental exchange.

'But tell me, Mr Twist,' said Sir Ebenezer in a more business-like tone, wiping his tears away, 'why on earth was this scoundrel Trench so intent on killing me. I didn't know the fellow.'

'He is associated with your other son, Jeremiah, whom I gather owed Trench a considerable sum of money...'

'Bah! That boy is always in debt. He's a wastrel. If ever there was a cuckoo in the nest it was he.'

'Well, he has gone to ground, out of Trench's grasp and so it would seem he had a crazy scheme to murder you in order that Jeremiah would inherit your fortune, thus bringing him out in the open again. With Jeremiah becoming a rich man that would allow Trench to leech off him for many years to come.'

'The devil. Where is Jeremiah now?'

Oliver shook his head. 'I have no knowledge of his whereabouts.'

'Well, if he does appear, he can be assured that I will disown the bounder. I have my good son now who will carry on the Throate dynasty with dignity and grace.'

'You must not be too harsh on Jeremiah, father,' said Lightwood.

'Oh, yes, I must. That boy has been no son to me and I will not weep if I never see him again.'

Sir Ebenezer Throate did not know that when he did see his son Jeremiah once more, it would be on a slab in a dark and gloomy mortuary and that he would shed some tears for his wretched and dissolute son.

* * *

Later that evening, Roger Lightwood sat in his room at his little desk penning a letter with great fervour and excitement.

My Darling Felicity,

I have the most remarkable news. My whole world has been turned around in a miraculous fashion for the better. It is absolutely incredible. I feel as though I am living a dream and yet it is reality. The changes in my fortune have removed all barriers to our happiness together...

About the same time as Roger Lightwood was penning his missive, Felicity Waring was about a similar task in her own little room in London.

Dearest Roger

You will not believe what happened to me today. Indeed I find it hard to believe it myself. Only a few days ago I was a penurious companion and tonight I am the heir to a considerable fortune. I am living a fantasy. Wealth means little to me, but the changes in my fortune have removed all barriers to our happiness together...

It was nearing midnight and Sir Ebenezer Throate was still awake. He was sitting up in his bed, a guttering candle nearby and a glass of brandy in his hand. He knew that sleep would not come easily to him that night: his mind was awhirl with all the events that had occurred that day. He had long ceased to love, or indeed care about his wife, but he would miss her – miss her as one did a tooth that was extracted because it was giving you pain. He was sure that she would be feeling the same about him if he'd had the misfortune to tumble from the roof.

The drama with Trench preyed less on his mind. In a stoical fashion, Sir Ebenezer had accepted his fate when the villain entered his bed chamber and thrust a knife to his neck. The Lady of the Manor had gone; it looked like it was his turn now. Well, someone had already tried to make mincemeat of him and now it looked like this grotesquely masked fellow, like a renegade from a gloomy novel, was about to complete the deed. The drama that enfolded was theatrical in the extreme: the two young legal chaps acting in unison like a well-trained circus act performed a miraculous feat, disarming and disabling the murderous felon. What brave men they were. He must remember to present them with a small reward before they returned to London with a letter of gratitude and praise to pass on to their employers.

But, and what a huge and glorious 'But' it was – But the real joy on the day was finding his son again. A son whom he had been harbouring under the roof of Throate Manor for some time. He was a young man of whom he was already naturally fond. He was a boy he respected and admired and he was his father. He beamed with joy at the thought.

It was at this moment, when he was about to take a small sip of brandy to add to his natural inner warmth, when the door of his chamber opened and a figure slipped inside. For a moment, all ease evaporated from his body and he slithered down into the bed full of apprehension.

'Tis only me, Lizzie,' said a voice.

Sir Ebenezer relaxed again and pulled himself up into a sitting position.

'I have heard the news. The wonderous news,' she said.

'Oh, my goodness, my dear, I have been so wrapped up in events, I forgot to come and tell you myself. What a marvellous boy you gave birth to.'

'It is so strange to think that he was here under our noses and we didn't know it.'

'Fate was playing a trick with us, no doubt. But in my ignorance I grew fond of the fellow without being aware that he was my own. And rest assured I will do all in my power to make up for my cruel and stupid behaviour of years ago when I… when I abandoned him.'

Lizzie sighed. 'For different reasons, I abandoned him also. It is a parcel of guilt that I shall carry with me to my dying day.'

'No, no. You must not feel guilty. I was the one to blame and anyway it was your 'ghostly' performance that prompted me to seek him out.'

She nodded sadly. 'So, my work here is done. I will leave by the end of the week.'

'You will do no such thing. You must stay. I insist.'

'I cannot.'

'Why not?'

'I … I don't know.'

'You are his mother…'

'No. No! He must never know. I beg of you. He must not be told. I could not bear it. I am happy he has been brought here. Throate Manor is his rightful home. That is all I wanted'

'Then stay and watch him grow and develop. Become his loving friend. You can help me guide him along the path of life. I will keep your secret as long as you want me to. Please, I beg you.'

She hesitated, casting her head down. 'I don't know,' she said at length.

'How can you bear to abandon him again? He is your flesh.'

His words lingered in the air like motes of dust.

Lizzie Barnes fought back the tears. 'Yes. You are right. You are right. Very well, I will stay and do as you ask on the condition that you swear that you will never, *never* reveal my real identity.'

'As you wish. I will respect your decision. But I suspect that you will change your mind.'

* * *

The tap at the door was recognisable. Jack Dawkins had a way with his knuckles and wood that was as identifiable as his grating laugh. He didn't wait to be asked to enter, but slipped into Oliver's bedroom, carrying a bottle and two glasses. 'I got this claret from the sideboard in the dining room. I reckon they won't miss it. More importantly I also reckon we deserve it. We did save the master of the house today, after all. You'll have a drink with me, Oliver, won't you?'

Oliver grinned. 'How could I refuse?'

Jack poured the wine and raised his glass. 'To us and Fagin's

Diversion.'

Glasses were clinked, smiles exchanged and glasses drained.

'What a lark it's all been, eh, Oliver. Been great fun, hasn't it?'

'I wouldn't quite say that, but this has been a colourful detour from our usual routes.'

Jack whistled. 'My, you do have a way with words. No doubt you will become a very famous lawyer in time, baffling the opposition with your eloquence.'

'Pour me another glass and I'll see what else I can come up with.'

Jack did as he was asked. 'I reckon old Gripwind & Biddle will make you full partner after this lark. Sir Ebenezer is very pleased with the outcome. He's sure to put in a good word for you.'

'We'll see.'

'You always were a cautious one, Oliver. Except today with the old FD. You were as quick as a whippet.' He guffawed loudly and Oliver joined in.

'I must say,' said Jack, pouring them both another glass, before lolling back in his chair, 'I haven't enjoyed myself as much in years. This Throate business has been a real tonic. Colour, excitement mystery and drama. Like a real melodrama. It's a pity we don't get involved with more larks like this.'

'Well, you never know,' said Oliver softly, taking a long drink of the rich red wine. 'You never know.'

ABOUT THE AUTHOR

David Stuart Davies is an author, playwright and editor. His fiction includes six novels featuring his wartime detective Johnny Hawke, Victorian puzzle solver artist Luther Darke, and seven Sherlock Holmes novels, the latest being Sherlock Holmes and the Ripper Legacy (2016). His non-fiction work includes Starring Sherlock Holmes, detailing the film career of the Baker Street sleuth. David is regarded as an authority on Sherlock Holmes and is the author of two Holmes plays, Sherlock Holmes: The Last Act and Sherlock Holmes: The Death and Life, which are available on audio CD. He has written the Afterwords for all the Collector's Library Holmes volumes, as well as those for many of their other titles. David has also penned three dark, gritty crime novels set in Yorkshire in the 1980s: *Brothers in Blood, Innocent Blood and Blood Rites*. He is a committee member of the Crime Writers Association and edits their monthly publication Red Herrings. His collection of ghost and horror stories appeared in 2015, championed by Mark Gatiss who said they were 'pleasingly nasty'. David is General Editor of Wordsworth's Mystery & Supernatural series and a past Fellow of the Royal Literary Fund. He has appeared at many literary festivals and the Edinburgh Fringe performing his one-man presentation The Game's Afoot: an evening with Sherlock Holmes & Arthur Conan Doyle. He was recently made a member of The Detection Club.